Praise for *Empire of Wild*

'Deftly written, gripping and informative. *Empire of Wild* is a rip-roaring read!'   Margaret Atwood

'*Empire of Wild* is doing everything I love in a contemporary novel and more. It is tough, funny, beautiful, honest and propulsive ... Cherie Dimaline is a voice that feels both inevitable and necessary'

Tommy Orange, author of *There There*

'A blend of close-knit emotional bonds and ambiguous menace ... Dimaline's novel is able to take the plot to some unexpectedly phantasmagorical places without losing sight of its emotional core ... Stories and their telling run throughout this book, from official histories to tales of uncanny and mythic creatures whispered about late at night ... Dimaline here turns an old story into something newly haunting and resonant'   *New York Times* Review of Books

'*Empire of Wild* is a small book. But it is not a slight book. It is close, tight, stark, beautiful – rich where richness is warranted, but spare where want and sorrow have sharpened every word. And through multiple narrators (including free-floating, disjointed chapters from Victor which haunt every major angle of the plot), disconnected timelines, the strange geographies of memory and storytelling, Dimaline has crafted something both current and timeless, mythic but personal. It is the story of Joan and her love. Joan and her loss. Joan and her family. Joan and her monster'   *NPR*

'Sharp'   *New Yorker*

'Wildly entertaining and profound and essential'

New York Times

'Exhilarating'   *Lit Hub*

'Revelatory ... Gritty and engaging, this story of a woman and her missing husband is one of candor, wit and tradition'

Ms.

'Dimaline trusts her readers. Her characters reiterate the importance of heritage, culture, and representation to their careless and dismissive youth, but she uses language that compels everyone to take heed – native or not; old or young ... Dimaline has written this narrator as if she is moving from room to room, traveling through the pages: yes, she has seen and survived it all and when it comes right down to it, Dimaline makes it clear that when it comes to standing up for her people, she is wildly excited about the choreography of a damn good fight'   *Chicago Review of Books*

'The novel is at times sad, at times humorous, and at times terrifying. Smartly written with believable characters, a tight plot, and breathtaking sentences, this is a must-read literary thriller'   *Publishers Weekly* (starred review)

'Canadian writer Cherie Dimaline blends fantasy, monsters and contemporary First Nation struggles in a powerful and inventive novel ... *Empire of Wild* seamlessly mixes realistic characters with the spiritual and supernatural. As much a literary thriller as a testament to Indigenous female empowerment and strength, *Empire of Wild* will excite readers with its rapid plot and move them with its dedication to the truths of the Métis community'   *Book Page* (starred review)

Y039003

The item should be returned or renewed by the last date stamped below.

Dylid dychwelyd neu adnewyddu'r eitem erbyn y dyddiad olaf sydd wedi'i stampio isod.

Newport
CITY COUNCIL
CYNGOR DINAS
Casnewydd

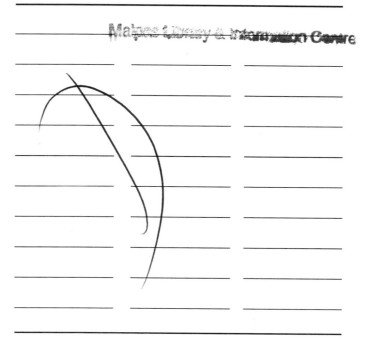

Malpas Library & Information Centre

To renew visit / Adnewyddwch ar
www.newport.gov.uk/libraries

EMPIRE
OF
WILD

CHERIE DIMALINE

WEIDENFELD & NICOLSON

First published in Canada in 2019 by Random House Canada
First published in Great Britain in 2020 by Weidenfeld & Nicolson
This hardback edition published in 2021 by Weidenfeld & Nicolson
an imprint of the Orion Publishing Group Ltd
Carmelite House, 50 Victoria Embankment
London EC4Y ODZ

An Hachette UK Company

Epigraph excerpted from: *Self-Defence for the Brave and Happy*, Paul
Vermeersch, published by ECW Press Ltd., 2018. Used with permission.

Text design: Terri Nimmo
Cover design: Terri Nimmo
Cover image © Wendy Stevenson / Arcangel Images
Interior image © Shutterstock/Thomas Sandberg

The right of Cherie Dimaline to be identified as the author of
this work has been asserted in accordance with the
Copyright, Designs and Patents Act 1988.

ISBN (Hardback) 978 1 4746 2158 8
ISBN (Trade Paperback) 978 1 4746 2159 5
ISBN (eBook) 978 1 4746 2161 8

Typeset by Born Group
Printed and bound in Great Britain by Clays Ltd, Elcograf S.p.A.

www.weidenfeldandnicolson.co.uk
www.orionbooks.co.uk

For Jaycob,

the boy who chased the monsters away

We went to the best motels,
which is like sleeping
in unfinished novels. We slept
soundly amongst the teak
and twill and plaid and brass.
We left the window open
just a crack.

—PAUL VERMEERSCH, "Motel"

"Just shut up, you; and listen."

—MY MERE, EDNA DUSOME, 1913–2006

A NEW HUNT

OLD MEDICINE HAS A WAY of being remembered, of haunting the land where it was laid. People are forgetful. Medicine is not.

The town of Arcand was a church, a school, a convenience store, a bootlegger and a crowd of stooped houses leaning like old men trying to hear a conversation over a graveyard of Greniers and Trudeaus. Sundays were for God, though most people prayed out on the lake, casting Hail Marys with their fishing lines into the green water, yelling to the sky when they didn't get lucky or when they did.

Parties were held in kitchens. Euchre was a sport. And fiddles made the only sound worth dancing to. Any other music was just background noise for storytelling and beer drinking and flirting. Or for providing the cadence for fight choreography when you just had to beat the shit out of your cousin.

The people who lived in Arcand were brought from another place, moved off Drummond Island when it was handed over to the United States in 1828. They were halfbreeds, the children of French voyageurs and First Nations mothers, and Métis people who had journeyed from Manitoba. The new colonial authorities wanted the land but not the Indians, so the people were bundled onto ships with their second-hand fiddles and worn-soft boots. They landed on the rolling white sands of the Georgian Bay and set up their new homes across from the established town that wouldn't welcome them. At first they were fine on their own, already flush with blacksmiths and hunters, fishermen and a hundred small children to toss stones into Lake Huron. If they had known then how each square inch would have to be guarded, how each grain of sand needed to be held tight, perhaps they would have stacked the rocks instead of gifting them to the lake.

Over the years, without treaty and without wealth, the half-breeds were moved away from the shorelines where million-dollar cottages were built in a flurry of hammers on lumber, so many at one time it was as if the shore was standing to an ovation. Family by family, the community was pushed up the road.

Catholic by habit, they prayed on their knees for the displacement to stop, for the Jesus to step in and draw a line between the halfbreeds and the new people. Those among them who carried medicine also laid down coarse salt as protection against the movement. This salt came from the actual bones of one particular Red River family, who drew their own boundaries when the hand of God did not reach down to do it for them.

Eventually, inevitably, the shore belonged to the new-comers who put up boathouses and painted gazebos and built docks where sunburnt grandchildren would cannonball into

June waters, calling for someone to watch what they could do. And the halfbreeds? They got the small settlement up a dirt road. They got Arcand.

Some of the people managed to hold on to the less desirable patches of waterfront, areas with no beach or too many lilies like the decaying fingers of a neglected woman pushing out of the muck. These were the older people, who refused to head up the road to Arcand. They kept rickety docks where the fishermen tied their rusted boats in exchange for some of the catch. The heavily wooded acres that bloomed out from Arcand toward the highway and the smaller roads with hairpin curves snaking down to the occupied shore, these areas, too, remained up for grabs. In any halfbreed home there were jars of coins and a wistful plan to buy back the land, one acre at a time if need be.

On these lands, in both the occupied places and those left to grow wild, alongside the community and the dwindling wildlife, there lived another creature. At night, he roamed the roads that connected Arcand to the larger town across the Bay where Native people were still unwelcome two centuries on. His name was spoken in the low tones saved for swear words and prayer. He was the threat from a hundred stories told by those old enough to remember the tales.

Broke Lent? *The rogarou will come for you.*

Slept with a married woman? *Rogarou will find you.*

Talked back to your mom in the heat of the moment? *Don't walk home. Rogarou will snatch you up.*

Hit a woman under any circumstance? *Rogarou will call you family, soon.*

Shot too many deer, so your freezer is overflowing but the herd thin? *If I were you, I'd stay indoors at night. Rogarou knows by now.*

He was a dog, a man, a wolf. He was clothed, he was naked in his fur, he wore moccasins to jig. He was whatever made you shiver but he was always there, standing by the road, whistling to the stars so that they pulsed bright in the navy sky, as close and as distant as ancestors.

For girls, he was the creature who kept you off the road or made you walk in packs. The old women never said, "Don't go into town, it is not safe for us there. We go missing. We are hurt." Instead they leaned in and whispered a warning: "I wouldn't go out on the road tonight. Someone saw the rogarou just this Wednesday, leaning against the stop sign, sharpening his claws with the jawbone of a child."

For boys, he was the worst thing you could ever be. "You remember to ask first and follow her lead. You don't want to turn into Rogarou. You'll wake up with blood in your teeth, not knowing and no way to know what you've done."

Long after that bone salt, carried all the way from the Red River, was ground to dust, after the words it was laid down with were not even a whisper and the dialect they were spoken in was rubbed from the original language into common French, the stories of the rogarou kept the community in its circle, behind the line. When the people forgot what they had asked for in the beginning—a place to live, and for the community to grow in a good way—he remembered, and he returned on padded feet, light as stardust on the newly paved road. And that rogarou, heart full of his own stories but his belly empty, he came home not just to haunt. He also came to hunt.

1

JOAN OF ARCAND

Searching for the one you lost feels like dying of exposure again and again and again. You are bloodless, single-minded, numb around the edges of the panic and loss. Fingers exist only to dig, legs to pump you forward on blistered feet.

You look.

You look.

You look.

You push granola bars between your teeth to get some fuel into your stomach. So you can keep going. You piss in the woods to save time, but only after meticulously checking the ground for evidence.

You hold your breath when you spot tracks and then you follow them. Any small sign that he may be close slams electricity into your nerves so that everything is on fire. You are a fever in the woods.

But then a broken shoelace is just a shoelace and nothing

more. A clue is not a clue, just a dropped barrette, a drunken stranger sleeping it off, a used condom.

And your blood recedes like a red tide and your fingers close tight around another shitty cup of coffee. They rest over a broken heart held careless by inadequate ribs.

You look some more.

Joan had been searching for her lost husband for eleven months and six days, since last October when they'd fought about selling the land she'd inherited from her father and he'd put on his grey jacket and walked out, the screen door banging behind him. She'd pored over that small sequence of movements and words every hour for eleven months and six days until the argument had distilled to a scream and a dash, then the door.

"Going to check the traps," he'd thrown over his shoulder and into the living room where she sat.

"Yeah, good," she tossed at his back from the couch. "Go enjoy the land you want to sell out from under us. Why not?"

Then she'd half laughed through her nose so that the last sound he heard from her was a derisive, mocking exhale. That was the punctuation at the end of their collective sentence, that horrible noise. Maybe he hadn't heard her. She hoped that he hadn't.

She couldn't remember what it was to eat and sleep and dream. She couldn't make herself cum and she couldn't ease her lungs enough to sigh, which, she thought, was almost the same thing. Without Victor, Joan was half erased. Was he dead somewhere? Had he run off? She couldn't grieve like a normal person—cut her hair, cry herself to sleep and wait for a day when she could live with his absence. The only thing she could do was search.

She was born in Arcand, like generations before her. Unlike them, she'd lived other places before moving back, in cities and towns around Ontario and once, years ago, in Newfoundland when she'd hooked up with a cod fisherman. Growing up in Arcand had made her itchy and absent-minded. She had to see what else was out there. There had to be some-place where she fit. As it turned out, the fisherman stopped being verbal and she couldn't figure out how to play a decent hand of 120s like a respectable islander, so she'd made her way home.

Between Leading Tickles, Newfoundland, and Arcand, Ontario, she met Victor.

"Watch yourself," Mere had warned when she heard Joan was taking the Greyhound. "Some fellow cut some other fellow's head off on one of those things." Her faraway voice on the phone was quick with concern.

"Don't worry about bus murderers. With my luck, I would end up dating him." Joan was only half kidding.

Mere clucked her tongue. "You just get home. Never mind about dating anyone."

"Yeah well, once I get to Arcand, I can't date anyone. They're all related to me."

She had a two-seater to herself for most of the trip, a good book, a bag of snacks and smokes, and eighty dollars left over from her cheap fare. So when the bus squealed and burped into Montreal with a four-hour layover until her Toronto connection, she decided to hit a bar near the station.

She climbed down the steep steps and hopped out of the bus onto the slushy asphalt in inadequate shoes, her backpack over one shoulder. She looked up into a sky layered to navy past the greasy halo of city lights. Snowflakes tumbled down so huge and slow it was as if they'd been cut from folded paper by a pair of delicate shears. The parking lot was a poem about white. The neon bar sign for Andre's was a Christmas tree, all dressed. And the fat, black Harleys out front were eight little reindeer all in a row.

Joan ordered the first beer listed on tap and settled in at a corner table away from the loud regulars circling the bartender like thirsty seagulls. Drinkers hunkered over a couple of pool tables on the far side of the room, illuminated by a stained glass fixture of ships at sea. The tables were filled with bodies, spilling out clipped French like a burst pipe. She drank quickly to push back the anxiety of being alone and uncomfortable and ordered another beer when the waitress breezed by. Coming back from the ladies' room after her second, she stopped by the bar to order another, armed with temporary confidence.

It was late now, almost eleven, and her bus was leaving at half past midnight. The front door opened often, blowing in mostly men but a few women too, and swirls of the constant snow. At some point, she was sucked into a group conversation about Osama bin Laden's death. She lost track of drinks and details, speaking free and laughing easy with the security of a near departure. But then she saw Victor, beautiful Victor with his sharp cheekbones and old-fashioned tattoos of swallows and pin-ups and knives stuck in thick-lined hearts, Victor with his smart mouth and kind eyes whose colour was indefinite, and she knew she wasn't getting back on the bus.

Though the next afternoon she was back on the road. Only this time she was riding shotgun in Victor's Jeep and they were on the way to New Orleans.

Arcand had a way of slipping itself around a person and applying subtle pressure so that you settled back into its groove, somewhat conscious of being swaddled but mostly comfortable with it. Bringing Victor home was not easy. They had spent almost a month driving to Louisiana, bumming around with his friends and then taking the long way home, tracing the puzzle-piece perimeter of Florida. After that, they'd holed up in Montreal for two months until his loft lease was up, fucking and wandering the streets with song and wine and skin bruised from so many kisses. Then they'd packed his life into three cardboard boxes and headed for the Bay. Like any small community, Arcand demanded familiarity and loyalty. It pushed outsiders out like splinters, and it tried its best to eliminate Victor in this way.

When Joan's father died, the house she'd grown up in was handed down to her. Joan's mother couldn't stand to be there anymore and, between her and her brothers, Joan was considered the most in need of stability. Since it had been sitting empty while she had her Newfoundland fling, Joan had moved

Mere from her apartment to the house. Which meant the first obstacle she and Victor had to face was her grandmother, Angelique. Not generally judgmental, Angelique was moody when worried, and Joan's track record with men definitely caused her to worry. Her reaction to Victor's sudden appearance took the form of silence, which Joan tried hard to break.

Victor's father is a Boucher—didn't you know some Bouchers back in school?

Victor likes to hunt. You should tell him about how the deer used to be around here, back when Grandpa was around.

Me and Victor are going into town for groceries. You want us to bring you to bingo?

Most of Joan's overtures were met with mumbling, half in Michif. Joan only understood enough to know none of them were real responses. Mere spent more and more time in the silver Airstream she'd parked out back, down by the creek, the place where she kept her medicines and best tea set and liked to do her puzzles. Eventually, she started spending nights in the trailer. And finally, she stopped coming up to the house for anything but to shower and use the landline.

Victor refused to give up. He baked bread and carried it down to the trailer, wrapped in a checkered dishcloth. He invited Mere up for cards every time they were about to play. He landscaped the whole property and planted sage by the birch trees. Only when he told her a dick joke while she watered the garden did she finally begin to relent. Mere liked a good dick joke and appreciated a man who could tell one.

Joan's brothers and mother were less measured in their show of disapproval. The first time she brought Victor over for Sunday dinner at her mom's, her brother George took his plate of Shake 'n Bake to sit in front of the TV, Junior went to the workroom and Flo went out on the porch. Joan was hurt and embarrassed, but not surprised. She'd wasted their goodwill on a lot of goofs over the years. Now here she was with the person she was going to marry, with the man who was where she finally fit in the world, and they were refusing eye contact.

This went on for months.

Victor held her when she cried about it, gently, like her bones were broken just under the skin. He said, "I'm a stranger to them. Of course, they're overprotective." But she knew it was getting to him too. They weren't being overprotective; they were being assholes. She went back to work with the family contracting crew but was silent while they shingled roofs and sullen when they put in decks. She started calling her mother once a week instead of daily and showing up for dinners and baptisms even less.

The stalemate ended in their second winter, when Junior got into a fight at Commodore's over someone calling someone an Indian and then a bottle was broken on the edge of a table. Victor had stopped in at the bar after work with a new guy on his framing crew. When the shouting began, he excused himself and ran toward the fight, shedding layers of flannels as he went. He threw down for Junior without question— popping jaws, taking a kick to the ribs, yanking raised pool cues out of callused hands. Then the police showed up and shooed everyone home.

He and Junior rolled up in George's truck at three o'clock on a snowy Saturday morning, then all three staggered to the house, arms around each other. Joan opened the door and Victor beamed so big it was clear he'd lost an incisor to a fist of heavy knuckles. It was also clear that he and her brothers had become buds for life. It was a good thing Mere was down in the Airstream. She would have beat them black and blue again just for getting beat up. All in all, it was worth the cost of the dental implant.

Victor grew on people, one by one, especially after the wedding when it was clear he intended on sticking around. The first week he didn't come home, everyone looked for him. Even Marcel, the Québécois logger, went out to help search the woods, even though he was the one who famously carried the tip of Victor's tooth embedded in his right hand after the fight at Commodore's. But by the end of the second month, it was only Joan wandering the township like a broken-hearted ghost. There were days she couldn't remember how she got to her patch of land or out to the dump. She just ended up there, putting one foot in front of the other down narrow paths and over mounds of wrecked furniture and wet newspaper.

Eleven months and six days and she was still a distracted driver, checking out every person walking down the side of the road, looking into each car that passed, or else so lost in thought, so tired, she was prone to drift. Even ferrying Mere and her cousin Zeus to Sunday dinner at her mother's house, she was caught up in her thoughts.

"Dieu, Joan. Pull over," Mere shouted. "We can walk the rest of the way to your mom's." She was braced for impact, holding on to the dashboard with two hands, her top-handled purse propped up on her lap like a small, white dog. Her seat-belt was pulled tight over her low breasts, her back straight against the seat. "I'm not ready to see the Jesus just yet. And Zeus, him, his voice hasn't even cracked."

From the back seat Mere's great-grandson chimed in. "Don't kill a playa before he even gets to the game, Auntie."

"Sorry, guys." Joan sat up and put both hands on the wheel—ten and two—steering the Jeep back over the yel-low line and firmly into their lane. She'd been thinking about the ditch on the side of Highway 11 between Barrie and Orillia. Had she checked both sides? Might be worth another trip out.

"Long summer this year," Mere remarked, watching the sailboats in the Bay out her window. They cut slow across the dark water like children gliding on an ice rink, all pastel coats and white toques.

"They call this Indian summer, Mere, when it goes on into October," Zeus remarked.

"Who does?" Mere craned around to frown at him. "Who?"

"I dunno, *they* do." He shrugged.

"Who's that, then?" She loosened the belt and shifted so she could turn enough to stare at him.

"Uhh, just them, Mere. People."

"What does that even mean—Indian summer? Can't be nothing good if *they* are saying it." She turned back to the front, crossing her arms over her chest.

"Well," Joan joked, "there is such a thing as a white Christmas, so maybe fair's fair."

"Hmm." Mere folded her hands over her purse. "You could be right." She clucked her tongue and looked back out the passenger window. "Might all be part of this reconciliation thing."

Joan caught her little cousin's eye in the rear-view mirror and they shared a smirk.

Florence Beausoliel's house was small and tidy, like its owner. Joan's mother was barely five feet tall in steel toes, but she ran the construction crew herself, each member of which she had given birth to. She didn't stay in the office either. At sixty, Flo was the fastest on the roof, jumping joists like a jackrabbit through clover. She could eyeball blueprints and see the finished project in three dimensions in the void.

Flo had renovated her two-storey cabin herself. It wasn't the house where Joan had grown up; that's where she, Mere and Victor lived now—well, she and Mere, who had moved back up to the main house from the trailer after Victor went missing. Flo bought this place by the marina after Percy died and the kids moved out. But then Junior got divorced and moved in with her. Shortly after, the youngest, George, got kicked out of university in Waterloo and returned to his mother's house loaded up with laundry and student debt. Flo had even offered up the living room pullout to Joan, considering what she referred to only as "her situation."

Joan would never move back in with her mother. One of them would be dead by the end of the first week, and she wasn't sure which one it would be. Her mother had serious moves. She'd seen them. The whole town had, that time one of the new elementary school teachers in town tried to dance with Percy at a bush party. People still made karate noises at her when she walked down Main Street. "Hi-yah! Here comes Kung Fu Flo!" Joan thought her mother could have worked a little harder to get them to stop.

No, Joan had always been Percy's girl. After her father died, for a lost and sometimes scary time, she'd been anyone's girl. And then she had been Victor's girl. And now she was just a girl, a thirty-seven-year-old girl who drank too much and tried to stare into the sun until she went blind as an offering to the universe for the return of her beloved.

With twelve-year-old Zeus and ancient Mere, along with her two brothers and her energetic mother, converging in one modest space, Joan was claustrophobic as soon as she'd taken her shoes off at the front door.

She squeezed onto the loveseat beside her older brother in the room left by her mother's ridiculous collection of over-stuffed pillows. He was watching the tiny TV their mother refused to replace, as that might compel her boys to stay in the nest even longer. "Jesus, Junior, when are you getting your own place?"

"Don't know. When are you gonna take a shower?"

She rammed her shoulder into him and he lifted his arm across the back of the couch, pulling her in and dropping a kiss on the top of her head, his eyes never leaving the game.

"It's just, it would be nice to be somewhere where we could smoke something other than meat, you know what I'm saying?" Joan tried to speak low, jabbing a finger into his newly soft gut.

"Weeds are legal now. Why you gotta be all whispery over there? Gladys Trudeau uses it for her bad hip. And Ajean, she's been smoking pots for years." Mere said this from the kitchen, where she was peeling carrots with a thin knife and plunking them in the giant enamel stewpot. "I think I might get some next time Junior drives me in to the pharmacy for my pills."

"Holy fuck, Junior, you better not get Mere drugs."

Her brother just laughed and shrugged. "Like, I can control her?"

Flo was carving up a thawed slab of moose, frying the cubes in a greased pan. The meat spit and hissed like a quick temper.

"Hey, did you know it's Michif summer?" Mere asked her daughter.

"How's that?" Flo said.

"*Indian* summer, Mere. Indian summer," Zeus corrected. He was at the counter mixing up some Kool-Aid.

"Well, hell, I gotta have a status card to have a long summer now?" Mere glared at him. "Halfbreeds like the sun too, you know."

Zeus stirred the powder crystals into the water in the jug in silence.

When dinner was ready, they crowded around the small table in a nook between the kitchen and the living room, George on the little stool Flo used to reach the high cupboards so that only his head and shoulders were visible when he sat up straight. They ripped off pieces of bannock and used them to soak up the stew broth. Zeus already had a bright orange ring around his lips from the Kool-Aid, and seemed happy just to be at a sit-down dinner. His mom, Bee, rarely cooked and when she did, they ate in front of the TV.

"You finish the MacIver roof?" Joan asked, between bites of moose.

Junior nodded. "Just in time for the end of cottage season. It won't be leaking for next summer, anyways."

"We would have been done weeks ago if you showed up once in a while," George said to Joan.

"Georgie, shut up, you. You know your sister's situation." Flo shook the salt container so hard her trick wrist clicked.

"Yeah well, it's been a year. How long do you need for a situation, anyways."

Flo slammed the shaker on the table. There was silence, like she'd snapped off the volume.

"I'll be around next week," Joan finally said. "What are we doing?"

"Marina needs a new tool shed." Flo went to the fridge to grab the margarine and settled back in her seat at the head of the table. "Shouldn't take more than two days. Then we start slowing down. A couple decks. An addition on Longlade's boathouse."

"Come November we'll need to look for winter jobs. Maybe I'll go north, to the mines." Junior caught his mistake too late and readied himself for the rebuttal. It didn't take long.

Mere dropped her spoon. It rattled against the bowl like a miniature alarm. "The mines? You gonna work for thieves? That's going from making things all day to taking things all day."

Junior stepped soft around his grandmother's ire. It was slippery and quick and, if you weren't careful, before you knew it you could find yourself getting soft-shoe stomped. "I'm worried about going from paying my bills to not paying them."

"You find something else, not the mines, that's what you do. You can't work in town? The Friendship Centre doesn't need anyone?"

"The centre doesn't pay the way the mines do."

"It also doesn't steal from us, ignore our rights and mess up the land. How bad do you need that pay?" She had abandoned her food—never a good sign.

Zeus tried to be helpful. "I mean, you live with your mom, anyways."

Since Zeus was an acceptable target where Mere was not, he bore the brunt of Junior's frustration.

"Shut it, Zeus." It wasn't enough. Junior was still angry. He looked his cousin up and down. "Fuck, you're fat."

"That's it." Flo stood up and leaned over her table. "I'll have no more of this bullshit at dinner. Mom, relax a bit on the Elder politics, would you? And Junior, apologize to your cousin right now. He's less than half your age."

Junior took a moment to calm himself down, then reached across the table and patted Zeus's chubby forearm. "I didn't mean it, buddy. I just got upset. Sorry, little man."

Zeus shrugged.

George was laughing behind his hand so hard his glasses were fogging up. Joan was just trying to concentrate on getting more food into herself before anyone made a comment on how skinny and haggard she looked lately. There had been too many of those kinds of remarks lately.

Mere had stood up when Flo sat back down and had gone into the kitchen. She opened the cutlery drawer, and the tinny ring of metal on metal filled the small space.

Flo let her head drop and ran one hand through her hair. "Jesus, what now?" she muttered. Then she spoke louder. "Ma, what are you looking for? Everything should be on the table."

No answer. Another minute of clanking metal and then the drawer closed. Mere walked back to the table but didn't take her seat. She was coming up behind Junior when George yelled, "Yo, she's got the scissors, bro."

Mere reached out, pretty deft for someone legally blind with arthritis in her fingers, and snatched hold of Junior's braid hanging down the middle of his back.

"Mom!" Flo yelled.

"Mere, no!" Joan jumped up so fast her chair tipped over.

Junior tried to get away but Mere gave his braid such a yank he sat back down, hands up as if he were being robbed at gunpoint. "Mere! What are you doing?"

"Me? I'm getting you ready for your new job at the mines." She sounded calm, jovial, even. "You need to fit in with all

the others and none of them will wear their hair traditional."
She opened the scissors.

"Hold on! Hold on a minute." Flo was almost climbing
over the table.

Joan felt like she was going to throw up what she had
managed to eat. Zeus took another sip of juice. He may have
even smiled a little.

"Okay, ma mere, please, s'il vous plaît, let's talk about this
some more. I'm listening. Seriously."

Junior was ready to bargain. His grandmother was not.
"There's nothing to talk about. All my seniors group has been
doing at shrine on Fridays is talking, mon Dieu. It's time for
action. We can't support companies that don't support us
right back. We can't let our young people work for such
places. I refuse!" She raised the scissors to the sky like a halfbreed Evita, holding her grown grandson by the hair. Junior
looked on the verge of tears.

"Okay, okay, I won't go. I promise, I promise."

She lowered the weapon and used his braid to pull him
close and kissed him on the top of his head. "My boy, you're
too important to lose."

Once the scissors were on the table beside his napkin,
Junior was much too relieved to be angry. He wrapped his
arms around his diminutive mere and took all the petting
and kisses she handed out.

Flo, who didn't have a braid to lose, was angry. "Great,
Mom. Maybe you and the seniors group can come by this
winter and help us out with our loan payments and the hydro,
eh?" She plunked herself back in her chair and reached for

more bannock, but she was not done. "Sometimes we have to do what we have to do, even if that means working in the mines. What are we supposed to do? Stay poor? Would that prove to you that we're Indian enough?"

"No, my love." Mere was serene now that she had successfully made her point. "We are supposed to stay right with community. That's how we know we're Indian enough. The companies are out to take it all, you know. We shouldn't just hand it over."

"Oh Christ, can we just finish the damn meal, please." Flo shook her head. "It's the goddamn Assembly of First Nations in here every Sunday."

"Excuse me." Joan got up from the table and headed for the bathroom. She locked the door behind her and sat on the closed toilet lid. Maybe if she stayed here long enough, counting the damask patterns on the linoleum floor, picking at her hangnails, bouncing her legs on the balls of her feet until her teeth chattered, people would settle down and she could finish her stew or at least make it look like she had. She wanted a cigarette. She wanted a drink. She wanted to sleep or run away or cry or fall into a coma—she wasn't sure which, and these days never was. Since Victor had been gone she felt like whatever she was doing wasn't the thing she was supposed to be doing. Nothing was right. Everything was knocked slightly askew, like a house on a cracked foundation. New tilts and slants made her nauseous at the most mundane times, like grocery shopping. Unexpected fractures threw her completely off balance, like eating Sunday dinner with her argumentative family. She flushed in case anyone was paying attention, splashed her pale face with cold water, smoothed back her long, brown hair with wet hands and opened the bathroom door.

Her phone vibrated in the front pocket of her jean shorts. She pulled it out. It was a text from her cousin Travis, who lived two towns over.

Come and watch Netflix and drink with me and be sad. Joseph and I broke up! Come now SOS

She sent back a thumbs-up emoji and pocketed the phone. Halfway back to the table, she heard raised voices and realized she hadn't stayed in the bathroom long enough.

Her mother's voice. "If you're so traditional, why are the seniors meeting at the shrine, anyways? Shouldn't you be in a lodge or something?"

As Joan sat down, both her brothers were taking small bites of their food, trying not to be noticed.

Mere let rip. "We're Métis, you fool. The church *is* the lodge. And besides, it's better to be close to the enemy than far away. Keep an eye on things. I'm tryna organize the old people to take a stand. We're not letting the community leaders sign no agreements with nobody."

"Like agreements for jobs, you mean?" Flo was pissed off her meal was ruined and now her boys would be unemployed for the winter, and she wasn't going to let it go. "And just how exactly does the church figure into this conspiracy theory of yours?"

Mere was patient. "The more the people stay off the land,

the more vulnerable the land is." She nudged Zeus, who was fiddling with his old CD player, duct taping the sprung cover back down after switching discs. "Pour your old Mere some juice, there."

Joan cleared her throat. "I'm going to head over to Travis's place for the night. Can someone drive Mere and Zeus home, please?"

Junior raised his hand, not yet willing to risk speech.

"Good enough."

Joan slipped into her sneakers by the front door and edged out, carefully turning the latch and easing the door shut behind her. She felt lighter leaving the burden of young and old relatives behind, lighter and without boundaries. It was scary to feel this weightless, to be this unheld. She slid behind the wheel and lit a cigarette, cranking the window down, then backed out of the driveway as quick as she could.

The early evening air was warm enough for bare limbs, the sky streaked with uneven slashes of orange and pink like a child had mashed a fistful of highlighters into a blue wall and run down the hallway. Kids screamed and laughed from cottage backyards, fearless. Two teenage girls from Arcand were walking on the side of the road, sharing a smoke between them. Joan raised her hand to return their shy waves. Everywhere she looked she saw not-Victor. Victor was not in line to leave the marina. He was not at the pumping station refilling the water jugs with drinking water. He was not part of the crew repairing the heritage barn that had half burnt down last month, its old planks crumbling to ash in the heat of young fire.

She smoked slowly, leaned back in the seat, the picture of someone taking a leisurely drive around the Bay into town. Even still, she was tempted to veer off the road at Concession 5 and crash into the wide oak at the corner, smashing her chest to bits. Because inside the dark of her thin body, her heart was beating against bone like a wing trying to find the sky. It would be a small mercy to grant its release.

2

THE RESURRECTION

Joan was so hung over she thought she might still be drunk.
She'd left Travis on his couch, curled around a half-empty
box of wine, with his phone on the coffee table where it had
sat all night just in case Joseph had a change of heart. It wasn't
the best way to be at noon on a Monday, deathly hung over,
walking across a Walmart parking lot under a sun like a spot
rubbed clean and thin on the sky. But she needed coffee and
food before attempting to drive home, and this place was the
closest spot to Travis's apartment where she could find both.

In front of her, a freckled child came out through the sliding glass doors with a jumbo freezie in his red fist and pointed.
"Mom, look, a circus!" Joan turned and saw a tent in the
corner of the lot. At first she thought it must be one of those
sad carnivals that pop up in small towns for no real reason
or occasion. But there were no sketchy rides or rickety game
booths around it. And the tent was just white, with no flags
or signs or colour. The prospect of cold cuts eaten straight out

of the package in an air-conditioned aisle was a powerful incentive to keep going. But a low, thick hum—from some joyful machine?—was escaping through the gaps between cloth and asphalt. She couldn't resist.

As she walked across the lot, the tent seemed a mirage wavering just past the shopping carts scattered like camels in the desert. It took forever. She grew dizzy in the bright heat and thought she should at least have grabbed a bottle of water.

She was almost there when the humming stopped, breaking off into a dozen individual voices, then winking out one by one. Before she could push aside the canvas flaps, they opened and a wave of people poured out, breaking around her, then curving back to a single stream in the concrete sea. She stood still while they passed, holding her nausea in place. There were a lot of people, and none of them were carnival-boisterous.

Being surrounded by all these good, sober souls reminded Joan that, at the moment, she was neither. She shouldn't have hung out with Travis. She'd been partying too much lately. It was the only way she knew to fill up the hollow hours when she wasn't searching.

As the herd thinned, she deked around the last of them and into the shade of the tent. No smell of popcorn or cotton candy or animal shit, just a soft undertone of summer sweat and fresh sawed wood. The tent was much bigger than it looked from the outside. The ceiling was high enough to be forgotten. Hundreds of folding white chairs went on forever, one after the other like crocodile teeth. At the front was a low wooden stage holding a simple podium and a wooden cross about nine feet high, painted white and barbed with clear

Christmas lights. It was crisp in here, all shades of pale with clean corners at ninety degrees. The only thing out of place was a high-backed armchair on stage, upholstered in pallid green velvet. It seemed a mistake, like it had been put down for a moment on the way to somewhere else and forgotten. It was soft folds of mould on smooth white fondant.

When she realized she'd wandered into some kind of old-timey revival tent, Joan put her hand over her mouth and giggled, turning on one red Converse to take in all the weirdness. Suddenly the white walls and carpeted runner leading up to the stage, even the folding chairs, seemed unusual and singular, like weapons from a dead civilization displayed in a museum.

Shit, why hadn't she brought her cousin? Travis would have loved this. The scene was so strange it begged to be shared. She took her phone from the back pocket of her jean shorts and started filming.

A voice entered the tent, just behind her. "Excuse me, miss. Can I help you?"

She turned to find a pleasant-looking kid, about twenty-five, clean-shaven with blond hair parted on one side with such fierce exactness a ruler had to be involved. He smiled big and genuine, and Joan felt ashamed of her small mockery and shoved her phone back in her pocket.

"I was just curious. I was, uh, walking to the store there and saw the tent." She pulled a fallen bra strap up over her shoulder and hastily tucked in the wrinkled back of her tank top.

"So you were drawn in, were you?" He clasped his hands in front of his khakis, still smiling like his life depended on it. His angles, too, were all ninety degrees. The sun muscling in through the open canvas flap behind silhouetted him beatifically.

"Uh yes, I mean, no. I was just curious." She laughed nervously, making her way around him in two steps, heading for the exit. "Guess I'm just a cat that way. Not that you're gonna kill me or anything, uh, ha ha . . . You know, curiosity and the cat . . ."

"Well, we're done for the day. But I have good news." As she turned politely back to him, he threw his hands up and spread his fingers to demonstrate the reach of such good news, opening his eyes almost as wide. "We don't head out of town until tomorrow evening. Perhaps I could interest you in one of tomorrow's sermons?"

"No, no. I'm okay." She touched a palm to one cheek as if to make the assessment physical. She turned away and stepped out of the cool shadows of the tent into the glare and uneven geometry of the world.

And then she heard him.

"Jonathan, we good to start stacking chairs?"

She looked back and, over the smiling blond's shoulder, a second person came into focus standing on the stage: a man in a black suit and grey fedora in this improbable heat, his red bow tie the colour of shock and murder. He lowered himself into the armchair, unbuttoned his suit jacket and slouched into the comfort of the cushions.

If her heart was a song, someone smashed the bass drum and pulled all the strings off the guitar. Notes fell like hail, plinking into the soft basket of her guts.

She didn't know she'd fallen until her knees jabbed her.

She tried to stand and they spit out gravel and a small piece of glass. Blood trickled down her shins, fast and thin. She folded again, right back onto her raw knees.

"Miss, are you okay?" The blond was over her, reaching out to help her up, the earnest smile gone.

"I'm, uh, yes I'm okay, Jonathan." Fuck, she was dizzy. How did she know what this guy was called? Then she remembered the other man had said his name in her husband's voice. "Victor?" She blinked hard to make her eyes work, searching the blurry expanse for him. She used Jonathan's offered arm to pull herself to her feet.

"Ma'am, I think you maybe fainted? Maybe we should get an ambulance. Those knees are bleeding pretty bad." He didn't seem equipped to deal with this kind of non-religious crisis. A knee wasn't a spiritual thing unless it was being used to balance on in prayer.

Her head was swimming with impossibilities and stale booze. She pushed him out of the way, teetering the few steps back into the tent.

"Victor, where are you?" she called, as her eyes adjusted to the dark cool.

"I'm Jonathan, ma'am, not Victor. There is no Victor in our mission."

But the man who was Victor came down the aisle and stepped into the light streaming through the open doorway, his beautiful face illuminated like Jesus himself. Joan sobbed, once—a big gulp.

He removed his hat, revealing hair cut close at the sides and wavy on top.

"Oh," she whispered. "All your hair."

Holding his hat to his chest with one hand, he reached out slowly, as if approaching a wild animal, to touch her forehead. She felt that connection like electricity and her eyes fluttered. For a moment it was a perfect portrait of healing; the good preacher laying hands on the weak and ill, the latter swooning under his holy touch, the glowing cross in the background.

"She's a bit warm. Let's get her into a chair." He called over his shoulder, "Bring some water, Cecile, will you please?"

Joan was laughing now, delirious, relieved. "Where have you been?" She threw herself into his arms. "Oh my god, Victor, I almost didn't make it."

He gently shifted her away from him, patting her arms until they were back by her own sides. "You're going to be just fine now. We'll just get you situated there and get some water into you." He placed one hand on her back and guided her to a chair at the end of an aisle. He took a knee in front of her, concern on his handsome face. Her eyes pinballed from mouth to eyes to newly shorn hair.

She reached out to search the planes and hollows of his face, and he pulled back, just out of range. What was wrong with him?

A woman scurried over with a bottle of water. She put a hand on Victor's arm to get his attention, her yellow braid hanging over her shoulder as she smiled into his face.

"Thank you so much, Cecile." His tone was kind, familiar.

Joan noticed how their hands overlapped for a second on the cool plastic of the bottle, and jealousy stitched humiliation into her muscles with quick, sharp loops. She only realized how close she was to anger when she was shouting at him. "What the fuck are you doing here?"

Cecile and Jonathan, in their matched khaki pants reeking of innocence and clean laundry, each took a step back. Cecile even placed one hand at her collarbone as if there were a set of pearls to be clutched.

"We are serving the Lord, sister. We are here because He sees fit to bring us here." The Reverend's voice was all chrome and shine, no recognition in his vacant eyes.

"Sister?" Joan shouted, standing so fast she had to grab the seat back in front of her to stay upright. She leaned toward him so she could speak directly into his face: "What the fuck, Victor? I'm not your goddamn sister. Where have you been? It's been almost a year!"

Being this close to him made her whole body react. Lust elbowed rage out of the way, then slipped on the slick cold of relief. She was wrong—this *was* a carnival, a fun house, everything ugly and exaggerated.

Her legs gave and she sat back down. When he crouched in front of her, holding out the bottle of water, she wrapped her arms around him as tight as they would go. She pushed her face into his neck and breathed deep. Even though her nose was right up against his pulse, she could feel that something was still draped between his skin and hers. She couldn't pull him close enough, and then he was grabbing at her too, that sweet pressure of his fingers. Except he wasn't. He set his hands on either side of her ribcage and pushed her back into the chair. He picked up the bottle he'd dropped and settled it in her lap. Then he knelt in front of her again, at a distance.

"Miss, I really think you're confused. Perhaps too much sun or too much of a good time?"

Shame hit her hard in the chest. Of course, she stank like a brewery. Probably looked like death warmed over too. Was he trying to disown her, the drunken halfbreed? Maybe because he was with his new blonde girlfriend? Anger punched her again.

"And who's this bitch, then?" Twisting the cap off the water bottle, she pointed with her lips at the woman he'd called Cecile. She eyed the girl, who showed no fear on her face, only a kind of pity that hurt Joan more. She downed half the water in one long shot. Then she collected herself enough to say, "Is she why you never came home?"

"Cecile," he said, "I think we really do need to call that ambulance—and right away." And off she went.

"Look," the man pretending to be not-Victor said, "we're just trying to help you, Miss . . . ?"

"Joan, I'm Joan."

A brief light showed in his eyes and then was gone.

"I'm Joan. Your wife. Are you kidding me?" Tears gathered in her arid skull.

As she saw his confusion melt into practised pity, she finally realized he really didn't know who she was. Either that, or he was going for a fucking Emmy. He put a hand on her shoulder and, despite the familiar weight of it, there was no electricity this time. It was a dead connection. It was the most she'd felt in eleven months and one week—this devastating absence.

"I'd better go get Mr. Heiser," he said. "You stay here with her, Jonathan, please."

The Reverend turned and fled, slipping through a fold in the canvas near the back of the tent. Joan looked up at Jonathan, who gave her a tight smile, then down at her hands, still holding the water. She felt herself teetering between giving chase and crumpling to the floor. What the fuck was going on?

"I hear we have an issue out here." A clear voice cut the room. From the same slit where the Reverend had made his escape, a shorter man emerged.

His blue suit bore a subtle stripe and his pant cuffs hit his brogues crisply. His shoes clicked on the false floor like fingers snapping a simple military rhythm. His narrow tie and pocket square were both daffodil yellow, a colour that brought out the gold hue of his eyes, deep-set below groomed brows.

As he came toward her he extended his right arm to check the time on a wide gold watch. In the shift of fabric, Joan saw dark hair dense on his too-white skin. He met her eye and then smiled with so much sharp in it, something in Joan reacted like she'd taken a punch with the promise of more.

"Hello, there. I'm Thomas Heiser," the man said. "What can we do for you?"

Joan held her breath to stop a scream from rolling out. Her bladder pinched. Her stomach hitched up. It was clear her body wanted to flee.

Victor, she reminded her heart.

Victor, she scolded her feet.

We need to stay for Victor.

"I want to see my husband."

The man called Heiser put his hand on Jonathan's shoulder. "Why don't you give us a moment, please? See if the Reverend needs any help."

Jonathan hesitated.

"We'll be fine. The cavalry is en route and I can manage here. Go. Now."

He gave the boy a pat that sent him speed walking to the tent opening. There was such a bright flash of sun, she had to make a visor out of her hand to shield her eyes, and then the boy was gone and she was alone with Mr. Heiser.

He said, "Have you been doing any recreational drugs I should know about before the ambulance arrives?" In the moment she'd been distracted, he had taken a seat in the folding chair in front of her and was leaning close.

"Are you being serious right now? I know my own husband. Get him for me now." Something about the way he looked at her with those light eyes made her shift her gaze to her hands. "Please."

He placed a hand on her arm and she flinched. It seemed like she could feel the whorls of his fingerprints on her bare skin. He smelled wrong too. Like milk. "Your husband isn't here," he said, and moved his eyes around her face as he tilted his head one way and then the other. He squeezed her arm a little, then let go. "Your husband is dead."

She stood so quickly light burst behind her eyes. "No." She shook her head as she backed away from him and into the aisle.

"He's dead and you are losing your mind because of it." The man still wore that same sharp smile.

Why was he saying this? How could he know? Her thoughts were muddy and her chest hurt. She leaned over and threw up the water she'd just drunk in a puddle by the man's feet. He didn't even move out of the way.

She swiped at her wet lips with the back of her hand, looking up at him. "He's here. I saw him!"

He shrugged. "He most certainly is not here."

"Who are you?"

He gave a small laugh and calmly sat.

She screamed, the way she had wanted to when he first walked toward her on those clicking shoes. She pulled at her hair. Such grief and confusion demanded movement so she walked in short bursts, glancing at Heiser when she could manage it. He remained in the folding chair, watching her as if she were part of a play. How could he say those things to her? What did he mean?

Nothing made sense. She was insane. Or he was insane. There was humming in the room again or maybe just in her head. She launched herself at him, grabbing his jacket. "Go get him! Get him now!"

Then the paramedics arrived in the company of a single policeman who detangled her from the man. The paramedics sat her down in a chair and listened to her heart, looked into her eyes with a small light and stuck a thermometer in her ear. They informed her and the man in the yellow tie that her heart rate was elevated and that she was severely dehydrated. They asked them both if she normally suffered panic attacks.

Joan yelled, "Don't talk to him. He doesn't know me. And he's a fucking liar!"

Heiser opened his eyes wide like he was shocked and then he led the officer away, leaning in to talk. The medics urged her onto a gurney and asked for permission to start an IV. She nodded, needing something, anything. The fluid dripped cold and steady. It made her think she had to count, which she did, whispering, "twenty-eight . . . twenty-nine . . . thirty . . ." before she felt her muscles unclench. She closed her eyes for a minute. Just to get herself together.

Someone was gently shaking her. She opened her eyes and twisted in the bed—why was she in bed? She pulled herself up on her elbows, her head aching, and looked around her. She was being unloaded from an ambulance.

"Wait, what's happening?" Her voice was dry in her throat. Then she remembered and crisis bloomed in her guts.

"Where is Victor?" She coughed, trying to free her voice.

The paramedics ignored her, fidgeting with the collapsible wheels and the IV as they pushed her toward the hospital's glass entranceway.

"Excuse me? Can you tell me where my husband is, please?" She struggled to sit upright in the moving bed. She saw the cop from the tent talking to a nurse by the door. "Officer? Hey, officer!"

He jogged over.

"Mrs. Beausoliel, I'm Sergeant McAllister. We've brought you here to regional hospital to get you checked out." His uniform was crisp and new, but he'd taken his cap off and his voice was soft. His brown hair shone red in the sun.

Her head swam as she looked up at him. "My car. My purse." She had to get out of here. Where was maybe-Victor? "Wait, how'd you know my name?"

"Your purse is here." McAllister pointed to the brown satchel tucked in by her feet. "It's where I got your ID. Sorry, ma'am, but I had to grab info for the medics here. And your car is safe and sound back in the Walmart parking lot. Good thing too, because you were in no shape to drive. Be glad you passed out when you did." He gave her a cop-gaze over the rim of his not-quite-mirrored sunglasses. "Let's get you inside."

"Do I have to stay?" She tried to sound steady, which she was definitely not.

"How 'bout this: if the doctor gives you the all-clear, we part ways on good terms."

She was pretty sure he had no legal way to make her see a doctor, but like any good Catholic of a certain age, she was scared shitless both of authority and of making anyone feel bad. So she lay back down and allowed herself to be wheeled in, the cop keeping pace beside her.

They parked her in a room separated from an old man on a breathing tube by a green curtain that didn't quite reach the floor. She watched feet in soft, white shoes flicker by.

She asked the sergeant, "Did you find out who the man at the church was? Is his name Victor?"

"First things first. Why don't you tell me what happened today?" McAllister sat in a chair beside her gurney and took out a notepad.

She tried to explain herself. She told him about Victor's disappearance, the missing persons report, the search parties, the bed with the sheets that never warmed up. She told him about the Reverend, who was somehow that same missing husband. She told him about the blonds in their uniforms and Mr. Heiser and what he'd said to her about Victor being dead, and then about throwing up and feeling horrible, and then, next thing she knew, the paramedics were laying her down.

"Well, that sounds a lot like what I was told by the other party," McAllister said. "I did speak to the church members onsite, including the man you claim to be your husband."

"Is he here?" She reached for McAllister and the IV needle tugged in her vein. She winced and dropped her hand.

"No, he isn't, and he's not your husband, ma'am. His name is"—he flipped back in his notebook—"the Reverend Eugene Wolff."

Joan stared at him. "Are you certain?"

"Well, he is, ma'am."

"Any chance he's been, you know, brainwashed?" She knew what this sounded like, but it was all she had.

"He showed me his ID. He didn't seem to be confused or under duress. I also talked to a few of the others travelling with him, who said that the Reverend has been in their company for over three years, whereas your husband's been missing just under a year."

He spoke with compassion, which had the effect of pushing Joan into the thin mattress until she was sure her ribs would crack from the weight of her disappointment. She closed her eyes to block him out, to block everything out.

They discharged her early the next morning. She called a cab and asked the driver to drop her back at the Walmart in the cloying dawn. She felt tiny, weak. It took so much effort to close the taxi door. She approached her car, waiting like an obedient dog, dropped her heavy purse on the hood and walked the perimeter of where the tent had been just yesterday. There was nothing left but a few strips of black hockey tape stuck to the ground where they had held down wires, maybe even the ones that powered the lights that studded the cross. So much for staying another day. So much for the possibility of Victor.

She sat down on the pavement, trying to pull a clear image of the Reverend Wolff to mind, but all she got was Victor on their wedding day in his rolled shirtsleeves and best black sneakers, an arm around her waist on the dock, a bottle of champagne in his other hand. "We did it, kid," he had said, and kissed her just below the hairline.

Joan, cross-legged in the oily lot, touched the same spot on her forehead. Her fingers were shaky as baby birds. Then she stood, walked back to the Jeep, picked up her purse and climbed in.

What now?

She had to find the tent. There must be a website or at least a Facebook page? She dug her phone out of her purse and touched the screen. It lit up with multiple notifications—missed calls from her mom, from Junior, from Zeus's mother, Bee, a few unknowns. There were text messages too. She opened these first.

The last one was from Junior.

They think it was animals—dogs, maybe wolves. Call us. I need to know where you are right now.

"What the fuck?" She typed:

I'm at the Walmart on 11, by Travis' place. What happened???

She scrolled up to find a text from Bee.

Holy shit Joan, I'm so sorry about Mere. Can you believe it? People are freaking out! Come by the house—there's a lot of us here. Zeus is worried about you

Mom.

Baby CALL ME ASAP

Junior.

Where are you, J? Have you heard? I'm headed back to the house.

Mom.

Oh ma mere. Who? Why? Whatever you do, DO NOT go down to the Airstream alone. We'll go together as a family

Zeus.

Love you Auntie

Her phone vibrated in her hand. A new text from Junior.

We're coming to get you. Joan, Mere's gone. We're on the way to you. No more than an hour. Hang tight.

Joan chain-smoked in the heat of the front seat until her brothers came to collect her. When they got to her, they guided her into the passenger seat so George could drive. Even when they passed into territory as familiar as their own pulse, Joan wasn't sure where she was.

VICTOR, IN A TWENTY-SIX-ACRE CELL

Victor's mother showed him how to skin a rabbit when he was four years old. He remembers the thin connective tissue, marbled like the curve of a gum bubble, and the stick and pull of drying blood between his fingers.

"Don't hold it by the head to peel. A head's not a strong enough thing."

Victor nodded, twisting his own head to feel the flex and give at the base of his skull.

She cut the brown corpse, from the horizontal slash at its throat used to bleed it out, down to the tail, curving around the sex organs, the knife slanted to separate fur from meat.

"Keep your blade sharp. You don't want hair getting in." She pushed a finger into the opening left by the knife, her nail making a small crescent against the wet belly skin.

She broke bones away from joints. She split and yanked out the pink hindquarters, peeling them free.

Then she put the flesh in his hands, holding his fingers in position to show him exactly how to do it. "Tight. Don't let go." She squeezed his weaker grip for reinforcement.

The rest came out like a lady unzipped from a gown.

He thought of this now as a rabbit hopped by, inches from his head. At least, he thought it must be a rabbit from the skip-run of its passing. It was too dark to know for sure. He was prone on the ground, the deep cold of the soil making a bruise of his back. He remembered how good that rabbit tasted when his mother stewed it up, how each bite was a prayer of gratitude. He lifted an arm and dropped his hand over his belly. He made an assessment with his fingers, checking the curves, tapping the empty hollow, like he was buying a melon from the grocery store.

Nope, still not hungry. Though the memory of food was a kindness in this isolation.

And then there was something else. He turned onto his side and stretched out his neck toward it, his nostrils flared— there was a smell in the air under the density of wood, above the mineral wet of soil. A woman.

A face came to him, soft with laugh lines and with a ridge of small, brown beauty marks along her jaw like a constellation. Straight teeth, dark eyes, dark hair. Her name . . . it was almost there, it was rolling slow up his throat. He felt hunger for the first time in memory. He reached both hands out in the dark. And then the wind blew warm, pushing into him, making it hard to breathe. He opened his mouth and it worked its way past his teeth. It was like his throat was full of someone else's breath. The image of the woman's face with astronomy on her skin was being pulled out of him. He was losing her.

The trees in this place shook but made no noise, the leaves quiet like lush flaps of felt and hide. No noise except for a far-off song raising itself up from an unseen horizon. He sat up, squinting, fighting to hold on to her. She was speaking to him now, her mouth shaping what he knew were the curves and full stops of his name, but he couldn't hear her. There was only the drone of a far-off hymn like elevator music in this small patch of forest, obliterating every other sound.

He lifted a finger to his mouth, spit on it and touched the tip on the matte grey of a maple trunk. And he wrote, rewetting his finger when it grew dry. For a moment he saw her name, darker grey against the light, pulled from memory and ache and terror. And before the wind blew it away, he said it aloud, and it was his once more.

Joan.

3

PACK DYNAMICS

Heiser preferred blondes but settled for the redhead. She wasn't all that smart and was no great beauty, but she had something he valued more—discretion. It was getting harder and harder to find companions in the congregation who wouldn't gossip. He placed a hand on the back of her head and ruffled her curls a bit.

"There's a good girl."

She mumbled a response around his dick. It sounded like gargling.

"Shh."

He turned and looked out the car window. With every mile it was becoming easier to breathe. The reflection of the passing trees slid over the Buick like bars. They were headed north. There was safety in distance.

It was his own damn fault. He saw that now. He should have noticed how close the last stop was to Arcand. But he'd been too busy dealing with relentless PR for the new pipeline consultations: too many posed handshakes with men in head-dresses; too many dummy copies of agreements to pretend sign for the press as the real deals were being sweated out between lawyers in the backrooms.

He didn't like making mistakes. He laced his fingers into the girl's hair, massaging the back of her scalp. She moaned and pulled at the seatbelt that still held her in the seat beside him, inching a little closer so she could take more of him in her mouth.

Heiser's sharp intake of breath was a hiss through clenched teeth. He closed his eyes briefly, then resumed watching the fields and thin forest whip by. He put a little pressure on the back of her head, switching hands for a moment to check his watch. Nine a.m. It felt later. It had already been a long day and he'd barely slept last night.

He'd figured, since he had already fucked up on the logistics, he might as well take care of some things in Arcand. Fucking Métis never used to be an issue. No one gave a shit about the halfbreeds in these deals. But now, they were every-where, on everything. If he had to see another fucking sash or hear another goddamn fiddle . . .

And then this woman, this Joan, comes into the tent losing her damn mind? Thank god she had the courtesy to show up half-cut. Made it easier to shake her loose. Way to live a stereotype, lady.

Someone always has to lead, to be the alpha. He sighed. Might as well be him. He'd been a leader his entire life, something passed down to him from his grandfathers in the old country before Bavaria joined Germany proper and their culture was absorbed and watered down.

His own father, Heinrich Heiser, had emigrated from Munich to Edmonton with his moody wife, two suitcases of clothes and a working knowledge of the English language. Not enough to write poetry but good enough for janitorial work at the high school. Thomas had only been one and didn't remember much of the early years except for the dogs. They would break out of their own backyards to follow him to school and back.

"Opa Emo, he had lots of dogs too," Heinrich had told him as they walked to the park with their baseball gloves. Heinrich was determined his seven-year-old should learn baseball, like all boys in North America.

"I don't have dogs."

"Yes you do, just not any that you need to feed or bathe. All these are yours." He waved his arms to encompass the three that trotted alongside them and the others running parallel to him along the nearby street. "Emo told me the Heisers always had dogs, and before them, wolves."

"Wolves?" Thomas looked up at his father. Wolves interested the boy. More than baseball. More than his mother. She was a hard woman who kicked the canines that showed up on their doorstep, and dragged him to church too often. She was fascinating but only from a safe distance.

He stopped walking and grabbed his father's hand. "Please, Daddy, tell me about the wolves."

"Yes okay, okay." Heinrich detached the boy's fingers and held the baseball in front of his nose. "But only if you catch ten throws all in a row."

He tossed the ball at the boy and jogged ahead to the park. Thomas looked down at the ball at his feet. It would be near the end of the summer before he heard any stories about wolves.

In grade eight, he narrowly escaped getting his ass beat by two older boys because an Irish wolfhound bounded into the schoolyard and skidded to a stop over Heiser where he curled on the ground. In his senior year of high school, a couple of beagles and a chihuahua sat outside his Corolla while he lost his virginity, howling when he came.

Thomas had always been the leader of the pack, ever since those first gatherings of dogs. Eventually, he used his ability to dominate creatures in order to grow a successful consulting company. And now, of all things, he had a travelling Christian ministry to take care of. Not that it was all that hard. Christians were like house cats, really. Just leave out the sustenance and let them roam in a confined space where they think they're free. Having to do the dirty work was nothing new for Thomas.

The girl reached into his open fly, going for his balls. He slapped her hand away, but then found himself watching her mouth work, so much blood rushing to his groin that his head felt light. He overlapped his hands near the nape of her neck and held her there, red curls twisted between his fingers, then bucked against her face, pushing more firmly when she tried to pull back. That's when he saw the blood spatter on his shirt cuff.

He finished, quick and quiet, and released his grip.

The girl sat up, tits spilling out of her open blouse, fat and veiny. "Mmm," she said, and wiped the corners of her mouth. "That was good, baby."

He called to his driver. "Robe?"

"Yes sir."

"Stop at the next gas station. I'd like beef jerky. And a Gatorade."

"Yes sir."

"Not the orange kind. That shit is terrible."

"Yes sir."

The girl strained against the seatbelt to lean her head on his shoulder. He shrugged her off and pulled his pocket square out to clean himself. She wiggled as close as she could get, watching him with needy eyes. Christ. Almost time to find a new one. He pointed to her chest and said, "Put those away."

"On second thought, no Gatorade," he said to the driver. "I want milk."

4

GOD OF ALL THINGS FIERCE

Zeus stood on the periphery of the group of hunters while they planned and packed for the cull in the church parking lot. He was ready to step up if someone would let him. He could have argued that being named for the god who was responsible for werewolves should mean something. But when the guns were shouldered and cocked for a last check, he flinched. Then there was the fact that he couldn't push a scope up against his thick glasses in a way that didn't make them shift, which skewed his vision so that he wanted to puke. And he didn't have a father to argue his case. It would embarrass him in front of the men if his mother tried to do it. So he backed down before he could step forward.

The job they gave him was the role of oshkaabewis—a helper for the ceremony to come. In the community that meant a church funeral, then a giveaway for some of Mere's things, and then a party to rival all the fiddles and wine in heaven.

The hunters counted bullets and consulted maps and then

slipped into the nooks of bush still left in their territory, knotted along the boundaries of domesticated land. They needed to kill the thing that took the old woman—to put down the animal that had tasted human flesh. It was solemn work dictated by the black-and-white laws of grief and peace. And they were glad for the chance to be tested, to play out the role handed down to them through blood memory. Even with their GPSs and Bass Pro Shop Gore-Tex vests they felt a connection to this old work, and they were grateful for it.

This was one way in which they pushed back against the jobs that took them into town, into the city. This was how they healed from the humiliation of tags and fines and charges levelled by agents of the Ministry of Natural Resources. The hunt was prayer. A few of them hoped they wouldn't have to be the one to take the target down. The rest asked to be the one who did. These were the men who carried tobacco with them to offer to the animals' spirits.

Zeus got on his BMX and pedalled out of the parking lot, heading to Ajean's. She was the oldest person in the community—the one everyone would look to for what they were supposed to do now. She was the one who gave tobacco to the hunters. She was the one who prepared her old friend Angelique for burial. She was the one who told Zeus he had to keep a close eye on his auntie Joan now.

When he got to Ajean's place, without him even asking, she sat Zeus at her table and set a baloney and jam sandwich in front of him.

"She needs you, boy," Ajean said. "No one else can reach her." She waved a gnarled hand in front of her face. "She probably can't even see the rest of us. We're just ghosts to her." She waved her arms in the air as if she were floating around the kitchen.

He had his orders. So he finished the sandwich, left his number with Ajean in case she needed anything, and got back on his bike. He carefully clipped his old Discman to his waistband and clicked play. By the time he crunched up the gravel of Joan's driveway, the back of his T-shirt was soaked through with sweat.

He walked in the screen door and called, "Hello?" No answer.

He went to the kitchen and got a glass of water from the tap, gulping it down so quick he struggled to catch his breath. Then he leaned against the counter and looked around. The house was small by most standards, just a living room crammed full of one-off furniture, a kitchen clattering with columns of china teacups and porcelain mixing bowls, one bathroom and a bedroom. The mudroom attached to the front doubled as both a laundry area and storage for camouflage snowsuits, fishing poles, boots and toboggans. Outside, the house was surrounded by a coven of birches pointing branches to the sky, their thin fingers linked in supplication, bark white as new dentures. The creek that ran behind them whispered eight months out of the year, telling anyone who would listen the best way to sit still. This was where Mere's trailer was. That's where he decided to head, refilling the glass with water to take with him.

The screen door bounced in the frame behind him as he stepped onto the back step. "Auntie?" he called.

He heard a constant swishing noise that didn't sound like the creek and followed it. The silver trailer glinted through the trees like a big fish, the water sparkling beyond it. He held the glass aloft and carefully made his way down the incline. He found Joan in front of the trailer with a bucket of soapy water, scrubbing the rocks around the firepit with a wire brush. The water in the bucket was pink.

"Hey, Auntie." He stood over her, his wide shoulders blocking the sun.

She looked up, still pushing the brush. "Hey."

"Can I help?" He did not want to help. He was exhausted from his bike ride. But he was a helper so he felt he had to offer.

She shook her head, dipping the brush and rinsing it.

"I can go get the hose?"

"No." Pink scum floated on the surface of the bucket.

He walked to the picnic table on the opposite side of the pit and climbed up to sit on the top. "Want me to call my mom? She can come over."

"No."

Zeus wondered whether the blood would ever come off. Mere loved these rocks. She'd picked and placed them herself. She called them grandfather rocks, round and grey with stripes of dark and lots of sparkle.

He jiggled his legs. There was a quiet panic in the movement. It made him feel exposed to see his auntie this broken. She was the one adult he knew who always stood in front of him, keeping bad things away as best she could. His mother wasn't much in the way of protector, and his father? Well, he wasn't really in the picture.

Bee was always stressing how she didn't abort any of her four kids. Then she'd tell you about the sleepless nights and the state of her nipples after six years of breastfeeding. She'd say, *My whole life is for those kids and I'll never fit into another pair of jeans as long as I live.* That she'd given everything she had to give. Zeus had heard this more than anyone else.

Joan was not a mother, but she seemed to understand that it was all fine and good to give everything, but being a mother also meant sometimes you had to create more just so you could hand it over. Find meals in the dust, build solutions out of napkins, conjure worlds from blood memory and then hand it all to your children as if it came easily. So you wouldn't burden them.

He knew his mother wasn't a bad person. She was funny and loud and made Christmas into Disneyland. But she had limits. Zeus lived in a small camp on the other side of Bee's limits. This had a lot to do with his father, Jimmy Fine.

Zeus had been told, time and time again, that Jimmy Fine was Bee's first real love. She already had Artemis with a guy from town. Art was about three when she met Jimmy, old enough to shit on the pot and eat a sandwich by himself, and so, old enough to go to a sitter's overnight. Art was quiet, content, a good sleeper, one of those first babies who trick their mother into having more kids. Later on, surrounded by his three brothers, all squalling and needy, Bee would call him the original con man.

The year that Art was old enough to be babysat and Bee had her boobs back, the reserve that sat on the island just off their bay hosted its first competition powwow. Indians of all shapes and sizes flooded into the territory. Corporate types who worked for the federal government showed up in their suits, shiny around the knees and elbows so you knew they were policy advisers at best. Teenagers with braids so tight they couldn't manage a complete blink and athletic wear two sizes too big crowded the ferry. Old women in long skirts and the kind of fingernails that were both rounded and ridged like tree bark found each other under the shade of trees. Married couples, carrying new babies in fully beaded cradleboards, dragging wild toddlers with broken sandals and runny noses, parked their jam-packed cars near the powwow grounds. And then there was Jimmy Fine.

He drove a burgundy 1979 Impala with the seat cranked way back so that he manoeuvred from a reclined position, arm straight out to grip the wheel. Beaded ropes, three faded pine air fresheners, an eagle feather on a leather string, a cheap white rosary and a baby picture of himself all dangled from the rear-view mirror. He had a big forehead that shone like a freshly greased pan and thin hair pulled into a narrow braid that fell to his waist, split ends like eyelashes exploding out of it. He might have been handsome if not for his teeth.

He had generous lips and a wide smile. But his teeth? It was like God put a bunch of potentials in a Yahtzee cup and tossed, thinking, *Fuck it, let's just hope for the best*. Vain hope.

But none of that mattered because in the trunk of Jimmy's dented Impala was the most beautiful, fully beaded traditional regalia the Ontario powwow trail had ever seen: side drops emblazoned with spirit bears and deep slashes of lightning; a vest, heavy with geometrics in glass beads, that closed with silver Indian-head nickel buttons; moccasins Jimmy resoled every fourth week so that the aphrodisiac scent of buffalo hide wafted when he passed by, copper ankle bells singing his steps like a goddamn wedding march. All this and the biggest, fullest eagle bustle you could imagine, plucked from the kind of eagle that hadn't existed since dinosaurs two-stepped the Earth.

When Jimmy swayed by during Grand Entry, raising his dance stick strung with bear claws in her direction, Bee, sitting on the bleachers, a scone-dog in one hand, a du Maurier Light in the other, felt her eggs vibrating in her ovaries.

In maudlin moods, Bee insisted that she had tried hard to be the kind of girlfriend Jimmy Fine wanted. She let him park the Impala in her driveway and wash it twice a week, even when he left the hose out afterwards along with the buckets of brown water and used sponges. She left Art at her mom's place for days at a time because it was hard to get romantic with a three-year-old demanding you examine each blade of grass and every flyer that was shoved through the mailbox. She cooked meat the way Jimmy liked it— overdone—and tried her best to appreciate powwow music in the car, on the living-room stereo and on his iPod when they lay in bed at night. She couldn't bead but she threaded his needles and bought him the things he needed to keep his legendary outfit crisp—tri-cut beads and sinew and hide and replacement bells when he danced them off. Sometimes she drove to Six Nations, two and a half hours away, to pick up supplies. She travelled with him to a new powwow every weekend, meeting his friends, making coffee runs for him and his cousins, chain-smoking in a lawn chair under his awning. She made sure his registration number was pinned on his regalia so that it wouldn't obstruct the best parts of his beadwork and that his bustle was tied up safely on the awning when he wasn't wearing it, staying nearby to keep passersby from handling it. She became smaller, quieter—living for Jimmy Fine and the ways she could be a better Indian through him. This was important for a halfbreed born of other halfbreeds.

Then winter came. Jimmy stayed on at Bee's, when he wasn't in Manitoba taking care of his mother. He slept late and then left the bed to move to the couch where he could watch TV and eat plates of fried spaghetti and bread balanced on his off-season belly.

Bee was seven months pregnant with Zeus when she met Jimmy Fine's wife.

Clarice showed up on a Sunday afternoon when Jimmy wasn't around. She told Bee that Jimmy already had a son, Jimmy Jr., who had been born with a malformed spine and would never walk. Clarice told Bee that this was why he was with her now, a baby on the way. All Jimmy wanted was a child to dance with him in matching regalia as he travelled the open road. Clarice said she didn't blame Jimmy and she certainly didn't blame their son. She was too busy caring for them both to cast blame.

The two women confronted Jimmy that night. He cried, then got angry at them, then cried again. At last, he told Clarice he wanted to stay in Ontario with Bee, that he felt like he needed to be here for the new baby. When Clarice drove off in her old van retrofitted with a wheelchair ramp, Bee felt that she had won. That she was actually grateful, and not on her way to jail for attempted murder, spoke to her diminished state.

By the time Zeus was two, though, Jimmy realized that his new son would never dance. The boy was deathly afraid of the drum. What his father didn't know was that after nine months in utero, hearing the drum echoed by his mother's anxious heart, the sound caused him acute claustrophobia. Bee did everything she could to persuade Zeus to dance, bribing him with food, with love, with her attention, and when he still refused, smacked his ass red.

Four months after his second birthday, Jimmy Fine sent Bee an email from Manitoba, where he'd been for the week visiting his first-born. In it, he explained that Clarice was pregnant with a little girl and that he'd had a dream about her being a champion jingle dress dancer. He told her he needed to stay there for the new baby. And that little girl did dance, like she was created for that very purpose. Jimmy Fine never came back.

Bee was humiliated as much as she was devastated. Humiliated by both losing her man and actually still loving the fuck. And she never forgave Zeus, even though she moved on from Jimmy, marrying Rocky, a kind, quiet man she'd grown up with. They had twin boys, Hermes and Hercules, and Bee turned all her attention to them. Her love for Zeus was a painful thud at the bottom of her broken heart—still there, still strong, but surrounded by a rattle and wheeze that made it difficult to hear.

And so Joan became the person Zeus needed to survive. Once, he heard his mother describe the ideal partner as a soulmate, someone who knew what you needed before you did and provided it. Someone who was happy you were there, even on the bad days. Joan was his soulmate.

And now she needed him. He put the glass down on the picnic table and stood up. "I'll go change the water."

He carried the sloshing bucket to the side of the trailer, careful not to get any of it on his grey jogging pants. He poured it out in the tall grass, watching red rivulets dash toward the bank of the creek looking to rejoin the stream. He made the sign of the cross. *Amen.*

He scooped up clean water from the creek and carried it back to the firepit. Joan was sitting back on her heels like a robot on pause with the brush still in her hands, her head down. Then she started her work again. He stayed by her side, quiet and observant, until she was done and the sun had moved to pull the trailer's shadow over them like a sheet.

"Wanna head to Flo's with me?" Joan asked him.

"Is she cooking dinner?"

Joan shrugged. "Probably."

"Let's go, then." He dumped out the bucket without being asked. The water was clear enough that this time he poured it directly into the creek.

They let themselves in and took a seat at the kitchen table. Flo was in the living room not really watching a rerun of *MASH*. She got up without a word and joined them, stopping to put the kettle on. Her eyes were red-rimmed and her hair was messy. She wore a T-shirt with the company logo and a pair of pyjama bottoms.

"Zeus, you been by Ajean's?" she asked.

"Yeah. She was headed to get Mere ready for tomorrow."

She sighed. "I know. I took her to pick out clothes and jewellery this morning."

"Mom," Joan cut in. "I really need to talk to you."

Flo and Zeus exchanged a look. Flo was right there at the table. Joan picked up a cardboard coaster and started bending the corners.

"When George and Junior came to get me, I was at the Walmart near Travis's place." She spoke fast, breathing hard, like she was running down a hill. "I found this tent there, a preacher's tent. The gathering was over but I went in. I don't know why, but I did. And there was a man there, and it was Victor. It was him—his eyes, his body, his voice." She sat straighter, refusing to look her mother in the eye, to see her doubt. Not yet. She had to tell the story, to get it all out first. "Except he was a reverend. And his hands, the way he walked—he moved different. I kept calling to him, talking to him, and he kept telling me he didn't know who I was, or even who Victor was. But it was him!"

She was growing frantic with how impossible it was to describe everything.

"And then he left me and there was this other man, a horrible man who told me Victor was dead. How would he even know? I mean, who says that? And he kind of laughed at me. He also called the ambulance and the cops."

She told her mother about being taken to the hospital, how she'd spent the night there and had been released the next morning. And then about taking a cab to find her car, and the tent was gone, and then finding out about Mere, and her voice hitched to a stop.

Flo listened all the way through in silence. Normally, she was one of those people who would stop a story to tell you the outcome it should have had if you'd done things right, which was always the way she would have done things. So the quiet was unusual.

Now she stretched once, running her hands through her short hair, which was still dark on top, though the sides had silvered. Then she leaned across the table and patted the backs of Joan's hands. There was a small pile of ripped coaster bits beside them.

"Ahh, my girl. There is too much on you right now."

It was clear her mother was more comfortable with the idea of Joan's irrationality than any kidnapping and brainwashing theory. Joan didn't blame her. Zeus stayed quiet.

Flo pulled her hand back and wiped the corner of her eye. "First Victor leaves you and then Mere. It's too much. It's just too much. There's no way to make sense of everything." She wiped her eyes again. "You know, it's not like everything was perfect with you and Victor."

"We had one fight!"

"Sometimes that's all it takes. Especially about something as big as this."

It was something big. But nothing could be big enough to tear them apart. Victor was the one person Zeus knew mattered as much to Joan as he did.

Flo had started in a few months ago with the subtle hints about how Joan had to move on—that "burying an empty coffin doesn't mean you need to jump in it yourself." Joan hated it every time her mother got onto that idea.

Flo softened a little at the look on Joan's face. "Love, do you really think your missing husband has somehow changed everything about himself and taken to the priesthood?" She folded and refolded the faded red-striped dishcloth beside her placemat. "And in a revival tent, no less? Jesus, at the very least he'd end up at the shrine proper and not in a parking lot."

It was so like Joan's mother to call Victor a hallucination and then criticize the hallucination's choice of career.

"Walmart? Victor? No way." Flo slapped the wooden table-top with the dishcloth. That was her halfbreed gavel—decision rendered. "Let me make some sandwiches. Then we should all have an early night. Funeral's tomorrow and we need the rest." She got up and went to the fridge.

Joan looked like a balloon with a leak, slouched in her chair. Zeus wanted to hold her, restore her shape, but the air was too heavy with words said and unsaid.

"And love," Flo said over her shoulder, "maybe don't talk about this, uhh, episode, to anyone else. It wouldn't be the best thing for your love life or the company. No one wants a crazy woman building their house."

Later, Zeus and Flo ate their ham sandwiches in silence. Joan picked at hers. They heard Junior drive up and Flo got up to take their plates to the sink. "Nothing about this to your brother, eh?" she warned. "He has enough to deal with right now. We all do."

"I have to get going, anyways. Lots of cleaning up still to do." Joan stood and Zeus did too and followed her out the door. They passed Junior on the porch and they all nodded at each other. The drive home was silent. Zeus didn't even listen to his Discman but kept his headphones in his lap. When Joan took the corner onto her dark street, Zeus glanced sideways at her. She looked tired, the kind of tired that comes with sick. Her shoulders were slumped but her hands were white-knuckle gripped on the wheel.

"You'll get him back," Zeus said. "I'll help. I'm a really good helper."

Joan smiled, for the first time since she learned about Mere, because this boy was so certain of his promise.

They parked the Jeep in the driveway and then both of them went down the hill to the trailer where a wild animal had killed Mere in the night, to finish cleaning. They even peeled swatches of red-splashed bark from the shaken birch trees, revealing underneath the resilient glow of something new.

5

NAMING THE BEAST

"You know what a man and a dog have in common?" Ajean asked Joan over tea at the round table in her small kitchen. Empty bottles and full ashtrays crowded every surface in the place.

Joan shook her pounding head, sore from whisky and tears, both of which were a bad idea to indulge in all night.

"Fucking." Ajean laughed hard and deep.

"Gross." Both the idea and the word seemed awkward coming from a toothless mouth. Why was Joan still here with the old woman?

"S'true. They even have a way of doing it named after dogs." Ajean leaned conspiratorially over the table, the tip of her grey braid dipping into her milky tea. "It's when the man is in behind, you know."

"Yes, yes, Ajean, I know what doggy style is. I don't know why you're bringing it up, though." Joan dug around in her purse on the wooden bench beside her and mercifully found a bottle of Tylenol. She unscrewed the cap with difficulty and fished out three. It hurt to swallow.

"Never mind, you. I could still have my choice of snag."

Joan glanced at her. Ajean could be telling the truth. She was lacking teeth, but she had the thickest braid in the over-sixty set and a beautiful tan face with wrinkles permanently etched into smile lines even when she scowled.

Last night's wake would go down in community legend. It started off with soup and bread and ended in a jig-off between old man Giroux and the Longlade widow. A tie was called and they went off to the bathroom to make out.

Joan was so worn out with her grief she gladly accepted the bottle when it passed her way the first time, and the second time, and soon she was hogging it all to herself. She'd woken up on Ajean's crochet-covered couch with a blinding hangover.

She didn't like being so vulnerable. Sure, Ajean had been ancient for about a hundred years and Joan was related to her in that way that almost everyone was related in Arcand, but to be so horribly hung over and broken open in front of her? That was uncomfortable. Also, why was the woman insisting on talking about sex over their morning tea?

She prayed to the gods of Tylenol to hurry up and get to work. "We don't need to talk about, you know, relations right now, do we?" she said.

"Relations?" Ajean quirked a brow at her. "Oh, you mean *fucking*." She laughed again. She raised the heavy mug to her thin face with a shaking hand and took a sip. Then she set it down and crossed the short distance to the fridge, pulling out a plate of sliced cucumbers lying in a pool of vinegar, dusted with salt and pepper, which she brought back to the table.

"There is no one right time to talk about men and women, it's all the time. And I'm only telling you so's you know what to do about your old man."

Joan's eyes snapped open wide and too much light got in, which was like being hit with a Taser in the middle of the forehead.

Ajean popped a cucumber slice into her mouth and gummed it a bit, watching the shock and embarrassment slide over Joan's face.

"Yes, yes, you wouldn't shut up last night, you. After everyone left, you talked a blue streak."

Joan was seized by a sudden urge to use the washroom. But dread filled the spaces left in her guts and she was unable to move.

"Did I?" She ran a hand through her long, tangled hair. "Did I, uh, talk to anyone else about Victor?"

Ajean shook her head. "You saved your confessional for me." She sucked the vinegar and salt off her fingers. "You just yelled at the others about leaving too early and then chased them into their cars, trying to wrestle the guitars from their hands. Then you sent them to the devil, spat in their headlights and said you could do it yourself, anyway."

She slapped the table and laughed. "Oh boy, could you ever. You took off your pants and sang Johnny Cash on the front stoop in those men's underwears of yours until Rickard from next door threw a boot at you like you were an alley cat."

If the table wasn't so hard and far away, Joan would have

dropped her head. "Christ." Johnny Cash, of course. That was thanks to Zeus. Because the man had called himself almost a full-blooded halfbreed in an old interview, he played Cash on repeat at all hours.

"That's okay, that's okay." Ajean patted Joan's shoulder. "But maybe you can go out there and try it again tonight. I wouldn't mind if he threw the other one so I had the full pair." She glanced over at a shiny rubber by the door. "Good for fishing, them."

She laughed real big, letting the puffs of sound fall between them.

"Listen, Ajean, I don't know what I said last night, but I'm not one hundred percent sure it's him."

"As if. You *know* it's him. What more do you need?"

Joan felt these words on her skin as much as in her ears, they fell with such weight. "But my mom——"

"Listen girl, your mom's a good worker and she's got them good boobs and all. But she don't know about these things. Now your mere, on the other hand, if the Jesus had spared her for a bit longer, she'd be able to help you." Ajean made the sign of the cross. Joan noticed that one of her work-whittled fingers was smothered by a family ring with two rows of cloudy birthstone gems. Probably an Avon special; all the grannies around here had them. It was an enormous source of pride to accumulate the most gems. It was also a feat of Herculean strength that their tiny hands could support such a weight, never mind that their small frames had supported so much life.

"Jesus had nothing to do with her staying or going. That was all devil." Joan didn't even realize she'd said these words out loud until she felt the back of Ajean's hand with that same heavy ring connect with her upper arm.

"What a thing to say. No devil could catch up to Angelique Trudeau. Don't say his name aside hers."

Joan bent her head, spending a minute examining the faded fruits printed on the placemat in front of her, waiting out Ajean's anger. "I'm sorry," she said at last.

"No, my girl. Your man—and it is your man to be sure, even if he doesn't know it—"

Joan interrupted. "He's sure he's someone else."

Ajean was quiet a moment. When she spoke again, all the teasing and mockery was absent. "Hunters came back with nothing."

"I know."

"That's because the killer already left the territory."

"I thought it was a pack that got her?" Joan asked.

"No. I cleaned her with cedar and dressed her myself. It was no pack." She sipped her tea. "It was just one."

"One dog?"

Ajean shook her head.

"A wolf, then?"

"Of sorts."

Ajean took another sip of tea and then turned the cup clockwise on the table in two full circles. "Rogarou came for her."

Joan stared at her. She had heard enough rogarou stories growing up. Tales of a human-sized black dog that guarded the roads were a good way to keep kids from wandering too far alone. She felt the piss wanting to exit her bladder even now when she heard the name. Maybe every kid from around here felt this way, but for Joan, there was something more to the terror. Leave it to Ajean to scare her in the midst of her grief. At least it was distracting. "A rogarou? No one noticed a giant dog wandering around."

Ajean was solemn. "Don't pretend you don't know about him. You came in this very room not so long ago, screaming over it."

Joan blushed. Yes, she had her own rogarou story. "I was a kid," she said. But she remembered the smell of it even now, the way that wrong scent had pulled all her nerves to the surface of her skin like a magnet. She'd come across that same smell not too long ago. Her skin crawled, remembering.

"Ajean, is it just halfbreeds who have a rogarou?"

"We don't have just one. There's lots of ways to become one." She counted on her fingers. "Being attacked by a roga-rou, mistreating women, betraying your people . . . that's the ones we know around here, anyways."

"But is it only us?" Joan interrupted.

Ajean used a teaspoon to scoop up the sugary syrup from the bottom of her cup and deposit it on her tongue. She swallowed, eyes closing on the sweetness, then said, "When I was in school, one of the grey nuns told me about these wolf men, stories from her home. Sure sounded like Rogarou. Almost. Less style. And I don't think they could dance like he does."

"The nun, where was she from?"

Ajean laughed. "Oh shit, she was mean. Fat and mean. She came from Germany. I got beat once when she caught me making fun of her. She had a good left hook, that one."

Joan put both hands flat on the table, holding herself upright. "I know who it is."

"You do?" Ajean leaned in.

"The rogarou. He's the goddamn rogarou."

"Who?"

"Mr. Heiser."

"Who the hell is that?" Ajean scrunched up her face. "Never heard a man of that name around here."

"No. He's not from a community. He works at the tent. Where I found Victor." She stood, her thoughts coming too fast. "Could that be why Victor is all fucked up?"

Ajean smoothed out the placemat in front of her. "The Jesus tent? Gee, I don't know. Don't know anything about those wolves from other places."

Joan got up and paced the small kitchen, knocking over a collection of empties near the fridge. "Why, though? Why would he come for Mere? Why would he have Victor?"

"Who knows why they do what they do?" She rubbed a finger along her gum, then picked up some spilled sugar with her wet finger and popped it back into her mouth. "Are you sure?"

Joan nodded. She was sure. "It's him, it's got to be. I know that smell. What the hell else would smell like that?"

Ajean thought for a second. "Death."

Joan felt the word slip into her stomach, making her queasy. "It's him."

"Well then, you know what you have to do now."

"No. I don't."

Ajean looked at her, serious and direct. "Go get your man from that wolf."

Before she fell asleep in the moonlight pushing through her window, Joan thought about their fight.

When her father, Percy Beausoliel, died at Commodore's halfway through a Labatt 50 while watching the Habs beat the piss out of the Leafs again, he was not a rich man. He'd spent a lifetime building houses for other families up and down the Bay, mostly gabled cottages with two-car garages. Over time, he had managed to purchase small parcels of land on his traditional territory. He wanted not only to keep some of it out of the hands of the dickholes from the city but also to build four homes: one for himself and his bride, and one for each of their children. By the time he slid off his stool and smashed his flushed cheek on the foot rail, felled by an aneurysm, he had amassed just under eighty-six acres in total. Sixty acres sat in one parcel about forty miles north of the Bay just past Honey Harbour. A trickle of a creek wound its way diagonally across it, ending in a small, deep pond just before the concession road in the southeast corner. The solitude and the water made it home to a number of deer families, wild turkeys, ducks, even some beaver. Joan's brothers, George and Junior, took that parcel together, vowing to one day put up a monster of a cabin. For now they were content to hunt the land.

Flo was more than happy with her small cabin by the marina that could be cleaned in less than an hour and where she could watch the boats moving back and forth between the islands. She didn't want any of it. So the other parcel of twenty-six acres, out past Lafontaine, went to Joan.

Joan wasn't a big hunter. After puberty set in and her interests diversified beyond those of her father, she didn't even really fish. But her land made her happier than she could have imagined. Her plot was less densely wooded than her brothers', with a central, small, open field greened by ostrich ferns. Black birch trees peeled and perfumed the shaded undergrowth. The Chicken of the Woods fungus climbed trunks and fallen logs like fleshy scaffolding for industrious squirrels. Reddish soil underfoot was knocked loose in spring by the new growth of fiddleheads and later by morels, like sweet, brittle claws. Walking there in summer was to be surrounded by the tiny flutter and flicks of insects that fed the birds, who in turn sang into the soft down of their nests. The place reminded her who she was.

She thought Victor loved it just as much as she did, until the night he suggested selling it to developers. He even brought home the paperwork.

"Look, babe, let's just discuss it. This is a shit ton of money—life-changing money!" He laid the sheets of paper on her lap. She refused to pick them up, but she did see the number. Six hundred thousand. It knocked the breath out of her lungs, but she turned the whoosh into a sigh.

"It's not up for discussion." She wiggled into the back of the couch so that the papers slipped off her knees and onto the floor between her socks and the coffee table.

He bent down and retrieved them, then read bits out loud, as if literacy were the problem. "A one-time payment in full of $600,000, if accepted within 40 days of offer, after which time the offer will be null and void. JT Development Corp will cover all costs associated with survey, legal fees and contracts. This offer is $180,000 over the assessed property value."

He stopped and searched her face. She pulled a foot up and tucked it under her thigh. "Victor, I am not selling my dad's land."

It was his turn to sigh. "But that's just it, Joan. It's not your dad's land anymore; it's yours. And I thought it was ours. Besides, you'd still have your brothers' plot in the family."

She shot him a look. "Yes, it is *ours* to enjoy, to build on. It's not *yours* to sell." She returned her gaze to the TV. She couldn't recall being more disappointed in him, ever. So she told him just that. "I can't believe you would even ask. It's like you don't know me at all. That makes me feel really lonely, Victor."

He stood up, tossing the remote onto the cushion beside her. He refolded the pages and tucked them into his back pocket, then walked to the front door, where he grabbed his grey wool jacket off the hook.

"Where are you going?"

"Going to the traps. Since you're already lonely, you might as well be alone."

That was the last time she'd seen him until he turned up as the Reverend Wolff of the Walmart Ministry, or whatever the fuck it was called. She'd got up and watched him out the window as he walked away from their home, his back a small wisp of grey against the blast-orange sunset that was all emergency and warning.

6

THE ROAD

Joan had grown up with stories. They'd covered her childhood, expanding and connecting until they tucked around her like a patchwork quilt. She didn't mind them when she was very small, but at around age seven they started to feel like the worry of old women with more time than teeth. The hours she was stuck spending with her mere and great aunts, in between euchre and rushing down to the shore to jump off the dock with her cousins, were the boring bits of the day. The year she turned thirteen, she decided she was too old for stories.

Two months after that monumental birthday, on the first day of summer holiday, her mother drove her and Mere over to Auntie Philomene's. As the Ford Fairmont bounced over the back roads, she leaned her head on her grandmother's smooth shoulder. Mere still smelled to her like Chantilly perfume and Ivory soap and safety. Flo drove away as soon as she'd unloaded them, back to the job site. Summer was busy season for the crew.

Philomene's apartment was all wood panelling and framed pictures hung according to a dozen different ideas of what was level. Her great auntie and Mere were already at the kitchen table, with mugs of tea and a deck of cards laid out in front of them, when Ajean came over from next door.

"Holy, Joan, you sure grew up," Philomene remarked, scanning her. Then she picked up the cards to shuffle.

"Got boobs and everything, my girl," Ajean said, without a hint of tease in her voice.

"Taking after your favourite auntie, then," Philomene said.

The old ladies looked at one another. These kinds of changes caused them new concerns, and they needed new ways to keep her safe.

Joan went over to the door, quietly pulling her sneakers back on. She had to get the hell out of here.

"Hey, come sit." Ajean patted the chair next to her. "You can deal the first hand."

Joan stayed where she was. She wasn't going to start her summer vacation the same way she'd been doing since forever, hanging out with old ladies doing old lady things. "I'm gonna walk over to Tammy's."

Tammy was the one cousin who would understand that thirteen meant something different was going to happen this year. And she lived near town, another bonus. "I'm probably going to stay at her place. So we can do stuff."

Her aunts and Mere looked at one another. Joan clarified. "*Fun* stuff."

"You shouldn't be on the road by yourself," Philomene said. "Summer people are around and we don't know them.

Plus, Dorothy said people saw a rogarou out there by Pitou's place."

Of course. A rogarou. It wasn't enough to imagine a man being turned into a vicious dog, she was also supposed to imagine that he was haunting the road into town. All the other kids from her class were no doubt at water parks or loitering at the mall, not having to deal with stories about monsters and the old women who told them.

"Here." Ajean held out the ace of spades to her.

"Jeez, Ajean, we need that to play." Philomene tried to snatch it back, but Ajean pulled it out of reach.

"If you're gonna go walking all over the Bay, you need to take this with you," the old woman insisted, flapping it at her.

Joan stayed by the door. "Why would I need an ace?"

"Not just any ace, the ace of spades. It makes the rogarou weak, gives you a chance to get away to try to switch him back."

Joan looked at her mere, who nodded, supporting Ajean in this.

"No, I think I'm good," Joan said. She pushed against the screen door and then made a break for it, calling back to them as it slammed, "And I'm not a little kid anymore."

The road curved as it climbed around the water's edge and past the small church where her parents had been married. The trees hung limp in the heat. Joan soon grew sticky with sweat, crunching along the gravel at the road's edge. Like lazy flower girls, birds too hot to fly rustled their wings and threw half-hearted chirps at her.

For the first time in memory, she felt completely alone. No pedestrians, not even any sidewalks. No friends, no grand-mother, no aunties. She felt her independence in all her limbs and stretched in the dusty heat. She was a grown-ass lady and she could do what she liked, and what she liked was to take a casual stroll to her cousin's house. She hummed her free-dom under her breath, stopping here and there to lop the heads off downy dandelions with a thin stick.

A sudden cloud covered the sun and immediately the breeze ran cold. And just as sudden, she didn't feel so alone. She walked faster. Why hadn't she called Tammy and asked her to meet her halfway? She came to the split in the trees where a dirt road led to old Pitou's boat shed. On a scratched post, a mailbox leaned precariously. And beside it, watching her with marble eyes, was a black, short-haired dog.

Jesus! She shuffled back a step. The creature didn't move. Didn't shift its gaze. Was it a statue? One of those weird cement animals that people decorated their garden beds with? It was glossy, vivid, not weathered at all. She stepped forward and reached out an unsteady hand toward it. "Good dog." Her brain screamed from somewhere in the back of her skull: *No one's lived at Pitou's for years. What's a dog doing here?*

And then the creature dipped its head, tucking its narrow snout into its chest. In a moment its legs unfolded, covered in dark fur and bent like a dog's, but much too long. It stood up on its rear paws, which were the size of an adult's splayed hand, revealing a torso that was sleek and wrapped in fur but without the barrel of protruding canine ribs. This chest was flatter and wider, muscled like a man's. The face was dominated by glint and wet—bright yellow eyes rimmed with a pink third lid, and a mouth rammed with splintery teeth, too many to comprehend.

She took in all these details in the nanosecond before she ran like the devil himself was at her heels, her arms pumping, dust in her lungs, ice at the back of her neck. She didn't stop until she got to Dusome's Garage, closed because it was Sunday and Dusome saved his Sundays for fishing. Joan huddled there, in front of the padlocked door, catching her breath, eyeing the road for the impossible black dog.

Each rustle of branches sent her spinning to check all around her. Eventually she began to pace in the driveway. Tammy's was too far to go it alone. She'd be easy prey. He'd chase her down with ease. How was she going to get home? She thought about heading back to her auntie's, but then she'd have to pass Pitou's again. A rogarou could tear you to bits. She'd heard countless stories about him, hungry for lone travellers—a dark emergency born of any number of transgressions. So many stories. And that's where she went now, looking for an answer.

Ajean had told her once when she was really little that there was a way to disarm Rogarou. "Remind him he is a man under it all. You can do it by making the thing bleed. Make him remember."

Joan found one of Dusome's old wrenches rusted to ruin at the back of the garage, tested its weight in her hand, even swung it a few times. Convinced it was a formidable weapon, she started back down the road to her auntie's. She was sure she saw the rogarou's shadow stretched across the pavement, his fur stiff even in the breeze.

"Alright then," she said out loud. "Let's see if I can jog your memory."

From behind her came the sound of a car. She watched it pass, wondering if she should call out to warn them, or better yet, to ask for a ride back to safety. It slowed down as it passed her, then came to a rolling stop. She picked up her pace, striding toward the shiny black door. Just then, a man stuck his head out the passenger side window. The way he looked at her, the way his lips curled into a cruel smile, caused her to stop walking, raise the wrench and square her shoulders. After a few seconds more of staring at her, the man pulled his head back inside and the car drove on.

When it made the turn onto Marina Road, she took off running, not pausing to more than glance at Pitou's lopsided mailbox where it stood alone and harmless at the side of the road. She fell twice because of the awkward swing of the heavy wrench as she ran, got back up and kept going, refusing to drop her weapon.

When she pushed into the kitchen, out of breath, the old ladies were still seated at the table. They didn't ask her about why she was back. They didn't question the wrench she put down by the shoe rack. They just dealt her into the game and started a new story. When she'd had some tea and her heart slowed enough for words, she told them all about it.

She'd since told herself many versions of that afternoon—it was a dog, it was her imagination, it was shadows. Eventually, those hours walking around the Bay, running into the rogarou, became so blurred they were lost to her conscious mind.

But like many things forgotten in childhood, they lived on in the way she behaved. She never walked alone. She thought she'd been told Pitou's was haunted and so she avoided that side road as much as she could. She feared men in unknown cars.

But now, the rogarou was back and very, very real. And like all things real, it could be killed.

☙❧

Two weeks later she got the call that set everything in motion.

"What time did the churchies show up?" Joan asked, her cellphone held to her ear with a shaking hand. She bent her toes around the metal railing of the kitchen stool, and her knees bounced in quick, nervous bursts.

"Rocky says they pulled into Hook River around two," said Bee. "He called while he was having lunch. I made him stop eating fast food on the road. He has to at least find a Denny's *and* get a salad instead of fries. It's why so many truckers are fat, you know—eating on the go like that." Bee's TV was loud in the background. "Hey, Wendy Williams got a new weave. You should see it, all ringlets and hairspray like your grade eight picture. Man, that shit was horrid. Remember?"

Joan let the comment go. Bee could have that one, a small payback for her diligence. Joan had been asking everyone she knew to let her know as soon as they heard anything about holy rollers in the area, telling them she was looking for a long-lost friend. It wasn't a lie, not really. So when Rocky noticed people in the next booth talking about a Jesus revival, he called Bee.

Hook River was a three-hour drive away. "What time can you be by to pick up Zeus?" Joan asked. Zeus had been stuck to her tighter than usual since Mere was killed. "I want to get on the road soon."

Bee ignored the question. Joan could hear her other three kids crashing around in the background. Apparently someone took a Lego to the eye. She asked, "Why are you so interested in getting religion now, anyways?"

"I'm looking for something."

"*Shut up, youse kids! Hermes, I swear to god, if you throw one more* . . . Like what, Joan? Jesus? All you're going to find in that tent is crazies with loose change to throw around. Come to think of it, maybe I should go. I could use a sugar daddy."

Bee could pry all she wanted, but Joan wasn't going to tell anyone else about Victor until she was sure. She glanced into the living room where Zeus had his headphones on and a book in hand. "I'll be gone overnight, so you should really come grab him."

"Yeah, but with Rocky on the road, I don't have anyone to watch the kids. And you know I can't drive; suspended licence and all. I could call around . . ."

"No, it's okay," Joan said, wearily, "I'll drop him off before I go."

"Thanks, Joan. You're the best." The kids started hollering for their mom. "Seriously, maybe I should come with you. I can be someone else's salvation for a change."

Joan hung up on her and sat a moment under the yellow kitchen lights. They hummed and flickered just enough to make the black-and-white linoleum vibrate. Out of habit, she counted Mere's thimbles on the wooden wall racks. Twenty-two. Who needed twenty-two thimbles when you only have ten fingers? She reached across the counter and grabbed the rack, shaped to resemble a barn, with twelve individual slots so each thimble had its own room like a lonely child. The final room contained only a circle on the bottom where the dust hadn't settled. Its thimble had been lost since the day of Mere's wake. She'd searched for it under the fridge, in the crack of the baseboard, but it had disappeared. The holder looked unfinished. Joan thought of what Mere had told her about beadwork.

"Do your lines straight, thread tight. But always include an odd man out, a different colour—like red in a sea of white, or blue cut glass in a line of turquoise seed beads. That's your spirit bead. It's a prayer for improvement."

Eleven thimbles. She'd been alone now for eleven months and twenty-eight days, she thought, as if her solitude was a toddler that required incremental milestones. She could organize her grief this way: one thimble for each month alone, a separate pewter divot to push her solitary moments inside of like a crumb of playdough.

She walked to the living room and tapped Zeus on the shoulder. He sighed dramatically before closing his worn paperback and pulling his headphones off.

"Yes?" He rolled his eyes until they met hers. "Can I help

you?" He gave her an exaggerated, tight-lipped smirk undone by the roundness of his cheeks.

"Listen, man, I really appreciate this fifteen-year-old-girl attitude you're trying out, but can you grab your stuff? I have to hit the road, so I'm going to drive you home."

He shrugged. "Fiiine." He placed the headphones back over his ears and opened the book. "But I really don't think Flo would be okay with you being on your own, especially not on a road trip. Not now. I can call her and ask? Maybe she'll want to go with you."

"You little shit."

He shifted the duct-taped Discman to his lap and pressed the volume button up three clicks. He'd carried that poor thing around since his dad gave it to him and Joan always checked second-hand stores for any new discs he might like. So far Johnny Cash and Willie Nelson were at the top, with "Folsom Prison Blues" and "Whiskey River" duking it out for his favourite song. He sang them both in a high soprano when washing the dishes or knitting one of his famous extra-long scarves.

She leaned over and kissed his shaggy, dark head, popping his headphones off his ears. She kicked at the full laundry basket by the TV stand. "Pick through this, because there's some of your stuff in there. Grab enough for two days in case we stay an extra night, or in case you shit yourself."

"Ha ha, Auntie. Very funny." He smiled despite himself, and began rifling through the folded stack.

"And call Bee and tell her you're coming with me. I'll be right back."

She left through the back door, the now familiar adrenaline stitching into her chest when she saw the birch trees. She watched her feet shuffling through the grass as she made her way down the hill. Head down was the only way to keep moving forward these days. A breeze came in off the creek and lifted the edges of her hair, causing a shiver down her spine. Passing the firepit, she glanced at the clean barrier rocks.

The trailer door was unlocked. It opened with a stiff yank, and chimes made out of small souvenir spoons tinkled. She stepped inside and was greeted by the smell of sweetgrass, then a heavy kind of emptiness.

Mere had spent her time here doing jigsaw puzzles or else preparing food and medicine. On the day after their fight, day one of Victor's absence, Joan had sat at the table while Mere worked in the kitchen.

"Here, my girl, wrap that string around the base." Mere was holding a bundle of small, leafy stems over the tiny sink.

Joan took up a spool of red twine and unravelled it against the stalks like she'd been shown, not too tight or the stems would bruise, not too loose so they didn't escape.

"It's just, I mean, why would he think it was okay to even bring it up? It's my land." Victor hadn't come home and Joan was sick with worry and electric with anger. She was still in her pyjamas—an old Pabst Blue Ribbon shirt three sizes too big and a pair of black bicycle shorts.

"Victor, he's from out west, isn't it? He didn't grow up in community, yeah?"

"He did when he was little, with his mom, but then he

went with his dad to Winnipeg." She cut the twine with a small pair of sewing scissors and knotted it.

"Sometimes we forget what's real. For him, he sees a different way of being secure, I suppose." Mere touched some of the smaller leaves thoughtfully with her pointed fingernail, appreciating the architecture of the plant. "It's not bad, just not right."

Joan sighed, sinking back into the built-in bench around the table. "I guess. But why didn't he come back last night?" She felt a twinge of embarrassment. Couldn't even get her man to sleep at home. That's the way Bee would put it. She'd heard her say it about other couples before. But she was more worried than embarrassed. He'd never done this before. What if he had fucked up? What if he'd got drunk and ended up with someone else and was too mortified in the sober light of day to come home?

Please don't let it be that.

Mere was quiet. She hung the bundle on the thin, white curtain rod over the sink, pushing the lace curtains out of the way. The rod was cheap but it could hold the weight of medicine. Most things could.

Joan went on. "I just mean, like, how do you not know what your wife would feel about something like that? Sell my father's land, Jesus. Why? Land's the only thing I would buy if I had money." She fiddled with her phone, opening and closing the main screen, checking that the volume was turned all the way up. The land wasn't the most pressing issue on her mind, but she didn't want to keep giving the other thing oxygen. Not out loud, anyways. Had he left for good? They never fought, but would he really walk away after one argument? How well did she know him if this was even a possibility?

"Can you track him?" Mere was pouring water over tea bags in chipped mugs.

"Like, through the bush? It's not like he went out on a hunt. And it's not like I'm all old-timey. Jeez."

Mere paused, the kettle held aloft. "No, dummy, on your phone, there."

"Holy shit!" She jumped up from her seat. "You're a genius! I didn't even think of that."

"Well, it's not like I'm all old-timey, jeez." She measured out sugar into the mugs and added, "Just kidding."

Joan slammed her phone down on the table a moment later. "Dammit, he has his turned off. It won't show me any-thing." She held her head in her hands. *Oh Victor, what have you done?*

Mere put the mug in front of her and sat opposite. "Chère, don't worry so hard. That man loves you. He's no fool—well, maybe about this land business—but with you, no. There is no woman alive that should make you nervous."

Now Joan stood in the kitchen, that same bundle of dry rasp-berry leaves bound with red twine hanging from the curtain rod, dry as bones, brittle as chalk. A thick rope of longing looped through her muscles, over and under her spine. *Mere, I need you so bad right now.*

She went to the back of the trailer, to her grandmother's bureau, and took three items: a deck of playing cards held by a length of red ribbon, a small nub of bound sage and the Swiss Army knife Mere had ordered for herself online. Boy, she'd been so proud of that. She'd waited for the Amazon delivery guy up at the road for days. Then she made her way back to the house to finish packing.

She checked the alarm clock on the nightstand—almost six. It might be too late to make the service in Hook River. But maybe she could wait out the groupies and the lonely lingering in the makeshift parking lot afterwards, along with the extra-holy who volunteered to clear the snotty tissues and boot-print mud cakes from the floor, and catch the Reverend on his own. And then she would know for sure.

She tucked Mere's three items into her bag and carried it into the living room, chucking the boy on the shoulder. "Come on, Zeus, we gotta hit the road."

7

THE MEMORY OF WANT

On the drive to Hook River, Zeus plugged Joan's phone into the stereo system so he could DJ. He'd introduce the songs, then pause them mid-stream to provide trivia. "Trent Reznor wasn't going to let Johnny Cash even do 'Hurt.' He thought it was too gimmicky. But after it was done he agreed the song belonged to Cash now—that he could never do it better."

"Good to know, Zeus."

"It's a big deal. He, like, sacrificed one of his most famous songs because Johnny just, like, marinated it."

"Marinated it?"

"Yeah, like he soaked it in Cashness and made it completely his own."

"Gross."

"It's true, though. You can't take the eggs out of a cake after it's been baked. Same thing. You can't un-Cash a song that's been Cashed."

"Just play it, you nerd. Or I'm going to put the radio on."

She reached over and made a half-hearted attempt to wrestle the phone from his hand.

"Okay, okay." He pressed play and settled back in his seat. An hour from their destination, he fell asleep.

Zeus's steady breathing was peaceful, and in that comforting silence, Joan remembered how much she liked the road. There were so many things to see and not enough time to overthink them. Out of the corner of her eye, as they passed a rundown bar with a hand-painted sign of a misshapen boar, she caught two women in sundresses slow dancing in the parking lot between a pile of firewood and a rusted-out pickup. Just as the sky swelled to the kind of deep blue that is velvet, a shooting star took its time swooning over the ragged dark of the trees. A family of deer on the side of the highway watched traffic with reflective eyes.

But the road also made her long even harder for Victor. Over the years, road trips were an excuse for them to be neither here nor there, free from their daily lives. Fucking in the back seat behind a Tim Hortons; tipping lamps off desks in motels that still had smoking rooms; enjoying the smell of themselves on each other's hands and faces while ordering breakfast at four o'clock in the afternoon at Denny's. They once parked on the side of the road just to run into a field tilled like corduroy. They drank red wine out of paper cups on the hood of the Jeep, watching waterfalls carve profiles into rock. And they stopped at every roadside attraction they came to, from a mystery hole in the mountains of West Virginia to a massive gunfight depicted by wooden cut-outs along a strip of dusty New Mexico highway.

She pushed the heel of her palm against the seam of her jean shorts, but that's not where the ache was.

❧

Hook River wasn't a river at all. It was a small community surrounded by patchy woods and rolling hills of grass and shrub, which had grown on the side of the reserve like a tumour. They arrived just after nine and she followed the posterboard signs to the gathering. When she parked the Jeep, Zeus stayed asleep. And so she got out on her own, closing the door quietly behind her. She lit a cigarette and took stock.

In the upturned palm of the valley sat the tent from the parking lot. Christmas lights had been strung around the door and along its seams. The whole thing glowed from the generator-fed spotlights that illuminated its insides—she could hear the hum from here. Vehicles from the reserve were parked outside, the passenger door on one F-150 left open so that the inside light wavered with the draining of its battery. She finished her cigarette and flicked it into the ditch, then crawled into the Jeep to change. She emerged in a tight skirt, heels and a low-cut sweater, and with a long, red coat draped over her arm. Rummaging in her bag for her knife, she found the bundle of sage. In the angle of her open car door, she lit the medicine. The flames undressed each stem in the bundle to thick smoke, which she pushed over her face and head, praying for whatever the hell it was going to take to get this done. She closed the door carefully, locked up the car so no one would sneak up on Zeus, pulled on the coat and lit another smoke.

She could hear the congregation singing from here, sound-
ing like a circle of wolves under the moon. Joan exhaled, listening for his voice among all the others.

Hallelujah . . .

The singing stopped and there was a burst of applause.
The tent started to empty. She inhaled, allowed the smoke to
roll over her tongue and fill her chest, then exhaled into the
navy night. She ducked her head to stare into the passenger
window to check on Zeus. He was still out. She started across
the field as people reboarded their cars and trucks and pulled
out of the makeshift parking lot in smears of light. As the
last of the cars swung up the road to her left, headlights
sweeping over the field, crickets replaced the choir. She
heard someone shouting: "Leave the chairs stacked at the
back for tomorrow." Then another voice: "Get those Bibles
into the bins."

As she drew close, Joan saw two men in blue shirts drag the
pale green velvet chair she'd seen on the stage at the Walmart
into a clearing at the side of the tent. They set it down on the
ground, then shifted it until the legs sat even.

And then the Reverend emerged from the back of the tent
and stared around the quiet expanse. He walked over to the
chair and settled himself, crossing his legs at the knee. He
wore a white suit and shirt, its stiff collar pushed together by
the clean knot of a black tie. He tilted his dark head back
against the worn velvet seat and seemed to be watching the
moon blow clouds from its full face. He lit a cigarette and put
it to burn in the crystal ashtray that rested on the wide arm, its
small light winking like a buoy. He was clearly illuminated in

that light suit under the full moon, but she couldn't do more than glance at him yet. She was trying to keep her guts from roiling.

If he saw her approach, he didn't let on. She hoped she could hold it together. She wouldn't try to persuade the Reverend that he was her husband, not straight on, anyways. If he was Victor and not her own madness, she didn't want to spook him. She searched the perimeter for signs of wildlife, especially those who could masquerade as man. He was alone.

He spoke first. "There are whole societies who based their science on the stars." He lifted a hand to gesture above his head. "As if these points were a manual of some sort."

The words and intonation were all wrong, but the voice . . .

She was so close that she could smell the good smell of his sweat, though it was mixed with something artificial, like cologne from a bathroom quarter machine. His dark hair was carefully combed, parted and oiled. There were no earrings in his ears, no tiny crucifix dangling from his neck, only a silver watch chain that stretched across his tailored vest.

She said, "And what's the better story? Some white guy on a throne held up by cherubs and weather?"

He pushed air out of his nose in a kind of laugh, tapped ashes off the end of the unsmoked cigarette and regarded her in the glow of the tent lights.

She fought to stand still under his gaze, then shifted her weight onto one leg and pushed out a hip. *That's right*, she thought. *Take it all in*. But if he appreciated the view, she couldn't tell.

"So nice to see you again. Joan, right?" He was being conversational. It hurt like hell. "What's it been, a month, maybe two? I've thought about you since that day."

Her rebellious heart leapt and she put a hand on her chest to hold it in. "You have?"

"Well, it's not every day someone comes into the tent claiming I'm her long-lost husband. Don't be ashamed, though, Joan. Addictions can be demon enough without the heat and lack of sleep. I hope you've been feeling better."

"I'm not a drunk." She reached into her coat pocket and fingered the tin of cigarettes, then the well-worn edges of softened playing cards. The other pocket held her Zippo. And her knife. She felt the weight of both but made no move toward either. She nodded toward the ashtray. "You smoke now?"

He looked down, almost surprised to see the lit cigarette there. "I enjoy the smell of smoke. I don't much care to inhale, but there's something about the smell."

She watched his hands, the way his fingers still looked callused even though the nails were neatly trimmed. She wanted to push those hands inside her blouse. Instead she spoke, struggling to keep her voice even.

"Maybe it reminds you of something. Or someone."

He didn't answer right away. Instead, he crushed the cigarette out and placed the ashtray by his feet.

"Could be." He smiled to himself, not her, then met her eyes. "Did you come to service tonight? It was a good one."

"No. I stay away from things that make me feel hopeless."

"Hopeless? How can a place of hope make you hopeless?"

It was her turn to half laugh. "A place of hope? How do you feel any shred of hope for humankind around a herd of sheep?"

Easy, Joan. Easy does it. What if he got up and left?

"Sheep?" He pointed upwards with both index fingers. "It's not such a bad thing to be sheep when you have such an excellent shepherd watching over the flock."

"Are you talking about Jesus here, Reverend? Or yourself?"

"I am a mere instrument, and lucky to be so. It's always Jesus."

She looked around in the dark, a slice of pale light from the open tent illuminating the space between them. "You have anything to sit on out here, I mean, besides your fancy chair?"

"Afraid not, I don't usually have company this late."

"Well, it might be a good idea to have another chair or two out here." She struggled to find a way in, then said, "Me, for one—I am a little shy of the crowd, but I like the idea of some private time with . . . God."

He checked her face for humour and found none. "I guess I could ask that a folding chair be brought outside, in case you continue to materialize out of the night." As he waved a hand, she noticed that Victor's gold wedding ring had been replaced by a wide silver band etched with the outline of a dove. Blood rose in her cheeks. He was looking up at the stars again, a slight smile on his lips. She decided to tell him a story. She needed to break his composure, remind him he had a cock or draw blood, as Ajean had insisted.

"The very first year my husband and I were together, we went south on a summer road trip."

He refocused on her. She shivered, having forgotten just how fixed a person felt in that stare. She was expecting a reproach, maybe a Bible quote to head her off at the pass, but none came, so she carried on, pulling the memory out into the night like a siren song.

"It was a hot summer to begin with, even here. The kind that makes you wish you could peel your skin back. By the time we got to Alabama, we were damn near crazy with it. I took off my pants and rode in my underwear and a tank top, with my bare feet stuck out the window. God, I remember my panties felt so tight in that heat, just a strip of cotton holding back this painful swell." She laughed low in her throat. "Victor was so distracted he almost drove us off the road. I was desperate to crawl onto his lap and kiss him."

The Reverend shifted in his chair. She reined the story in a bit. She couldn't get him to unforget if he refused to listen.

"We'd bought this ridiculous tent at a second-hand store on the way south, an old army pup tent." She laughed at the memory of it. They barely fit lying side by side and Victor couldn't stretch full out. "We had a twelve-pack of Pabst and a couple of bags of chips, so we were totally prepared to rough it for the night."

They'd headed for the abandoned set of a Tim Burton movie she'd read about, built on an island in a brown lake in the middle of the Alabama backwoods. Twice the GPS led them astray, but they got there just before dusk. An old man sitting in a basket-weave lawn chair by the bridge charged them five dollars for a camping pass and hand cranked the gate open so they could enter.

They'd found a secluded spot behind the gingerbread church, which was now a night pen for the goats that wandered the island. They set up their majestic tent and snapped a couple of Pabsts. It must have been forty degrees Celsius.

Joan lit another cigarette, watching the Reverend watch her lips as she did. She moved a little closer.

"We were so sweaty from the drive, we stripped down to our underwear and waded out into the lake. Victor was nervous because there were dead trees sticking out of it like skeletons, and he was worried their roots would be a haven for alligators, snapping turtles, anything. I mean, we were in the South. I swam out to the trees and climbed one of them. Above the water line, the wood felt baked, all dry and chalky.

"I looked back at Victor and it was clear he wasn't going to come to me, so I swam back to him. He was chest-deep in the water, so I just wrapped my legs around him where he stood, and pushed myself against him under the water."

Joan crossed the remaining distance between them and perched on the arm of his chair. He kept his eyes on her, watching her smoke. When she placed the cigarette in his ashtray, he watched her hand.

She had his attention now, but she had to go slow. She ran a hand along her skirt, smoothing the material over her thigh. She heard his breathing change.

"I felt like we were being watched out there." She lowered her voice so that he had to listen closely. "I could feel eyes on us but saw no people, just the skeletal trees and the brown lake. Victor, he had these big hands, you know. He held me up so that my face fit into that spot on your neck, just by your collarbone. My auntie Dorothy told me that spot was made specifically for women to rest their heads. That's how she knew Creator was a woman."

She took a risk here and reached for his collarbone to show him the exact spot. When he didn't flinch at the touch of her fingers, she laid her palm flat against his chest.

"So there we were, making out in the middle of a cemetery lake, in the absolute heat and quiet of an Alabama July, and I see a large, grey goat, real fat. Behind him, farther up the hill, are four more, probably his wives, though I don't know much about the romantic lives of goats. They're not moving, not even chewing. They're just standing there, watching."

She turned, hand still on him, and hooked her gaze into his eyes, trying to find her husband. She edged her fingers toward the buttons of his shirt. She just needed to undo a couple, to see his skin, to see the familiar lines of Victor's tattoos so she knew it was him for sure.

"The thing about goats is their eyes. They're all geometry. They remind me of cameras and screens, not living things. I know it's weird but that small audience, well, it made me kiss him harder, made me move against him a little more." She was whispering now and his head tilted toward her mouth, so he could hear her. She bit her bottom lip. "Just a little more—"

"Reverend?" The woman, Cecile, walked out of the tent. When she caught sight of the chair they both now shared, disapproval squeezed into her voice. "Oh, I thought you were alone."

Frustration made Joan's chest ache. She had to consciously push it down, find the seam and fold it into a small enough shape so that it wouldn't burst out of her. She didn't want to scare him off. But Wolff stood up in one quick, smooth movement. Her hand fell back into her lap, a bird shot out of the sky.

"Cecile." He walked over to the girl, who worked quickly to erase the hurt on her face. "I was just checking in with Joan here—our visitor from the Orillia meeting, you remember?"

"Who could forget?" Cecile said, staring at her. She glanced at the Reverend and sweetened her tone toward Joan. "We were worried about what happened after you went to the hospital, given the delusions you were suffering. How are you now?"

"Not delusional at all." Oh, this was torture. "Less delusional than most, I would say."

Joan stood, taking care to let her coat fall open to show how her heavy breasts wrecked the lines of her good blouse.

Cecile's smug face fell. She said, "Well, we're headed out for the evening. Reverend, let's get you back to the motel so you can rest. This is only day one here." She laid a hand on his wide back and turned him toward the tent. "Mr. Heiser doesn't like us to keep you out too late."

Joan's throat tightened at the name. She watched them walk away, trying not to run after him. Then he called over his shoulder, "You should join us tomorrow, Joan. I'd love to see you at service. We begin at six tomorrow evening."

Cecile was quick. She stopped and turned to Joan. "Yes, we would love to see you. We always welcome new worshippers."

Joan smiled, slow and wide. "I might just come see you,

then, Reverend. Save a seat for me." And with Cecile watching, Joan lowered herself back down on the arm of the plush chair, as if the Reverend were still there, swinging her leg so that a good length of thigh dangled in the light from the tent.

When she got back to the car, Zeus was playing a game on his phone.

"Jesus, took you long enough." He sighed. He was never good after naps. "Next time wake me up so I can go with you. Anything happen?"

Joan didn't answer, just shook her head. She drove thirty minutes back down the road and checked them in to the New Star Motel. She paid a hundred for the night in cash and parked in front of room seven. She unlocked the door and Zeus went in. Then she went back out to the Jeep, unloading her bag and locking up. Back inside the room, she heard the shower running. She was exhausted. She stripped down to her panties right away, pulling on one of Victor's old work shirts as a nightie, the grey one with the peeling eagle on the front and the cut-off sleeves. She went online on her phone until Zeus was done in the bathroom and had climbed into his double bed, then she went to clean up. It wasn't until she was washing her face that she realized she was smiling, hard. It made it difficult to get the makeup out of the lines around her eyes.

Tomorrow. Tomorrow she'd try to yank him free. She didn't need to see his tattoos. She'd seen her husband's eyes behind the Reverend's facade. She still didn't understand what had happened to him, or what a white man with a roga-rou in him had to do with all this, but at least now she figured she could get him back.

She did a quick check behind the headboard then, between the mattress and the boxspring, for bugs. Finding nothing but cobwebs and an old *Penthouse* magazine, she slipped into bed. The sheets were cold and she had to punch the thin pillows into comfort, but still she was happy—or at least, happier than she'd been since Victor walked out of the house.

Lying under the popcorn ceiling, listening to traffic on the highway wheeze metal and smoke, she tried to imagine what was going through Victor's mind right now. Was he with Cecile? Were the memories she'd shared with him beginning to take on colour? Was he touching himself at the thought of her? Or was he sitting in that ridiculous chair reading his stupid Bible?

She threw off the scratchy blankets and rolled onto her side. From the drawer in the nightstand she removed the paper-back King James version stowed there, with its onion-skin pages and a crisp, unopened cover. She got up and walked quickly over the questionably squishy carpet in her bare feet and yanked open the door. The parking lot was illuminated by weak lamps affixed to the motel wall, shining like dull coins in grey water. She stood there for a minute holding the unread Bible. The moon was a perfect hole in the sky, bleed-ing the edges of the night to silver.

Then she cocked her arm back as far as it could go and threw the fucking thing. The covers opened and the pages flapped a frantic kind of applause until it landed with a light thud, gold-lettered front face down. Just a book. She locked the door behind her.

She had the best sleep she'd had in a year, eleven months and twenty-eight days to be exact.

VICTOR AND A NEW SOUND IN THE WOODS

Victor was thinking of his uncle. Etienne Boucher had been a large and quiet man, who moved like a ship on open water. He wore double socks even in the heat of summer, especially when he was puttering around in moccasins. In the winter his boots left snowshoe-sized footprints in the snow. Young Victor had had to jump from one to the next when he trailed along behind him. The year he could match his uncle's stride was the year he decided he was a man.

Victor remembered his uncle and tried to make his footsteps just as steady and quiet as he walked in the bush. Because he was being hunted. He was sure of it. There was a new smell in the woods, wild and refined at the same time, like body odour on silk. Something was watching him.

And then he heard her voice from far away. There was no mistaking her.

"Joan!" he called.

The voice paused, but then the muffled lilt began again,

somewhere above or maybe below him. He strained to hear and caught the maddening sound of music, too far away to recognize the tune. He ran a small circle in the space he knew to be the eastern clearing, slowing every few feet to listen, to see if he had come any closer to her. Then he tripped and landed so hard on his chin his jaw shifted.

"Joan!"

He scrambled to his hands and knees, and then leaned to press an ear to the ground. Her voice was no clearer. He scraped handfuls of dirt out of the way, then stuck his ear in the hole. She wasn't down there.

He got to his feet and turned his face to the sky. Her voice was still far and small, but he could tell she was upset. He'd been with her long enough to know it was best to stay quiet when she was upset. But not now. Now he would take a verbal headlock just to feel her curses on his skin, to stop her words with his own mouth. He'd swallow them all.

He leaned against a tall pine and sighed. How long had it been since he'd seen her? How long had he been here on the land, walking the same twenty-six acres? No matter how long he walked, he never found the road. Never came across his four-wheeler or the adjacent tract of sugar bush or the wreck of old Dusome's Garage. There was just grey light and black dark.

Fuck.

When did he sleep last? Why wasn't he tired? He thought maybe it was time to bunk down, anyway, and he slid to the ground. His chin hurt and he wiped at it, feeling a thickening clot of blood. He must still be alive if he could bleed.

Joan.

He couldn't hear her voice anymore, and the music had hiccupped out of range. He felt half erased. Except for the longing for Joan, there was only the new fear cutting through his cloud of confusion. Because as sure as he knew it was Joan's voice, as sure as he knew the blood on his face was red without being able to see it, he knew that something was in the woods with him. Close by. He made his breathing quiet. At the base of the pine, he curled up to make himself small, less of a target. To become a part of the tree. To disappear.

Twigs snapped in the dark to his left, scaring small animals into the higher branches. And now a knock, as if on a door, on a nearby trunk.

He opened his eyes as wide as they could go and willed sight into the stew of black. If he reached out, what would his fingers find? He made fists instead and jammed them into his coat pockets, pulling his face down inside the collar.

Joan better find him soon. Before the something else did.

8

REWIRED

Joan woke up when Zeus turned on the TV.

"Looks like rain today," he reported.

She rolled over. The light coming through the sheer curtains was grey. "Better not go out. You just might melt since you're so sweet," she said in a high-pitched voice. A pillow hit her back and she laughed.

"It's ten thirty. Can we go for breakfast?" he said.

She yawned and pulled herself up against the headboard, trying to organize her thoughts. They had hours before they had to get to the tent for the next revival. "Sure, why not."

She threw the blankets off. "Need the bathroom? I'm getting in the shower." He shook his head.

She carried her makeup bag to the bathroom and set each item on a folded towel on the counter. She turned on the shower and made the water nice and hot. Her favourite thing about motel rooms was all the hot water, not like at home. She used the shitty motel shampoo but her own peach-scented conditioner. Then, with the conditioner still slicked on her head, she shaved her legs.

She turned off the water, dried off and wrapped herself in a thin towel. She blow-dried her hair, then plugged in the straightener, smoothing her dark hair until it gleamed. With any luck, she'd be bringing Victor here tonight before they drove home together. She'd better get an extra room for Zeus, she thought, because she and her husband had a lot of time to make up for. "Prepare for the outcome you want," she said to her reflection.

Getting dressed with the anticipation of sex is a different experience than just getting dressed. She smoothed the lace band on her underwear against her hips so it was without a fold or wrinkle. She snapped her bra on the last hook, then reached into each cup to jiggle her boobs upwards so that they sat together, making that nice line under her clavicles. She turned in front of the mirror to admire herself and then applied her makeup. It was exciting, after a year of mourning and regret, to be beautiful in panties and red lipstick.

She pulled on tight black jeans and an oatmeal-coloured, loose-knit sweater whose neckline draped low and wide. The skin was a little much, so she threw on a necklace, the one with the silver handgun charm that Victor had given her one Christmas. She held it in her hand for a moment to warm it up as she checked the time on her phone. Eleven forty-seven.

There was a Denny's just up the road. She'd take Zeus there, come back to the room for a final once-over, then get to the tent nice and early to grab a seat near the front. She wanted to be able to maintain the kind of eye contact with the good Reverend that was impossible to ignore. She glanced one more time in the mirror, then came out of the bathroom, grabbed her purse, her coat and the room key on its blue plastic tab.

"Ready?"

"Yup." Zeus turned off the TV and scrambled off his bed. He was putting on his shoes as she opened the door.

With a soft thud, a book, heavy with condensation, fell at her feet. It was the Bible she'd tossed—it must have been propped up against the door. Adrenaline pushed into her blood, cold and fast. She looked around the parking lot. Most of the cars from last night were gone, except for the Jeep and a sad hatchback leaning to one side.

Zeus was behind her now. "Let's go, Auntie."

She didn't move.

"Auntie?"

She used the toe of her sneaker to push the book to one side. She stepped out of the way so Zeus could get around her and closed the door, double-checking that it locked. Maybe it was housekeeping. But there must be forty rooms here over the two floors. How would housekeeping know which room the Bible belonged to? Unless someone saw her throw it.

She put a hand on Zeus's shoulder and kept her head up, scanning their surroundings on the walk to the vehicle. She looked in the window before she unlocked the passenger side door. The seats were empty except for his black hoodie. "Buckle up," she said after Zeus climbed in, slamming his door shut. She checked the top-floor balconies and the metal stairwell as she went around to her side. She slid in and pushed the door lock back down. She felt safer in the small space.

Zeus was watching her anxious movements. "Everything okay?"

"Of course." She set her purse at her feet, glancing at their room, where the soaked black book lay on its back under the window.

She put the key in the ignition and turned. Nothing.

She turned the key again. Click.

"Fuck." She took the steering wheel in both hands and shook it.

"What's wrong with the car?"

"No idea. I just got the damn thing serviced."

The Jeep was old, but it was reliable. And last month she'd had it fixed up, replacing the brake pads, changing the oil, repairing a small crack in the windshield. What could be the issue?

She watched the wind flip the cover of the Bible open so that the pages jumped and snapped.

What if someone had done this on purpose? The cab of the Jeep was too silent, like a breath being held. What if they were still in here? She pulled her seatbelt slack and craned around to check the back, as Zeus watched her curiously. Empty.

"Ridiculous," she said.

"What is?"

She shrugged and dug her cellphone out of her bag and called roadside assistance.

❦

"Well, here's your problem right here."

Barry, the CAA guy who'd shown up in a flame-painted tow truck, held up the ends of two wires. "Your battery connection has been cut."

"Cut? How would that happen?"

He scratched his ginger beard. "No idea, lady. You piss someone off?" He snort-laughed and dropped the ends.

She was glad that Zeus was back in the room, flaked out on the bed and preoccupied with a game on his phone. It was almost two o'clock—it had taken far too long for Barry to show up.

"So can you replace them?"

He leaned on her fender, like they had all the time in the world. "Nope. But I can tow you to a garage in town." He pushed the dirty brim of his baseball cap up and down as he spoke, as if fanning his overworked brain. "I'm just the knight in shining armour who can get you there."

Yes, because Joan's knight *would* wear jogging pants and a windbreaker that kept pulling up when he moved his arms, revealing the bottom slice of a hard, round belly. But what choice did she have? She nodded and he dropped the hood and headed to the tow truck to hook her up. She went to collect her bag and her nephew from the room.

As they were about to climb in, Barry moved aside his cooler and a stack of clipboards, newspapers and empty chip bags. He patted the bench. "There's more than enough room for you," he said. "Your boy can ride shotgun. Seeing as how you're so slim, you can squeeze in beside me." She ignored his flirty tone as best she could, careful not to kick the open juice box on the floor, pretending not to see the weekly paper on the dash folded open to the escort section. The Bible waved goodbye in the wind as the tow truck pulled out of the motel parking lot, her Jeep hanging from the back like a field-dressed deer.

The town was ten minutes down the road, one of those ugly clusters of gas stations and fast food restaurants that pop up on the side of the highway. They took a residential street lined with houses that looked condemned, yards littered with children's plastic slides and ride-on toys, to Sunny's Garage.

"I can't believe people live here." She hadn't meant to say it out loud.

"Yup. Just a couple hundred now. Not for long, though. They're extending the natural gas pipeline, so there should be some new jobs coming this way."

"Oh yeah?" It was 2:26 now. She started biting the skin around her nails.

"Yup. The company was here last month. Had one of those town hall meetings. Just need to get some permissions and then it's a go. I might give up driving for one of those jobs. Good pay, great pension. I'm pretty much a free man and can make that kind of change. You know, seeing as how there is no Mrs. Barry." He took his eyes off the road to look at Joan over the top of his mirrored glasses, which had bright red frames and looked like something a race-car driver or a douchebag would wear. She pretended not to catch his drift.

The clouds were pulling together and splitting back apart like a fist clenching across the sky. Joan's stomach mimicked the movement. She had to get to the tent. She refused to think about who might have cut the battery wires; that was for later, once she was back on the road and headed toward her husband.

Sunny's was a double garage with missing siding under a broken yellow sign. It was run by a diminutive man wearing overalls dark with grease and sweat, one leg rolled up to show the mottled shin of an underfed bachelor.

"Listen, honey, you got another problem here." He was on his tiptoes, head in the engine.

"What?"

"Well, basically your system is shot."

In her growing hysteria, she pictured a bullet hole. "Shot?"

"Well, not actually shot." Sunny giggled. "That was what you call a figurative speech."

"You mean a figure of speech."

"No, *figurative*." He snorted at her ignorance. "Looks like someone popped out some fuses. Straight up took 'em."

She shook her head. "Missing fuses? How in the hell does that make the system shot? Just replace them. It's not complicated—and not expensive."

"Ho ho." Sunny gave her an appraising look. "I love a little lady who knows cars."

She frowned. "It's common sense . . ."

"Listen, I'm not here to pass judgment," he waved her off with a greasy bandana in his hand, "but I think you made an enemy, eh? Foolin' around with someone's old man, maybe?" He giggled again, wiping his tiny hands on the bandana.

Joan leaned against the driver's side door and sighed. "I'm not even from here. And my car was fine last night."

"Well, I can replace the fuses but I may have to order in the wire. And there's people ahead of you in line."

Joan looked around the parking lot. Besides the tow truck and the Jeep, there was one ancient Beetle and a massive four-by-four with Sunny's logo on the side.

"So you're looking at tomorrow afternoon at the earliest."

The clouds pulled over the sun like a thread had been run through their edges. The wind grew colder and debris skidded across the lot. Joan kicked some small rocks by her foot, thinking hard about the fact that someone wanted her to be stuck and who that might be.

"There's no way to hurry this up?"

Sunny shook his little head, the tendrils of his comb-over shooting straight up in the wind.

Barry was still lurking, pretending this was the perfect time to clean out the cab of his truck and do some paperwork. Zeus stayed with him, somehow withstanding the heavy metal coming from Barry's radio even though it sounded like a bagpipe in a hay baler. Joan knew what she had to do. She told the mechanic to go ahead and dragged her feet over to the tow truck.

"Hey, Barry, what are you doing right now?"

❦

She paid for the ride to the tent site with conversation. She learned that Barry was a Sagittarius, that he was allergic to garlic and that he preferred TV to Netflix. ("I don't like some robot suggesting what I might like next. The TV doesn't tell me what to like.") She listened. Barry told her he liked Indians okay, at least he liked their tobacco and casinos. And his mother had raised him by herself, which is why he felt inclined to stay in the area until she croaked, as he put it.

He droned on, the sound of his voice the background track to the smear of yellow line, blur of ditch and browning field out the window. The earth was not yet frozen, but Mere's bones would have begun to sing their terrible ache of cold; you couldn't fool them with false summer. You couldn't fool any part of Mere, not even her damn bones, which lay in St. Anne's cemetery now, shrouded in a floral print SAAN dress of impossible blues, the kind of blues that could only exist in climates where cold made no dent in the air.

They pulled into the makeshift parking lot at 5:26.

"We really appreciate you taking the time to get us here," Joan said, turning to face him. Zeus, still wearing his headphones, gave him a quick nod and climbed out of the truck.

"See ya, little buddy," Barry said, and leaned forward to look at the tent out the windshield, whistling through the gap in his front teeth. He glanced back at Joan. "I never would have pegged you for a Bible thumper."

"Oh, I'm not. But I have to meet my husband here."

"Your husband?" Barry's posture changed, one shoulder at a time. He dropped the small Tow-to-Tow business card with the handwritten number he was holding onto the chip-strewn floor.

"Yeah. Thanks for the lift!" She slid across the seat and climbed down, then slammed the passenger door behind her. She waved him off with a smile. It wasn't until she watched him turn back onto the road that she realized that now they didn't have a ride back to the motel.

Shit.

She'd worry about that later.

9

JOINING THE FLOCK

There were already people inside, the front half of the tent full. They wore black T-shirts with tour dates of country music artists fancy-lettered across their backs. They wore jeans or long-sleeved dresses from Reitmans *circa* 1986. They had non-ironic overlarge glasses that magnified their dark eyes enormous, and they tapped Reeboks with support soles and Dollar Tree jelly sandals on the temporary floorboards of the tent. They were freshly washed in their uncomfortable best and buoyed by something Joan could not see, their brown cheeks gold under the string lights. They struck her as beautiful.

The white chairs, the white canvas roof and walls, the white lights, the white handlers all conspired to illuminate your chipped nail polish or uneven sideburns, yet at the same time, forgave you for them. They would overlook your short-comings because they were so much better than you.

"Excuse me, miss," said a man in a cowboy hat, who smiled as he pushed past Joan and Zeus where they stood looking around.

"Sorry about that," she said, elbowing Zeus down the aisle toward a row.

He pulled his headphones down and pocketed his phone. "This place is insane." There was actual worry on his face.

Clean, lovely youths like the ones she'd seen at Walmart were doling out pamphlets and hugs in equal measure—an army of khaki pleats, blue shirts and good manners. Could one of these holy assholes have fucked with her engine? It was hard to imagine any of them even knowing how, but if not them, then who?

Joan squinted but could see no sign of the Reverend yet. Or Cecile. Were they together right now? Was she bent over a table of collection plates backstage, her khaki skirt shimmied up over her hips, panties down to her white Keds with Victor behind her?

"Can I offer you some good news, sister?"

A helper was coming toward them holding out a pamphlet. She didn't recognize him, but he was beaming away at her and wore the blue shirt emblazoned with a small, white cross where an alligator or polo player should be. He was so clearly without malice, she found herself smiling back.

Zeus took the handout from him, saying, "Sure, I can use some good news," and turned into a row of chairs. Joan followed.

"Have a great service," the helper called after them.

Zeus sat and Joan settled beside him. He said, "Man, it

smells weird in here. Like farts and gym shoes," as he handed over the pamphlet. Joan gave him a nudge with her elbow and told him to shush.

She glanced at the front of the pamphlet, where, on a blue background decked with a bedazzled cross, were the words *The Ministry of the New Redemption.*

Inside were pictures of people who looked like they came from a stock photo search for "Indians: smiling, laughing." There were babies in frills and twin boys and old men in camouflage vests. The women were drinking tea together, the grannies with their kerchiefs tied under the bulbs of their chins, and the children were running carefree through tall grass or having their cheeks pinched. There was a whole panel featuring professionals measuring brightly coloured liquids in beakers, or holding clipboards, or speaking in front of other professionals with a screen in the background that said *PROGRESS* in bold letters.

She read the entire block of text:

THE MNR'S STATEMENT OF FAITH
We believe that the Bible is the only authoritative and
undeniable True Word of God for all persons on Earth.

We believe in the resurrection of the saved into everlasting
life in Heaven and the resurrection of the unsaved
into everlasting punishment in Hell.

We believe in Christ's Commission to the Church to go into all the
world and preach the gospel of Jesus Christ to every creature.

We worship Jesus Christ, not other spirits, or totems, or animals.
We do not condone any other forms of spirituality or belief.

"Who the hell is worshipping animals," she muttered to Zeus. He sniggered and a woman with a thin cloud of auburn hair turned around to stare at them. Joan smiled weakly and then concentrated on carefully refolding the pamphlet.

The room was almost full now, which was impressive considering the scant population of the area. She heard a flurry of whispers behind her and turned to see what was happening.

Heiser was happening, making an entrance looking confident in his grey suit, shaking his heavy gold watch down his wrist to give it a quick check. (Stock photo search results for "white businessman.") The helpers lined up like obedient kindergartners in front of him to receive a hearty handshake that shook their narrow shoulders and set the teeth in their smiles chattering.

"It's fucking Heiser," she whispered to Zeus.

Zeus lifted his eyebrows, watching the man clapping backs and hugging girls, then crossed himself.

Cecile jogged out from the darkness at the side of the stage and down the aisle to take her spot at the end of Heiser's greeting line. When she stopped, she fluttered her hand at her chest, as if willing it to stop heaving, then smoothed her long, blonde braid. Joan narrowed her eyes. She hated Cecile. Youthful, helpful Cecile with her thick hair and thigh gap. Together she and Heiser walked down the aisle, shaking a few more hands, clapping a few more backs, and took seats a few rows behind them.

A high, lonely note from an organ snaked up into the ruching of the ceiling, and exploded in a flurry of lower notes. The crowd hushed, the music clicking off their conversations like a switch had been thrown. Those still by the door found seats and the organ went on for several minutes in brilliant suspension. Even Joan's non-believing heart swelled with each new chord.

And then, cued by a sudden joyous burst of instrumental hallelujahs, the beautiful Reverend Wolff walked on stage.

"Holy shit," Zeus said. "It *is* Victor!"

Auburn halo turned around and scowled, one swollen finger against her pink lips, though shutting him up didn't make much sense since the audience had gone wild, clapping and shouting and stomping their feet. For a split second Joan was proud that this man was hers, before she remembered that he wasn't, not anymore.

He held up a palm to quiet them, and when they fell silent, he launched right in, reciting the belief statement straight from the pamphlet as a few dozen other voices joined in.

She felt stuck somewhere between lust and disgust. He was still tall and lean and strong, that much was obvious even under the nice suit, but he moved like a man who had just learned how to move, not like Victor at all. Victor swaggered.

After a shout-out to the volunteers, the Reverend moved to the front of the stage and addressed them all as if they were sharing a private conversation.

"My friends, as Indigenous peoples, we are uniquely positioned. As stewards of our land, we are burdened with an evil that is buried within it, but also gifted with the blessed good of it all."

People nodded in response.

"This evil that lies in wait has been called into being by the decisions that our forefathers made to turn away from the Lord, to shun His word, to renounce Him and all He stands for."

Oh, the ugly bullshit coming out of his beautiful mouth.

The crowd swayed when he moved his hands to punctuate his message. They leaned forward when he whispered and stamped their feet when he shouted, like he was conducting them out of confusion and into certainty, speaking each note directly, pulling sound from the quietest string.

"We have allowed ourselves to be led astray. Some of us in this room have followed false teachings, worshipped false gods." He smiled then, holding his palms up. "I'm not angry with you. I know you were told that's what we must do, to communicate with these weaker spirits, these so-called totems. We are told we have animal helpers, that the ghosts of demi-gods and ancestors live in our homes, that we belong to clans named for earthly creatures. I was once like you, led astray. I was lost. And my friends, that wrong worship, that pagan way of life, is exactly what laid me to waste—what has led our people, our *good* people, to waste. And because of it, we fell into a time of degradation and great poverty. Why have we, among all God's men, suffered so greatly? Why have we been left behind when it comes to enjoying the riches of His bounty? Why are our youth dying, our men in prisons at such a high rate, our women being murdered and going missing? We are paying for the sins of our fathers."

He paced the edge of the stage, pausing to make sure his words hit their mark. As they rippled out across each row, they burrowed where they could, chipped a surface where they could not. Finding some lack in their response, he doubled down until sweat glistened on his smooth forehead.

"Your so-called community leaders have been agents for a much darker power. They have led you away from the light with simple distractions. Like children, we have allowed ourselves to *be* distracted. A drum is not a heartbeat—only the heart God gave you can beat the right way. A sweat lodge will not cleanse you—only confessing to God can do that.

"We have been given inadequate tools and faulty plans and told we must build ourselves up. Why? Because Satan rejoices in it. What better entertainment for the beast than to watch a broken people struggle with broken tools? Especially when God has already provided a house for us—when He has promised to feed and love and protect us. What a joke!"

He watched the crowd for a long moment, walking the edge of the stage, his arms thrown open.

"It's a joke that I don't think is very funny. Not as a First Nations man of God. No, not at all. Why, brothers and sisters, would you worship an animal or put faith in a feather when Jesus has given you a path to the One True God who created every animal Himself?"

The crowd shouted back to him "*Yes!*" and "*Amen!*"

"*Before*, we were broken. *Before*, we were in pieces. We were fractured and separated from the truth. And now? Now we have the whole and the holy." He drew a circle in the air and when his hands met at the bottom, he laced his fingers together in prayer.

"These lands were given to us by the Lord Himself," he insisted. "They are ours to live on and prosper from. This entire wilderness is ours for the very purpose of celebrating and honouring the glory of God. *He* is the answer to our poverty, for how can we know poverty in His love? And in return we need to dedicate our success and wellbeing to His holy light."

The assembly raised their palms to the roof, waving them like heavy buds on thin stalks.

"This entire empire of wild is ours in order that we may rejoice in His name."

As the whole crowd climbed to their feet to shout their praises, the helpers moved to steady the feeble and the very old so that they, too, could stand, arms raised, hearts open.

"We must build churches, new homes, better schools, thriving businesses—all in His name. This is how we move forward. This is how we heal."

"Heal from what?" Zeus said. He and Joan were the only ones still seated, though Joan felt like a bee was buzzing around her ear. She ran a hand over her hair and grabbed her earlobe. Still the feeling remained. She turned around in her seat.

There was Heiser, two rows back, standing with the rest of the crowd. At his shoulder was Cecile. They both offered her smiles that didn't come close to reaching their light eyes. As hundreds of voices joined in a great swell of song, Joan stared at Cecile, who shifted her gaze to the stage, then closed her eyes and opened her mouth to sing.

Heiser didn't join in. He kept his eyes on Joan, like they

were alone together in a wooden boat with uneven flooring and uncomfortable folding seats, surrounded by rhythmic waves of song.

This man knew what she had come for. And despite the fear that scuttled around her guts at that realization, she knew that if he was so attuned to her, she must be a threat. Her chest puffed out under the thin, red coat. She couldn't be ignored. She had to be feared. As the song ended in the final crash, she was the one to smile at him. And then she mouthed the words *I know.* He narrowed his eyes at her, and she turned back around, satisfied that she had at least unsettled him. She imagined the dark hair on his arms bristling.

The people surrounding her and Zeus were now gleaming with fervour, eyes on the Reverend, chins up, their faces tilted to the cross as if it were the very sun in the sky.

Satisfied, the Reverend sat down in his plush chair and opened the worn Bible with Victor's long fingers. The assembly sat too, chairs squeaking on the floor. He stayed quiet a moment as people settled, regarding them like a preschool teacher at storytime, an uncommonly attractive preschool teacher, and then he opened the pages and read:

Come, everyone who thirsts, come to the waters; and he who has no money, come, buy and eat! Come, buy wine and milk without money and without price. Why do you spend your money for that which is not bread, and your labour for that which does not satisfy? Listen diligently to me, and eat what is good, and delight yourselves in rich food. Incline your ear, and come to me; hear, that your soul may live . . .

He barely glanced at the page as he spoke, planting each word row by row, carefully enunciating the peaks, rumbling through the tender bits. He turned the page and continued without pause:

> . . . and I will make with you an everlasting covenant, my
> steadfast, sure love for David. Behold, I made him a witness
> to the peoples, a leader and commander for the peoples. Behold,
> you shall call a nation that you do not know, and a nation that
> did not know you shall run to you, because of the Lord your
> God, and of the Holy One of Israel, for he has glorified you.

Joan was anxious. She hated this cheap version of Victor, filled with so many lies. She couldn't sit still any longer. She pushed back her chair so she could stand, and it scraped the floor with a loud squeal. The Reverend raised his eyes for a moment and saw her. She leaned into staring back, holding his gaze so that he couldn't sweep it away.

He faltered, as if he didn't know *Christ* came after *Jesus*, and glanced down at the book open in front of him, scanning the lines to find his place. Joan was tempted to glance back at Heiser, but she dared not look away from the man on the stage in case he looked at her again.

He picked up the passage in a different spot, haltingly. When he looked back up, his eyes were wild, jumping over the faces turned toward him, searching for something or someone. Joan stayed standing so he couldn't ignore her. The Reverend dropped the Bible and rose. The crowd started to murmur as he put a hand on the back of the chair to steady himself.

He tried to clear his throat, then said, "Uh, sorry. I ah, I need . . . water . . ." He stumbled to the side of the stage and pushed through the curtains.

After he left, it seemed like the crowd woke up, slowly and together. Some stretched, others yawned and a few bent-walked along their rows to the aisle and then out the tent flap to visit the porta-potties, trying to remain small so as not to be disrespectful. Whatever spell the Reverend had woven was broken.

"What now?" Zeus whispered.

Joan turned around. Cecile was gone but Heiser was still there. She smiled at him again, making the kind of full-on jackass face that would precipitate fistfights with her brothers when they were growing up. Heiser only sighed and, pulling a phone from the inside pocket of his jacket, began typing furiously.

Then Cecile was back, leaning over to whisper into his ear, and he got up and followed her up the aisle. They walked quickly to the front and disappeared behind the curtains to the left of the stage. A minute later, a blond ministry volunteer stepped out onto the stage with a handheld microphone.

"Ladies and gentlemen, we are going to take a ten-minute break," he announced. "Rest assured the Reverend is just fine. Please feel free to step out for some fresh air or to visit with your fellow worshippers until he returns. Bless you all."

There was polite clapping. Then people got up and obediently headed for the exit.

"We gotta get to him," Joan said.

"Okay," Zeus said. "Should we just go back there?"

"We've got to try."

Joan started down the aisle. Zeus stayed right behind her, but he asked a little shakily, "Auntie, is it a good idea to try and grab Victor now, with everyone around?"

"All we have to do is remind him he's Victor. Then hopefully he'll come along without the grabbing part."

"Can I help you?" A red-headed volunteer blocked their way through the curtains. She winked at Joan and whispered, "Porta-potties are outside, on the far side of the parking lot, darlin'."

"We're here to see the Reverend."

"Well, aren't we all," the young woman said and giggled. "He should be back out in a jiffy. In the meantime, help yourself to some coffee and biscuits." She pointed back to refreshment tables by the main entrance.

"He's my uncle," Zeus said, stepping around Joan. "He's expecting me."

"Oh okay, then." She put a hand on Zeus's arm to stop him. "Let me just pop back and let him know you're here."

"Uncle!" Zeus shouted. "Uncle, it's me, Zeus!"

Her cheeks went pink. "Just one minute, please." She disappeared behind the curtain.

"Thanks," he called to her back. He tossed his head to move his bangs off his forehead and then straightened his heavy-framed glasses on his nose.

The curtains parted and instead of the redhead, Cecile stepped forward. Joan squeezed the back of Zeus's neck.

"Oh, hello, Joan. I thought it might be you." She didn't bother to smile.

"Cecile."

"Reverend Wolff is not feeling well. You're gonna have to wait until the conclusion of service if you want to chat." She glanced at Zeus. "Like everyone else."

"Lady, I want to see my uncle now." Zeus took another step forward. He was barely an inch shorter than Cecile when he straightened to his full height.

She flipped her eyes from Joan to the boy. "That's sweet. You need to wait too." Something in Cecile's hard stare made him retreat behind his aunt. She smirked and called over her shoulder, "Marvin?"

A young man with a buzz cut came through the curtains. He was much taller than they were and seemed almost as wide as he was tall. Cecile told him, "Can you please ensure that no one disturbs the Reverend? He needs his privacy right now."

"Yes ma'am."

Cecile picked a piece of lint off Marvin's bright blue shirt. "Thank you so much. We appreciate your vigilance." Then she turned back to Zeus and Joan, folding her arms across her chest.

"Come on, Zeus," Joan said, and they walked back up the aisle.

"I probably could take that guy," Zeus muttered, but he was right on her heels. "What do we do now? Wait, like she said?"

Joan led them straight out the entrance into the cool dark of the field. "It's a tent," she said to Zeus. "How fucking hard could it be to break in?"

They turned the corner away from the worshippers, who were now huddled in groups outside, and jogged down the side of the tent, looking for entry points. The generators were loud back here. The interior lights made the canvas wall glow. To their right a line of dark trees turned into forest, quiet in the way only the woods at night can be.

"Did you hear that?" Zeus hissed from behind her.

"What?"

"Stop!" He sounded scared.

Joan turned to him. "What's the matter?"

And then she heard it. A low growl leaking out of the dark. Zeus's eyes opened wide.

It came again—a long, deep rumble resonating in a large chest. She pointed to the woods. Was it coming from the trees? Zeus shook his head and lifted a shaky hand to point.

Joan slowly turned, using one arm to tuck Zeus in behind her. Just where the tent turned the corner into the dark stood a hunched figure, head riotous with knots and tufts of hair or fur, its chest heaving in another growl.

Zeus turned and ran.

Joan stood her ground for a minute, trying to make out the creature's face in the dark. "Mr. Heiser?" she managed to say, trembling. "Is that you?"

She was answered by a snarl so shrill and hard it was like spit landing on her cheek, and she, too, turned and ran. She could hear it galloping after her, feel its heat as it got closer.

She caught up to Zeus and the two of them burst into the light of the parking lot, just barely avoiding bowling over a group of old women gathered under a string of white lights.

"Fuck me," Joan shouted, as she skidded to a stop, frantically searching the night behind them. Someone tsked over her language. A couple of grannies giggled at it. Zeus was shaking so hard, she grabbed his hand and walked the boy quickly past all the cars and trucks, both of them panting.

Once they'd crossed the parking area, they picked up the pace and ran, Zeus's hand tight in Joan's, all the way to the road.

"What are we gonna do now?" Zeus gasped when they got there.

"I don't know. I don't know." She'd actually forgotten about the Jeep. "Dammit!"

Zeus bent over, his hands on his knees. "Maybe . . . maybe we can hitchhike?"

She massaged a cramp out of her side and nodded. "Good plan. Let's head toward town." They walked up the road, toward a white vehicle parked on the gravel verge.

Joan was close enough to read the licence plate before she realized it was their Jeep. The doors were unlocked and the keys were on the driver's seat.

"How?" Zeus said.

"I don't know. And I don't care."

They scrambled into the car, scanning the shadows around them for movement. At first, she missed the small, cream card tucked under her wipers. She got out and grabbed it, waiting until she was back inside and the doors were locked before she looked at it.

On one side, in raised letters, was *Thomas Heiser, CEO, Resource Development Specialists.* On the other, in careful blue script: *Joan, go home.*

❦

They drove in silence, pulling into the parking lot of the New Star Motel without having said a word to each other. Joan turned off the engine and they sat there a moment in the quiet. Then Zeus's phone dinged. He unbuckled his seatbelt and dug it out of his pocket. His lips moved as he read, his face lit blue by the screen.

"Ajean says we have to get back. Now."

Joan lowered her forehead to the steering wheel, resting it on the cool moulded plastic. Not that it would matter if they stayed, since it was obvious they were grossly unprepared to rescue Victor.

"She says she has something that will help."

"The cure for amnesia?" Joan felt tears behind her eyes.

"Here's exactly what she wrote: *Come home now. There's things that can help. We'll go get some. So's you can trap the dog.*"

"Great." Joan opened the door. "Just fucking fantastic." She got out and slammed it behind her while Zeus scrambled out the other side. "That's what I want to do, catch a fucking rogarou. Let's get our stuff and get out of here."

VICTOR AND SUDDEN WEST IN THE WOODS

For the first time in God knows how long, Victor saw the sun. He didn't think it was the actual sun, but rather the suggestion of the sun, just enough so you could believe the sun was there.

Under this newly lit sky, Victor held his hands up in front of his face. It was reassuring to see where he began and ended. To be certain that he was more than breath and heartbeat and longing and loss.

Here were his fingers, a shade of burnt ochre in the dim light, with half-moons of maroon under each nail. Blood? Had he been bleeding? Was he lying in a hospital bed, having been shot by a careless hunter; was the prison of woods only monitors and morphine?

He splayed his hands on his chest and felt around for wounds. Nothing. Then he remembered falling and that his chin had bled. He touched that too. But there was no cut to feel, no bruise to worry. Had he dreamt it?

So why the blood on his hands? And where the hell was his rifle? He scanned the ground around him. Nothing but dirt and scrub and the varicose veins of old tree roots. He checked the trunks themselves, hoping to find the gun leaning on one of them. It wasn't there.

Then it occurred to him that if the sun was indeed setting somewhere, that somewhere had to be west. West. He had a direction. If he kept aiming steadily toward the light source, he could avoid the circles he'd been turning in. He might just find a way out.

He took off running toward the light, which began dimming as if it were a special effect on a sped-up film. He ran harder. He jumped felled logs and trampled ground ferns, hearing his own footsteps from a distance. The darkness behind him was absolute, the same darkness he'd existed in for his indeterminate internment. He could feel it on his heels like the velvet muzzle of a large dog.

Up ahead, the smudge of sun lowered itself gracefully somewhere behind the trees. He chased it, pushing low branches out of his path with blood-stained hands as they caught at his jacket and his braid.

Under the panic and the burn and the sprint was a swarm of excitement. Just ahead, maybe, or just behind, there was a familiar scent. Smoke, lotion, rose lip balm, peach and cotton. And the image of the curve at the bottom of her breast.

Joan.

Stitch by stitch, loop over loop, Victor was made for Joan. He knew that the day he met her in Montreal, in the bar, with her quick mouth and face flushed with drink, standing with a hip thrown forward, rubbing her eye to a grey smoke of mascara and bourbon. He could feel her now the same way he felt her that night—as inevitable, as necessary. His job was to exist so that she could keep running that mouth, keep kissing him with a thousand little kisses in the oddest spots: inside of the elbow, back of the neck, above the belly button, on the exact spot where the zipper on his jeans began. There was no other reason for him to exist. And it was enough.

Where had she gone? What had she done while he'd been trapped here? How long had he been here?

He ran.

Finally, at the end of his strength, he burst through the trees.

No. No! NO!

He turned in a quick circle, a mad movement with no purpose.

What the fuck?

He was back in the clearing where he began.

He screamed into the space, fists at his sides, leaning forward to project, to place blame or find release. And there, in the middle of the clearing, before the dark became complete, he saw it. A wingback chair, moss green velvet on a dark wood frame.

And then the black swallowed them both.

10

GO HOME

They pulled up to the house in the deepest dark of night. Joan prodded Zeus half-awake long enough to stagger inside and flop down on the living room couch. She pulled the uneven blue blanket off the recliner, one that Zeus had knitted for her as a Christmas present, and tucked him in. Then she dragged herself to the bedroom.

She was still awake as the birds began singing in the soft dark, their chorus growing louder as the sky lightened. She watched as a ladybug crawled across her window screen. Ladybugs loved wood, so they were always around while her family was working. She learned young that they liked to bite. They would land on her father and he would cup them in his callused hands and throw them into the wind or off a roof. But her brothers liked to crush them, releasing their distinctive metallic reek, and she would always cry out, "Leave them be!"

They'd laugh and smoosh the small, red bodies as close to her face as they could get.

One summer she decided to build a ladybug colony near the back shed where they would be safe and multiply. She collected as many as she could, depositing them into a Mason jar stolen from her mere's canning supplies, which she prepared by punching holes in the lid with a screwdriver and filling the jar with leaves crusty with aphids. The ladybugs were like pony beads in there, rolling around when they lost their grip, climbing stems.

The last week of that July, she and her family went to her uncle's island in Honey Harbour. She made sure her bugs had extra leaves and set the jar in the shade cast by the shed roof before she left.

When they got back on a Sunday evening, she ran through the house and straight out the back. Halfway down the lawn, she felt a shadow of panic that made her pick up the pace. She rounded the shed and was relieved to see the jar sitting in the long grass under the overhang, exactly as she'd left it. She sat down beside it, already determined to let them all go.

She picked up the jar. It felt heavier than usual. Raising it to eye level, she saw that it now contained three inches of murky water. It had rained while they were away and the air holes had turned into faucets. The bugs didn't have a chance. Two dozen round bodies floated on the top, clumped together and motionless. She'd killed them.

🦋

Joan fell into sleep at last with tears in her eyes, which was normal for this room these days.

"Auntie, wake up." Zeus shook her shoulder.

She sighed into her pillow and rolled over to find him standing over her, his arms crossed like a disapproving parent.

"What, for godssakes?"

"It's almost noon. You said we should get an early start." He sat down on the edge of the bed, his hair standing out on his head in sleep spikes. When she looked confused, he said, "Remember? The text we got in Hook River? From Ajean?"

She yawned. "So noon is early?"

"Not my fault, man. Someone tucked me in with a rad blanket with great sleep properties. I had to fight my way awake."

She had to smile at him. "Right, so let's pour some coffee into me and head over to the old woman."

Ajean was down at the shore when they arrived, sitting at the picnic table eating a slice of baloney straight from the package while three of her grandkids threw rocks off the dock.

When she heard them coming down the path, she turned and said, "Holay, you guys just get in?"

Zeus lowered himself onto the picnic table bench beside her and grabbed a slice. Joan lit a cigarette and sat opposite. "Sorry. We got in late and slept in."

Ajean pinched Zeus's cheek affectionately, then surveyed Joan. "You look like shit."

"Thanks. You look old."

The woman cackled. "Did you find Victor?"

"Kind of," Zeus said.

"Hmm. Did you find the rogarou, then?"

Zeus again answered, "Kind of."

Ajean grabbed the lunchmeat and tossed it back into the grocery bag. "Kendall, Kylie ... er ... the other one, let's go," she shouted to the kids. "Zeus, you okay to watch them for a while this afternoon? Me and Joan gotta go on a mission. No kids allowed."

"I'm not a kid," Zeus protested, but Ajean stared him down and eventually he nodded.

Ajean pulled a long skirt over her jogging pants and talked while she laced up her moccasins. "I don't know much about that magic from over there." She pointed with her lips randomly to the east, which Joan took to mean Europe. "But I don't trust it. I believe it, but I don't trust it." The old woman was bundled against the chill with a peculiar layering of sweaters. The top one was a child's crewneck with a faded Daffy Duck on the front, his beak open and fist swinging as if in the middle of shouting *Tthantasthic!* Her braid was tucked in but was so long it hung out the bottom of her sweaters, making it look like she had a wispy, grey tail.

"Wonder if the old white people in town know anything?" she mused, then answered her own question. "No, that's the problem, them—no connection, no living in their old stories."

She chewed her lips and paced the kitchen, clasping and unclasping her hands. Joan sat at the table. Zeus was in the living room, sprawled out on the couch while the three little girls danced wildly in front of the TV, which was turned to the top-ten video countdown.

"You heard of the salt bones?" Ajean asked at last.

"Salt bones? Is that what you put in soup to make stock?"

"What? No. Jeez, you can't cook, can you? Your mom shoulda spent more time inside the house instead of on damn roofs."

"Ajean, what about salty bones."

"*Salt* bones, moron. Salt bones. Angelique never told you about them?"

Joan shook her head.

"And you never grew nothing?" She lowered her voice, stroking her own arm. "Like, in your body?"

Joan sighed. "I swear, first my cooking and now with the lack of kids. I get it, I'm a bad woman."

"Dieu, no. I don't mean kids. Jesus, anyone can grow those." Ajean threw her arm out in the direction of her grand-daughters, each one concentrating on matching Nicki Minaj's twerking, each one falling far short of the mark. "I mean things, like new parts, bones, kind of."

"What the hell? No, I'm pretty sure I just have the usual amount of the bones."

Ajean stroked a single long hair that grew out of her chin, like an evil genius in need of a better goatee, as she considered. "I don't think your mother ever grew one, neither."

At last, she handed her tote bag, in which things rattled, to

Joan to carry and pushed the screen door open, calling to the little girls, "You kids be good, you."

They were past St. Anne's Church and halfway to Dusome's before Ajean said another word. Since she moved at a pace that stole Joan's breath, Joan was fine with the silence.

"Angelique, she took me with her to bury hers. That's where we'll go. Should be hers, anyways, if you don't have one of your own."

Joan was too winded to ask for more explanation.

They walked between the paved road and the dusty grass. Only one car passed them, driven by Sven, the Swede who'd bought the Jug City store up near the elementary school, by the last beach before you hit the gated community that used to be the halfbreed settlement before the land got expensive. He honked twice and gave them a wave out his window.

Ajean raised her middle finger. "Damn capitalists." She clucked her tongue. "Sure hope these jack-offs haven't built over the spot. If they have, I hope those scary movies have it right and building over old Indian stuff makes your kids disappear into televisions."

They walked up the hill and around the bend, and didn't stop until they got to Dusome's Garage. This was where Joan had run that afternoon of the rogarou, but it was also where she stopped for Popsicles with her cousins on long bike rides around the Bay, depositing their quarters into a plastic container that Dusome set out by the white freezer. He never monitored the kids. His attention was saved for those seeking his skills on troubled engines, the older the better. After he passed away, the garage was locked up. It had sat unused so long it now looked like a cardboard box left out in the rain, almost melted into the cracked asphalt. Ajean headed around to the back where the grass was scabby with gravel.

"Where in hell—" Joan said.

"Shh. This is holy land now."

"Dusome's Garage?" Joan had lowered her voice nonetheless.

"No, no, moron girl. Something has been left here. Something that can't forget itself."

Whenever the old people got quieter in their volume and more precise in their words, Joan had learned to shut the hell up. So she did.

They walked up the driveway, past a chair and standing ashtray, both rusted to sculpture, to the edge of a small woods saved from development by a rare owl who nested there. Ajean was bent over scanning the ground. She stopped between a huge willow and a greying birch, and knelt on a spot where the braid of shallow roots had left a hollow. "Hand me that shovel there."

Joan reached into Ajean's tote bag and pulled out a wood-handled garden spade.

"We just need the right hands to free it. We need the right words to sing it back. Magic is patient like that."

Ajean made the sign of the cross with the small shovel, her eyes closed. She bent over and extended her hand, dangling the shovel from the very tip of the handle. The breeze scattered ancient litter across the rocky ground—tin cans with old pop logos, crunchy papers, bleached cigarette butts like tiny scrolls.

"Amen," Ajean said when she was done, and she let the shovel drop. The pointed tip found purchase in the earth. She pushed herself up and then dusted her hands off on the front of her long skirt.

"Okay then," she said to Joan. "Dig."

Joan sighed. She should have known she was here for manual labour.

"What am I looking for?"

"Just shut up and dig, you."

She dug. The ground was hard and she had to chip away at it, pulling small clumps out and stopping to examine every rock. When Ajean said nothing, she'd continue.

She chopped through two smaller tree roots, releasing a meaty scent that made her feel a bit murderous. Then, when the hole was about a foot deep, she hit something different. Carefully shovelling away a little more dirt, she spotted a piece of old cloth. She stopped and Ajean peered in.

"That's it. Careful now. Don't yank it all crazy and spill it."

Spill it?

Joan gently dug around the wadded fabric until she had enough room to pry up the whole bundle. It was crusted and stiff, almost fossilized in places from groundwater and pressure, but it was definitely a tea towel. And it had belonged to her mother's family—she could tell by the distinctive crocheted loop with the broken button on the top edge so that it could be hung off a stove handle.

"Did you know, those bearded guys, the ones with the big ships and the horns, what do you call them again?" Ajean said as Joan laid the tea towel on the ground.

"Vikings?"

"Yes, Vikings. Those are the ones. Some of those Viking men wore wolfskins. The ones that were considered the best fighters, the most fearless—the ones who couldn't be killed." She clucked her tongue. "Lots of power in that wolf. Maybe because he's everywhere."

"How do you mean?" Joan was carefully picking away the dirt that sealed the towel into a solid clump.

"Well, Vikings. Germans. Us here. And there's a tribe in the Bible, one of the twelve tribes from Israel? One of them had that wolf as their symbol too. But that group disappeared. A lost tribe. But those wolves, them, they are just all over the world."

"You been on the internet with the seniors group again?" Ajean always came back from adventures on the internet with crazy stories, not understanding that not everything online was actual news. Joan wiped her forehead with the back of one hand and sat on her heels. "There, that's the best I can do. Should I open it up?"

"Not here. Get that tin there, out of my bag."

Joan fished out a round, blue tin that once held butter cookies. She opened it up, shook out the single button bouncing around the bottom and carefully placed the cloth bundle inside. Then she put it back in the tote and stood.

"No, no." Ajean smacked her arm. "Put some tobacco in that hole and close it back up."

Joan did as she was told. When the hole was filled and patted down, she picked up the bag and they started back home.

"Ajean, do you think I was an asshole for taking Zeus with me to Hook River? I keep worrying I should have left him at home."

"Always better to have children around, you know. They see things we don't."

"Yeah but, the rogarou. I mean, we got chased."

Ajean stopped dead. "Chased? Jesus H. Christ. With people around?"

"Not too far away."

"Brave fucker, this one." She touched Joan's arm reassuringly, then started walking again.

Joan followed. "How could we know what it would do? Besides, now we have Angelique's bundle." She patted the side of the canvas tote.

Back at the house, they found all of the kids including Zeus snoozing on the couch. The girls were curled up, one under his arm, another at his feet, the third under a blanket on the chair. Joan regarded his plump cheeks for a moment, wondering why he was sleeping so much these days: maybe he was on the edge of a growth spurt.

"Let's leave them be," Ajean said as she spread a sheet over the kitchen table and placed the tin in the centre. She went to the cupboard and took down a metal cheese grater with a red plastic handle and placed it beside the tin.

"What do we need that for?"

"Your brother, he grew one, out of his forearm."

"What in the hell are you talking about?" Joan sat down, finally exasperated by all this Indian shit.

"A bone. A salt bone."

Ajean opened the tin and carefully lifted out the bundle. "People from Red River, on your mere's side, have been growing salt bones for generations." She unfolded the tea towel, revealing a lopsided ball, like a baseball skinned out of its leather. It was dark yellow, almost brown in places.

"Your brother's started as a lump under the skin of his forearm. It swelled up real good and the doctors said it was a sliver, infected or something, then that it was a cyst—they weren't sure, those doctors never are. But Angelique knew. She tried to tell your brother but he wasn't interested, him. He wanted it out right away, but the hospital wouldn't move too fast. Said it wasn't life threatening so he'd have to wait. Pretty sure that's why it grew so damn fast, because it was going to be taken out."

Joan couldn't help it. "So this random growth had consciousness?"

"Listen, you." Ajean pointed the grater at her face. "Enough with this bullshit."

"Funny, I was about to say the same."

"Ask George how he got that scar on his arm. Think it just showed up?"

And then Joan remembered coming back from Toronto after a failed attempt to be free in her twenties to find that George had a new line down his left forearm, from wrist to elbow. It didn't look angry—actually more like a fold in the skin than a healed cut. When she'd asked him about it, he just shrugged and said, "No big deal." She hadn't pursued it.

"Anyways, one night it pushed right through the skin. Your mere got it the rest of the way out and put him back together. Not sure what he did with it. Hopefully Angelique put it aside for him."

"So whose is this, then?"

Ajean sighed. "You're no good at listening. This one is your mere's—it's Angelique's, for cripe's sake."

"People don't just grow extra bones, Ajean. Not like that." Joan pointed at the calcified ball on the table.

"You think you're born with every bone you live with, you? Babies grow new bones when they leave their mother. Your family just grows more later on, is all."

"Okay, so where exactly did Mere grow this—out of her arm like George?"

Ajean laughed. "No, no. Angelique, she had to always be different. She grew this one on her head."

"Fuck!"

"Yeah, imagine that. She had to wear double kerchiefs for a month until it fell off." Ajean stuck her tongue out in concentration as she lined the grater up against the porous surface.

Joan rubbed her hands along her shoulders and down her arms. What if she had extra bones in there now? She imagined tiny limbs like a centipede, or bony wings poking out of her shoulder blades, too stiff for flight. "Why grow anything at all?"

Ajean shrugged. "Someone figured out if you grind them up, they make salt. And you can protect yourself with it."

"With salt from bones." Joan pictured throwing bone salt in the rogarou's eyes and running away while it screamed and tore at its face. So her secret weapon could be beaten with a bottle of Visine?

Ajean started grating. The sound made Joan's teeth ache. "How do you keep unwanted things from coming in your house?"

"A lock?"

No answer.

"A shotgun?"

"No, stupid, with this salt. You put salt around your house and no spirit, no rogarou, can come in."

Ajean produced a pile of granules about an inch around and half an inch high. The exposed inside of Mere's bone was a lighter shade of beige and solid. Was there no marrow in salt bones?

Ajean nodded toward her sewing table. "Get me a piece of fabric." Hanging from the chair was a bag of scraps she used for quilting. Joan grabbed a red square and brought it back. Ajean tore a thin strip from one side. She carefully piled the gratings in the middle, then twisted it up and used the strip to secure it. Then she rewrapped the bone in the grubby tea towel and put it back in the tin. "When this is all over, you'll rebury this where we found it. For next time."

"Jesus, I hope there is no next time."

Ajean laughed. "You think all we have around here is good men and handsome women like me? There's just as many bad. We gotta keep it in balance." She twisted in her seat and tossed the grater in the sink behind her. "Someone has to."

Ajean got up and set the tin on top of the fridge where all the important things lived. She handed the little red pouch of bone dust to Joan, who took it reluctantly, trying not to imagine how it had grown on her grandmother's head.

"So, what do I do with this, then?" She held the bundle by the tie. It was almost weightless.

"You keep it with you. If you need to contain the rogarou, you put it around him. If you need to keep your house safe, you put it around that. If you need to keep yourself safe, well, same thing. It's like Indian Alarm Guard." She started humming a jingle from a TV commercial on home security, but for once Joan didn't find her jauntiness funny.

She pushed the little pouch into the pocket of her pullover and linked her fingers on the table. "Ajean, how scared should I be?"

The old woman chewed her lip, looked out the screen door and knitted her sparse eyebrows together. "You need the boy."

The boy? Joan felt like she needed a lot of things—a handgun, a plan, a destination, a miracle—but the boy?

"Why would I need Zeus?"

Ajean pulled her braid out of her sweater, flopped it over her shoulder and played with the end. "A child makes you think before you go acting out all crazy. The boy will remind you to come home."

Joan pushed back from the table and crossed to the stove, where she flipped on the kettle. She leaned against the counter, staring out the window as a small fox stuck its head around the corner of the church across the street, then trotted through the parking lot and into the trees.

If the Reverend Wolff really was Victor, as she believed, she had to manoeuvre around a rogarou, steal him back from the ministry and get their asses home to Arcand. And all she had on her side was a moody twelve-year-old, an old woman and a bag of bone dust that her grandmother may or may not have grown like a fucking unicorn.

"What the hell do I do now?"

Ajean shrugged, soft in her layers. "Not sure. How about make some tea."

Joan had convinced Zeus that it was time to put in an appearance at his own home, so she dropped him off and drove back to her place alone. She parked out front and sat in the Jeep. She missed Mere. Mere would have known what to do. Even if she didn't, at least she'd be waiting with the kettle on.

What in the fuck is going on? she asked the emptiness of the car. Where had her life gone, the one where she roofed with her brothers, drank Labatt 50 with her mom, drove into town to shop for new clothes once a season with her favourite cousin? The life where she was married to a good and helpful man who turned her thighs unstable when he so much as touched her hand.

Her house was a cold, quiet tomb. In the foyer the lights were off, just as she had left them. There was none of the old music, or Victor singing in the shower, no footsteps coming toward her after a hard day at work, saying, "Let me take that belt off of you."

He liked to do that: open the screen door for her and unbuckle her tool belt. Truthfully, she'd put it back on when she got out of her car—there was no way to drive with a hammer sticking out from your hip—but he liked taking it off of her so much, loving the idea of her sweaty and laden with tools.

"Mmm, poor baby," he'd say. "You look exhausted. Here, let me help you out of those dirty clothes." And she would obediently raise her arms as he pulled her T-shirt up over her head.

"Oh, look at that. You're going to need a shower." He'd run a finger down from her collarbone, along her sticky skin.

She'd nod. Yes, of course she needed a shower. "You too." He was always still in his work clothes, smelling like clean wood and hot metal blades. She'd help him out of his shirt, sliding it off sunburnt shoulders that told her he'd worked shirtless that day. This would make her a bit jealous—a pinch in her lower stomach as she imagined the appraising looks from women who wandered by the job site. Her beautiful Victor, stripped to the waist, standing walls that should have taken two men to raise.

He'd bend down to unlace her boots, looking up into her face from where he crouched, so close to her crotch she could feel his breath. He'd pull off each one, and then her socks. Standing up, he'd lift her, a hand under each buttock, and carry her to the bathroom, her breasts pushed up under his chin so that he had a choice of either rubbing his face into the bounce or admiring her sun-darkened face. Such a dilemma for a man.

They'd leave the bathroom door open. There was no one to interrupt.

Tonight she pulled off her own shoes and wandered to the couch, feeling her life's great emptiness like a weight that

would not yield, pushing down and down and down. She sat
and pulled Zeus's blue blanket up to her chin.

She woke before the sun rose, tipped sideways on the couch.
Her neck was sore where it had rested at an odd angle and she
rubbed it as she walked to the kitchen to get a drink of water.
She took a glass from the draining board and filled it with
cold tap water, downing it where she stood. She was refilling
it when he spoke.

"Hi, baby."

She dropped the glass into the sink, where it hit the bread
knife, a round chip the size and shape of a bottom lip flying.

She spun around to find Victor sitting on one of the kitchen
stools, a wide grin on his dirty face. She held on to the edge of
the sink to stay on her feet, all the air knocked out of her.

"Victor . . ." she managed.

"I'm really sorry about the other night," he said. "I didn't
mean anything by it. I just, you know, was thinking that
you keep saying you want to be able to get out of here. To
hit the road in an old van, remember? One of those Eighties
specials with curtains in the windows and La-Z-Boy chairs
in the back? But I didn't mean anything by it. I'm just happy
to be with you, no matter where."

Her knees started to buckle and she locked them, bone into
joint. "Victor, where have you been?"

He rubbed his scruffy chin. He looked past her out the
kitchen window and his eyes grew dark.

Joan kept hanging on to the edge of the sink, squeezing the cool aluminum against the meat of her palms. His T-shirt was torn. It was his favourite too, the one with the pin-up girl leaning against an old bicycle. He'd gotten it from Abita Springs at a second-hand store because they ran out of clean clothes and were too busy fucking to do laundry. *He's gonna be pissed*, she thought.

He stood and his shirt moved. Through the tear she saw the glaring white of bone.

"What happened to your shirt?" she asked, as if the fabric and not the bone were the issue.

"Listen to me," Victor said.

"I'm listening. I'm here." She moved across the space to him. "Baby, we had this crazy idea of a rogarou and you were somehow like, enchanted or kidnapped, I don't know. But it can't be true."

He reached for her, still looking out the window behind her head. When his hands found her upper arms, he held them, hard, then stared directly into her eyes. She watched the colour of his irises change, from black to light brown and then a yellow found only on the underside of storm clouds.

He looked up and out the window again, and screamed, "Babe, you have to RUN! RUN NOW! FUCK, HE'S COMING! OH JESUS, GOD NO, HE'S ALMOST HERE!"

Her arms, where he held her, were freezing. She tried to turn, to see what he was seeing, but he wouldn't let go.

And then the wind picked up, swirling into a smooth fist that punched up from the linoleum. Pots fell from their hooks. Plates flew out of the dish rack like Frisbees, smashing against the wall that held the thimble holders, which fell to the ground in a cacophony of tin and silver and porcelain. His hair—and oh, his hair was long again—blew around his terrified face and she went to reach for it, to hold it back from his face, but what she saw then, beneath the strands of tangled hair, made her stop.

Something about his jaw looked broken and his eyes were growing wider, the skin pulling apart at either end like surgical scars reopened. His hands were red with old blood.

"*Run!*" he screamed again, but his voice was farther away than where he stood.

She fought him now but had no voice to call out—the wind had scooped that out of her lungs. Panic rose in her chest like liquid. She pushed away, trying to move. Then, she felt the edge of Zeus's blanket in her hands and yanked it down, panting for breath.

She was on the couch, alone. She closed her eyes hard for a second and then reopened them. The room was empty in the pre-dawn light. She sat up and saw that the kitchen was empty. As always, she was alone.

She ran a hand over her head, then held it over her eyes to give herself a moment of dark. "Oh my god. My good god."

She stood up, throwing the blanket back onto the couch. "Stupid blanket. Christ!"

She walked into the kitchen. Truly empty. The clock was loud—was it always this loud? She glanced at it and saw that it was nearly five thirty. She reached for a glass from the draining board, but there were only plates. Though there was a glass in the sink, a pink one, with a chip the size and shape of a bottom lip broken out of the edge.

"Fuck you," she said to no one in particular over the sound of time ticking away on the clock. And then to one person in particular she said, "I'm coming. I'm already on the way."

VICTOR IN THE WOODS: OVERHEARD

I'm already on the way.

11

FOLLOW THE SIGNS

Since Hook River, Cecile had been keeping a close eye on Reverend Wolff. Not that she didn't usually watch him closely, just that now she had a reason to. No one could fault her concern. No one would dare gossip about her devotion. Migraine, he'd told them. He'd been unable to take the stage again that night. Two days later, the Reverend was still a little off, taking long pauses before he answered a question, and he had started smoking. She knew Mr. Heiser was worried.

They'd been heading north toward the next weekend's tent-up when he told them all to stop for a few nights at a Motel 8 off the highway, a low, sad building pushed in behind a Pilot gas station. He did this sometimes, changing their destination completely or calling a time-out as they worked out some logistics.

From her second-storey motel window, Cecile watched the Reverend walk into the trees beyond the back parking lot. He carried a rolled-up brown sleeping bag and a green army backpack. He wore a grey tunic and black pants—no jacket, no hat.

He slept in the woods when he could. He said that to be under the stars made him feel closer to God. She always tried to book motels that were close to some patch of wild for this reason. Tonight, though, he walked like a man twice his age. She feared perhaps he was having some sort of breakdown. Ivy's theory was that he was distracted by the voice of God speaking directly to him. But Ivy was an idiot. Cecile had often thought about inviting her to leave the volunteer group, but lately Mr. Heiser had taken a special interest in the girl. Beyond her freckled face and giant cans, Cecile just couldn't see why.

Wolff had now disappeared into the trees, and he wouldn't come back to his room till morning. Cecile decided that she couldn't wait that long to see him. She had been patient. Months of being at his side. Months of reading scripture with him in the evenings. Weeks and weeks of edging closer: making sure she sat beside him in weekly meetings, coincidentally showing up for meals at the same time as him, often ending up in the same elevator. She considered herself a godly woman. A patient woman. But she was a woman all the same. And she decided that tonight would at last be the night, even if she had to track him down in the woods.

She sang upbeat hymns in the shower, then applied the Motel 8 body lotion she found on the bathroom shelf and dried her hair with the loud dryer attached to the wall. As she looked through her underthings, Cecile tried to summon a little of the old Cecile, the woman from before the Ministry of the New Redemption, before rehab, back when she was sexually free.

At twenty, her hometown of Hamilton had felt stifling to her. Her mother was gone, things with her dad were complicated at best, and her grandmother—the only person who had really watched out for her—had died when she was fifteen. She spent hours locked in her room watching TV specials on Ken Kesey and his road trip with the Merry Pranksters, on the Beats and on Timothy Leary and all things psychedelic. She loved the freedom, the self-expression. These were people who understood the importance of truly being and not just existing.

She read *Siddhartha* half a dozen times and could recite the first three pages of "Howl" from memory. Her father told her she was a throwback, but she felt brand new, part of a revival, part of a generation who were bored and done with the excess of the eighties, the embarrassment of the nineties, the brokenness of the two thousands. California was the place she had to be. So she socked away all her money from working the till at the No Frills, finished one year at Mohawk College like she'd promised her father she would, then bought a plane ticket to LA.

She should have been terrified, or at least nervous, given that she knew no one in California and that everything she owned, or at least, what this new version of herself owned, was rammed into a blue IKEA bag stuffed in the overhead. But she wasn't. She was excited. She wore sandals and two shimmery skirts layered one on top of the other, and a cropped top from grade eight with "Beat It" written in bubble letters across her breasts. She'd wrapped necklaces around her ankles and sewed their metal links together to make them fit, then looped two hemp braids around her big toes and connected them. She'd flown with really dirty hair: she'd promised herself to get dreads once she landed and had started the process by not washing her hair for three weeks.

That first day in LA, sitting in a café social media said was sympathetic to gutter punks and New Agers, she met Sage, a man with glorious, blond, sun-bleached dreads that hung to his waist. She had no idea how old he was, maybe somewhere between twenty-one and forty-nine. His face was all cheekbones and freckles around an easy smile that showed a childhood of dental work and an adulthood of neglect. His bare stomach reached into board shorts in an impressive V that brought your eye down. He stopped to order a kombucha with extra bacteria culture from the bald girl at the counter and then slid onto the bench beside her.

Sage told her she was a vision. He claimed that he had literally foreseen her coming, hence his ease at approaching her. Since they were not strangers, he felt comfortable laying a drink-chilled hand on her forearm, which he slid to the small of her bare back as they talked. Soon he had convinced her that she should stay with him and his wives in a caravan in what he said was the last true free community in the world— Slab City.

"It's on public land. There's no fees, no rent, no worries. I mean, no utilities and no sewage, but no hassle either. It's a self-made town, the way things are supposed to be."

"Sounds perfect," she said.

"What's your kick, anyways?"

She leaned in close. "Ram Dass, polygamy and organic mind expansion."

"Oh dude, you have to come with me. Stay in LA and you'll be panhandling and prostituting in no time."

His truck smelled like cat piss. Empty Red Bull and Listerine bottles rolled around the floor when they took corners. She paid for enough gas to get them out of LA and he lectured on the downfall of capitalism into the desert. When she sucked his dick in a gas-station bathroom near Joshua Tree, she realized he wasn't kidding about not having running water. Finally, they pulled off the highway onto a dirt track, passing a rusty trailer and a man in a mobility scooter smoking a giant spliff. Sage honked his horn twice and called "Hey, Jetson" out the window. The man waved back. They passed chicken coops and a mangy donkey tied outside a shelter built out of crates, its roof a green awning. That first day he toured her through the settlement, where magicians and artists lived in trash-built homes where you could drop acid or write poetry. He took her down to the hot springs, where they took bum baths.

Sage's wives were vastly overweight or underweight and were preoccupied with scratching themselves in various places and rolling cigarettes they smoked down to ash. Soon, Cecile knew the magicians were mentally ill and the artists more interested in scoring fentanyl than painting.

By her second week in the caravan, she was smoking meth on special occasions—concerts and poetry readings held in the courtyard, the stage delineated by dollar-store candles.

By month two, she had a bad habit, smoking even on days when the heat pushed the residents out into the communal living rooms of broken furniture and plywood floors and people could see what she was doing. She became less discriminating. She hitched rides on Jetson's scooter, the seat replaced with a beer cooler, to the trailers where she knew she could score. She did odd jobs, like washing dishes, running errands for the diabetics who had lost limbs and giving hand jobs to the elderly, for cash.

After a forced miscarriage presided over by the wives, who dosed her with raspberry tea and performed a kind of massage that was really just two tweakers pushing her stomach to her spine, Cecile decided she had to leave. She called her father, who bought her a ticket, and then she was back in Canada and straight into a rehab centre. It took several rounds of penicillin to clear her of the gifts she'd received in her time as a Slabber. Not to mention the crabs and dog bites, and the black eye she got when Sage decided she had taken a bigger share from the baggie than was right.

Some people say they didn't know what they were looking for when Jesus came and found them. Cecile knew. She knew the moment she picked up the Bible from the rehab centre's library shelf that Jesus was what she had been searching for. She threw out the beads and the mandala print shawls, replacing them with simple, long skirts and blouses, and a rosary she found on a day trip to a second-hand store. When her counsellor suggested she was trading one addiction for another, she firmly disagreed. After she was out of rehab, she fought her father when he arranged weekly visits with a psychologist and then fought with the psychologist herself when she brought up the possibility that Cecile's rapid shifts of direction might be due to borderline personality disorder. No one could see that what was happening to her was not mental illness, it was her being called.

She'd gone back to her father's house, but she could not return to the life she'd had before California and rehab and Christ. There would be no more college, no more movies and certainly no books that weren't written by the Lord Himself. She went from church to church, looking for a sign that this was where she fit, that this was where she was needed. And then the ministry came through town.

It was a smaller operation back then. No tent. Instead they held meetings in community-centre basements and handed out literature at church bazaars. She'd volunteered right away and began to travel to each meeting, working hard to become indispensable: organizing the other volunteers, designing and printing up posters and pamphlets that helped deliver news of a better way to the First Nations people the ministry served. Mr. Heiser was as impressive as he was inspirational. Here was a man who wore five-thousand-dollar suits but ladled out macaroni and cheese at the soup kitchen. He always had time for volunteers and worshippers alike. One time she'd asked him how he found the time and energy for it all. "God had time to create the world in seven days," he said. "I guess after that, nothing looks impossible." Of course.

At last Mr. Heiser recognized how invaluable she'd become by assigning her the role of congregational coordinator. That was also the day she packed up her belongings and left home for good. She'd been travelling with the ministry ever since.

A year later, the Reverend Wolff appeared. He was charismatic and of the people and soon their congregation grew and their circuit expanded. Suddenly they weren't just showing up, but were being invited into communities. They purchased a second-hand tent from a wedding rental store and bought stacking chairs with a loan from Mr. Heiser's company. It was clear as the sweet morning light on that first day the tent was erected, all peaks and posture, that Cecile truly had found her calling.

And in the handsome Reverend Wolff, Cecile saw a second sign—one she hadn't ever expected to receive. Now she knew at whose side she was meant to stand. God bless Mr. Heiser and wherever he had encountered Eugene (a name she only dared call the Reverend in her head). What glory it would be to be the wife of such a powerful minister!

And so she put on her best underwear and one of her long dresses, modest yet flattering and, more importantly, easy to slide a hand under. She pushed crystal hearts on silver hooks through her ears and applied enough makeup to highlight her best features. She brushed out her hair and gave the top volume with some hairspray, leaving the rest loose. Then she put on her long, beige cape, slid the key card for her room into the front pocket and rushed down the hallway, her door banging shut behind her. She took the stairs to avoid running into anyone from the ministry in the elevator.

In the dusk she crossed the parking lot, then picked her way across the litter-strewn ditch and slipped into the trees.

He wasn't hard to find. The woods were sparse and he had lit a small fire.

He was lying on top of his sleeping bag, a cushion under his head and a blanket pulled up to the neck. It looked like he was already asleep. She stood over him, watching the small shadows cast by the flames move over his face. They painted and erased his features so that his very person seemed to change: from long hair, five o'clock shadow, defeat and sadness, back to the groomed perfection of her Reverend. The shift disturbed her in a way she couldn't quite grasp, given that it was all a trick of the light.

Finally, she took a deep breath, kicked off her shoes and lay down in the space to his right. She propped her head up on her hand, supported by an elbow, careful of the placement of her hair.

"Reverend?" she whispered.

No response.

She laid her other hand on his chest and applied a bit of pressure. "Reverend Wolff."

Then she dared it. "Eugene?"

Nothing. How could he sleep so soundly out here? What if a bear came along? His leg would be chewed to the knee before he stirred. She slipped her cape off and lifted his blanket, slipping underneath. The heat from his body was alarming, but his breathing was regular, untroubled. Maybe he just ran hot at night. She'd consider that when buying their sheet sets.

She edged closer, resting her head on his chest. When he still didn't stir, she lifted a thigh over his belly, then pushed it lower than that. As she moved it up and down, her eyes closed and her lips parted, as she was seduced by her own movements under the wool blanket.

❦

Memories live not just in the brain but also in the muscle and tissue where they are created. They sleep curled in cells and platelets, until the right touch wakes them. When a man kisses his wife, it's not necessarily the fresh contact that unsettles his heart rate, but the memory of her wet mouth on his neck and the click of her wedding band against his fly three decades earlier. Sometimes a familiar hand on a shoulder can shiver song into your spine and make you dance.

And so when the good Reverend Wolff—who indeed believed Cecile was an excellent candidate for a wife and companion, who loved her corn silk hair and considerable piety—opened his eyes and saw her eager face, heard her soft moan and felt her heavy thigh, he was unmoved in the way she sought. Still, he allowed her hands to search out the plane of his stomach and did not protest when they moved to replace the weight of her thigh.

The Reverend was not so much a man as the outline of one—a chalk drawing on a sidewalk. This is why he needed the solitude of the woods and the light of the moon, why he needed his sessions with Mr. Heiser: he had to be redrawn on a regular basis, so that his edges could contain the words of the Lord, could move with purpose, could serve. All his will and whims were for the church. He waited to see if

God would allow Cecile's movements to stir him. God did not. The Reverend wasn't troubled. He knew this was His bidding.

He shifted and she rolled onto her back, waiting for him to move over her. Instead, he gazed up at the architecture of the sky and shook his head.

"No," he said.

She reached for his zipper, moving her lips to his neck.

"Cecile, no." The Reverend pushed her hand away gently and flipped on his side, putting his back to her.

The rejection paralyzed her for a long moment. Then she edged out from under the blanket and stood on bare feet. The ground was colder than it looked. She picked up her sandals, wrapped her cape around her and ran out of the woods, rocks, shards of glass and broken sticks piercing her soft soles.

Back in her room, Cecile turned the shower as hot as she could stand it and stood in the stream in her underwear. When she was done, she dried off with a thin towel that left her skin raw. Then she pulled on her longest white nightgown and crawled into the queen bed. She'd forgotten to switch off the overhead light and when she turned toward the window, she was faced with her own reflection, alone in bed. What did she do wrong? Had she misread the signs? She closed her eyes but she didn't sleep.

The next morning Cecile couldn't face seeing the Reverend, so she feigned a stomach virus and stayed in her room. Humiliation is a kind of sickness, after all—acute and self-pitying. That night she saw Ivy walk the Reverend under the parking lot lights toward the woods.

What in the hell?

Her breath had steamed a circle on the window, her hand clutching the burnt orange drapes that framed her face. There was Ivy, helpfully carrying the Reverend's bedroll, gazing up at him as he spoke. When he took the sleeping bag from her at the ditch and placed a hand on her head in joint blessing and dismissal, Cecile laughed. She hoped Ivy would look up on her long walk back alone and see Cecile in the window looking down at her. But Ivy didn't look up. And at least that night, Cecile was able to sleep.

She woke to a summons to a breakfast meeting with Mr. Heiser, the Reverend and the other senior members of the ministry in the Motel 8 coffee shop—likely to discuss heading farther north where all godforsaken things grow: pine trees, Precambrian rock, reserves. She hated north: too cold, too empty. Maybe once she'd taken over more of the overall planning from Mr. Heiser she could steer them back down south, even across the border into the States. For a moment as she got ready to face them all, she imagined a triumphant return to Slab City, bringing Jesus into the trashy Flintstone huddle like a winged stallion of destruction and rebirth—stomping over greasy tents, scattering noxious gas-fed fires across litter-strewn pathways, as the scrawny maniacs fell to their scabby knees on the splintered pallets they used as front porches. Even the bedbugs would be transformed, maybe into butterflies, or moths at least, with large eye prints on dusty wings to keep them safe from Satan's crows.

She made her way across the lobby slowly, the holes in her soles covered in Band-Aids. Each step hurt, but that was good—it reminded her that she was walking alone, just herself and Jesus, another martyr with wounded feet. When she pushed open the heavy glass door into the coffee shop, only the chain at the top clinked to announce her arrival—no cheerful bell. A row of puffy, ripped booths cut the room in two. On one side was a counter that was no longer used for diners, and instead held stacks of plates and napkins, newspaper sections, a sweater and a handful of pens. The other wall was reserved for window booths looking out over the parking lot and the highway beyond, edged by half a dozen tables with wooden chairs. Everything looked sticky.

The others were already here, seated in a booth with cups of coffee. Everyone but Mr. Heiser and Cecile, who'd decided to go with a long, white dress, was wearing the blue MNR polo shirt. They all looked up at her as she walked toward them and she gave them a small wave. Greg waved back. Was she late? She checked the slim watch on her wrist. Yes, by a few moments. She blamed her consecrated feet. Then she noticed Ivy, perched on the end of one vinyl bench. What was she doing here? She wasn't a senior member.

"Hi all, sorry I'm late." Cecile waited at the end of the bench for Ivy to move out and let her slide in beside Mr. Heiser, her usual position. "I guess I'm still a little wiped from this stomach bug. But I'm here now, so we can get started."

But Ivy didn't slide out. Instead she moved closer to the boss, leaving the edge for Cecile. She smiled down into her cup, refusing eye contact.

What the good Jesus hell? Cecile lowered herself to the bench, where the jagged edges of the torn seat cover had been duct-taped smooth. Surely someone would point out that Ivy should move.

But Heiser didn't seem to mind the younger woman squashed up against him. "Good of you to make it, Cecile," he said. "Let's begin."

"Wait, where's the Reverend?" Ivy asked.

Good god, who was she to interrupt? But Ivy was right. He was not in the booth or anywhere else in the coffee shop.

"The Reverend is getting some extra rest this morning," Heiser said. "There's obviously something going around— maybe he's got the same thing Cecile had. But anyways, we don't need to bother him with these details."

A heavy-set waitress brought Cecile a black coffee in a beige mug, even though what she really wanted was a cup of hot water with a wedge of lemon. Still, she said a polite thank-you.

Mr. Heiser checked his phone, then pocketed it, giving them his undivided attention. "Ivy here has brought up a good point, which we should talk about before we plan the next event and review the budget," he said. He looked sombre, dumping little, round containers of half-and-half into his coffee. "Ivy, why don't you go ahead and share with the group, please."

She cleared her throat, pink in the cheeks. Cecile's own

cheeks were a little closer to red. Take one day off and the whole world goes to the devil.

"Mr. Heiser and I were talking about the Reverend's fatigue at the last sermon, and I suggested it might be a good idea for all of us to take some time off, just a few days. Maybe we could even do something fun."

"Fun?" Cecile hadn't meant to say it out loud. She sipped the acrid coffee to stop any more words from leaking out. It burnt her tongue. Another penance.

Heiser said, "I think we should consider it. Because, sadly, there is a bigger issue at play. Cecile?"

"Yes, Mr. Heiser?" Finally, the adults were talking.

"You remember the woman who staggered into the tent at the Orillia service last month? The one we had to call the paramedics for?"

"Of course I do," Cecile said. "She was at the last two sermons too, in Hook River."

"Yes, she was. Ivy, you saw her as well. She was with the boy who tried to get into the back area."

"Oh my!" Ivy leaned across the table toward Garrison. "They were so aggressive, you should have seen."

Heiser sighed. "I've hesitated to do this, but it's time you all heard some hard truths about our beloved Reverend Wolff. I don't usually share people's personal details. But it's become necessary in this case, so that we can better protect him and the ministry."

Cecile's feet throbbed with her quickened heartbeat. What hard truths?

Heiser leaned his elbows on the table and steepled his long hands in front of him. "When I came across Eugene, he was in a bad way. Drugs. Maybe other things—I can't be sure. He appeared one night outside the tent. I don't think he meant to be there, but just kind of stumbled in our direction. The Lord works in mysterious ways."

The table gave the obligatory amen.

Cecile thought back to her first sighting of the Reverend. They'd told the cop it had been three years, but Mr. Heiser had shown up with him just a year ago after being away from the congregation for a week on business. Wolff seemed smooth and confident from the first day. But, she supposed, she shouldn't be surprised. Everyone has a past. Even the holiest among us.

"I saw something in him," Heiser continued. "I don't know what it was, but it was something powerful. Something that didn't need to be led but needed to lead."

More murmurs and nodding.

"And I thought, Heiser, you hold on to this man. You guide him just the right way and he will bring us into new territory, new glory. And so I approached him like one would a wild thing. I offered him coffee, water and a clean shirt. He accepted nothing, just sat down and wept. Seems Jesus had gotten there before me, because he was already broken open."

Wolff should have grown bigger in Cecile's estimation for what he had overcome, especially given what she herself had overcome, but instead she realized she felt deceived. She clung to that feeling.

"So I listened," Heiser said. "Right there in the mud

outside the tent. Seems this man was trying to run from some pretty dark stuff. He'd met a woman in Quebec who had led him astray."

"Oh my." Garrison tugged on his beard. "Lead us not into temptation . . ."

"Almost sounds like a TV show," Heiser said. "Before he left her, she'd got him hooked on some pretty nasty stuff, all kinds of things, not the least of which was heroin."

"Oh no!" Ivy gasped.

Cecile knew addiction. She'd leaned on the power of Christ to save her. But the Reverend? She was starting to think the Lord had saved her in the woods—that perhaps He didn't want her subjected to a junkie, not now that she was healed.

"Pretty shocking, right? Still, I decided right then and there he had been sent to us." Heiser pointed up at the ceiling of the diner, draped with cobwebs and clotted with grease.

Garrison and Greg both smacked flattened palms on the table, shouting "Yes!" and "Amen!" Spoons jumped and rattled and the waitress thought it was a signal they wanted more coffee. They waited her out while she poured.

Heiser picked up the story. "So I brought him to the city first chance I got. Got him into a good rehab clinic, then introduced him to a theologian I know over at the University of Toronto who thought he had tremendous potential. And so, he trained there, living like a monk.

"He worked hard and every minute of sacrifice was worth it, because he has become the most effective, godly minister we have ever had."

"Praise be," Cecile and Ivy said at the same time. Cecile avoided making eye contact.

"But now it looks like his old life isn't done with him yet. In Orillia, the woman found him again. She was drunk and crazed. The Reverend handled it, rightly or wrongly, by insisting that she was mistaken and that he didn't know her. Afterwards he was a mess. I took him back to the city with me for a whole week just to make sure he didn't relapse. Remember that, Cecile?"

She nodded. After that woman had gone off in the ambulance, Heiser had bundled a shaken Wolff into the back of his Town Car. She said, "This stalker did not like me one bit, not when she saw me trying to help the Reverend."

"Well," Heiser said, "he made me promise, begged me actually, to make sure she never got to him. He knows that she is his weakness. She led him astray once and he was frantic that she would be able to do it again. So I promised our good, pious Reverend that we would protect him at all costs. That we would make sure this woman, this Joan, never gets to him."

Greg said, "At least she doesn't know where we're headed. Maybe we could just keep outrunning her. Maybe look into a restraining order of some sort?"

Heiser sighed, unfolding his hands and dropping them to his thighs. "Actually, guys, I agree with Ivy. I think the best way we can handle this is to take a little break from tent-ups. When our mission calls us out onto the prairies, which I think will be soon, the problem should solve itself."

"How long a break?" Ivy asked. Cecile realized this was more than Ivy had bargained for.

"Just for a week, seven or eight days to be safe. Think of it as a kind of family vacation."

"What do we do if the stalker finds us?" Greg asked.

Heiser leaned over the table toward him, eyes crinkling in a wide smile that was all teeth. "Don't you worry. I'll handle her myself."

12

SOUL COLLECTION

Ivy wiggled her skirt back down, fished out her panties from under the bed and started talking as she threaded her pointed toes through the leg holes. "I think maybe Cecile knows about us."

Heiser hadn't even put his cock away yet, but had his phone in his hand, checking emails. "Ivy, you're going to have to be a little more specific." He set the phone down so he could tuck himself into his pants.

She sat on the edge of the made bed. "She's being mean to me."

"Jesus Christ, I do not have time for this." Heiser bit his lip and lowered his head. "Please excuse my blasphemy."

She nodded, as if he were apologizing to her personally. What a pretty idiot this one was.

"Cecile is a very busy woman," Heiser said. "Sometimes she becomes irritable because of it." He turned his back to Ivy and sent a quick text to his driver. "Part of the reason I like her is that she's so driven, even if it does make her crazy sometimes."

"You like her?" Ivy folded her arms over her chest.

Heiser sighed. "Ivy, I don't have time for this." He put the phone down again and reached over and lifted her chin. "Play time is over."

He excused himself and went to the bathroom to clean up. "Also, please look for an ideal retreat location, somewhere out of the way." He paused at the bathroom door. "Preferably off our current trajectory." Cecile would be pissed he'd asked Ivy to organize this. He honestly couldn't care less as long as it got done.

He turned on the tap and regulated the water to warm, but not hot. He dropped his trousers and leaned against the counter, flopping his dick over the edge of the sink. He chuckled to himself. Oh, Ivy. She was proving to be fun. Though he knew he really shouldn't be letting her distract him right now, when there was so much going on. What with his project contracts and now this bullshit with Wolff, he didn't have a spare moment.

Lately, the church was taking up more time than he liked. Still, it was one of his better ideas. It was a gamble to be a consultant—the gaps between clients, the reliance on the success of his last job to secure the next, especially when navigating Indigenous relations in the energy sector. He'd vastly improved his odds by bringing the word of Jesus into the territories he had to sway toward resource projects. Once God was in there, especially as portrayed by the beautiful Reverend Wolff—one of their own—people were less worried about protecting their traditional lands. He dried off, zipped back up and regarded himself for a moment in the mirror.

He never could have imagined having this life when he was a young man. An immigrant, an atheist, the son of a janitor—now here he was, fucking whomever he wanted, running a Christian ministry and raking in the big dollars from industry and government alike. The Reverend had brought in the masses, making the work of coming in behind to get project approvals so much easier. People loved seeing a reflection of themselves in the pulpit. Wolff was gold and Heiser would not lose him. But he was not worried: this Joan was no match for him.

Thirty years ago, Thomas Heiser had not yet truly understood what he was. So dogs liked him. So what. Other than a part-time summer gig as a dog walker, it hadn't changed his life in any way. Straight out of college, he'd taken a job as a low-level adviser for the federal government. He was first stationed in Saskatchewan as part of the legal team sent out to assess treaty adhesion claims. When he wasn't in his depressing cubicle, he travelled with two more senior advisers in a rental car. They stayed at a Days Inn while they took meetings in the band offices of surrounding First Nations.

It was early spring and he was at the rickety desk in his small room, typing up his handwritten notes on a heavy word processor. Part of his job was to carry that monster around.

Instead he usually left it in the motel and took shorthand at the meetings, notes he transcribed in his room.

That first night, he noticed an odd smell, a swampy organic rot. And then he had the sense that he was being watched. He finished typing up the page, stopping only to rub the back of his neck where he felt eyes on him. Then he turned toward the window.

Looking at him through the glass was a furry face, matted with hair and wild with debris and spit. The creature's eyes were overly bright under a heavy brow, and its long snout ended in a large nose that was the colour and texture of sand. At first he thought it was a dog, a huge dog, front legs up on the sill, staring in.

He saved his report to the disk drive, placed the handwritten pages in a pile at his elbow and snapped the lid back on the processor case. Then he took a deep breath, stood, pushed in the wooden chair and walked to the window. It was all very methodical. He'd always been calm.

As he got closer, Heiser noticed the width of the thing's shoulders and the immense height of it, even stooped as it was, shoulders rounded, neck thick to the point of grotesque. It opened its mouth and growled, a sound he heard through the thin glass as a slow cracking. Its front tooth was broken and brown.

Heiser's scream came up as bile. It choked him and he doubled over. When he looked back at the window it was empty, save for a gridded smudge on the glass from a greasy nose pushed against the screen.

He managed to carry on with his work for the next two days, running on such tiny naps they felt like nothing more than long blinks. Finally, he had to know just what the thing was, why it had appeared to him and what it wanted. So on the third night, he brought a bag of A&W back to his room and left the cheeseburger outside on a paper plate just under the window ledge. He locked his door and sat in the stained fabric chair with the lights off, slowly eating a small order of fries, watching out the window.

Just after midnight, it arrived. He heard it sniffing as it came around the corner. He got up and went to the window and watched as it stepped onto the cement walkway on the balls of its back feet, its hind legs without a canine haunch. It was covered in dense, black fur from head to toe. Heiser saw a glint at its waist—a silver belt buckle. No pants, but still, there was a belt. It peered into the cars and sniffed each in turn, avoiding the weak circles of light thrown by the bug-caked fluorescents in the roof overhang and the blue glare of TVs from the uncurtained windows. Heiser breathed shallow and quiet, watching as it made its way to his room, passing by his window without looking in. He waited for it to grab the burger, curious to see if it would use its hands like a human or gobble like a dog. It did neither. It stepped over the plate carefully, almost with grace. Then it walked up to the red motel door and politely knocked.

He didn't answer and eventually it went away. For the rest of the week, he locked himself in his room after the last meeting of the day. Each night he watched the parking lot through a small gap in the closed curtains. And each night the creature came, sniffed its way to his room and knocked at the door. On the eighth night, he let it in.

❦

Ivy had let herself out, as she always did. Good girl.

His phone dinged. He grabbed it from the dresser and opened a new email. Attached were half a dozen images of Cecile on her little foray into the woods. He wasn't naive enough to leave Wolff without a watcher, especially not now, with Joan lurking. He selected a photo in the middle of the stream—Cecile with a leg thrown over the Reverend, her eyes closed, her mouth open.

"Perfect," he said. He just had to dig up Joan's email address. Perhaps the only person who could keep her from her mission was Joan herself, and he was all too happy to help that cause.

There was a knock at the door, and he went to answer it. His driver stood there with his dry cleaning.

"Ah, thank you, Robe," he said, standing back so the man could hang the suit and shirts in the small closet.

"No worries, sir."

"And thanks for the email." He held up his phone and shook it. "These are just what I was hoping for." He laughed.

Robe smiled wide and took a small bow, snickering through his broken front tooth.

13

HIDE AND SEEK

Zeus sat at a long table on the second floor of the library. When Joan wasn't around, this is where he went. It felt calming to be surrounded by stories but no voices. Home was full of voices—too many of them, and none of them saying anything he wanted to hear. He was already dreaming of escape: college in Toronto or maybe Vancouver. It's why he worked so hard at school. If his dad had cared about him, he would have already moved in with him, away from the chaos that was Bee. But there was no room at his dad's house for Zeus.

Jimmy Fine had made his last trip through town five years earlier. One day he'd shown up unannounced in the same Impala, though the rumble of the engine was more wheeze than balls. He still wore his hair in a single, long braid, so thin now he had to loop the elastic around the end six or seven times. Two of his front teeth had fallen out, but maybe that was for the best. He had a quick, heated conversation at the front door with Bee, and then she pushed Zeus out onto the stoop and closed the door behind him, leaving him alone with his long absent father.

Jimmy shook the boy's reluctant hand. "Hey, son." Zeus saw Bee watching them through the window drapes with narrowed eyes.

"We're on our way from a powwow, you know?"

No, Zeus thought. *How would I know?*

"And well, I just thought you'd like to meet your sister. She really wanted to meet you. Her mom told her all about you."

Her mom? Zeus stayed silent, trying to make sense of the man. *Why would her mom mention him?*

"Anyways, she's over in the car, there." Jimmy started walking back to the Impala. Zeus just stood there in his white socks, hands shoved deep in the pockets of his basketball shorts, not saying a word.

Jimmy was at the car before he looked back. "Hey now, don't be shy. This is your little sister." He waved him over. "Come on."

Zeus took each step slowly, with his head down. He watched the way his toes moved when he stepped. He counted the ants he saw—six of them. He wished the driveway went on forever. When he got to the car, the little girl opened her door and sprang at him, wrapping her long arms around him. Maggie was beautiful—slim, deep brown, her long hair let loose from serious braids. A line of glitter from her powwow makeup still clung to her hairline. She was sweet and friendly. But why shouldn't she be?

"Gee, you're real big." She laughed as she let him go, not meaning any harm but cutting to the bone the way children can do. "I can't even fit my arms around you!" She tried again, though, squeezing him around the middle, nuzzling her face into his T-shirt, just above the round of his belly, just under the weight of his breasts. He kept his hands in his pockets.

"Well now, that's nice," Jimmy said. "Maggie here took first today over on the Island. Youngest in the Junior category too. She's a champion, this one." He put his hand on her shoulder as she let Zeus go, beaming pride bright in her face like the goddamned sun.

"The island?" Zeus asked, the first thing he'd said. The island was a ten-minute ferry ride away. They'd been ten minutes away for the whole weekend?

"Yeah well, once you're over there, you know how it is. And the contests go late. And the ferry is unreliable. But anyways, next year, maybe you'll come with us, eh?"

Zeus nodded slightly. He felt his guts roll over and lie heavy. He put both hands there. When he got upset, his stomach was the first place to know it. He squeezed his butt cheeks together, humiliated and confused in front of his father and his beautiful sister.

"I better go," he said. It was barely a whisper, but his father pounced on it.

"Oh yeah, okay then, son."

This was the worst thing of all: worse than the fact that his stomach was now carbonated by burning bubbles, worse than the fact that they had been so close for an entire weekend and only bothered with him now, worse than the absence of his father itself. The worst thing was that Jimmy Fine looked relieved when he said it, like he agreed that Zeus really had better go. It would be the best thing for them all.

"Anyways, your mom just told me I missed your birthday last week. Sorry about that. But here." He opened the back door and rummaged around in a cardboard box behind his seat. He picked out an old flashlight, then threw it back in and fished out an old Discman held together with a piece of masking tape and attached to a pair of foamy earphones. "Take this, son. It's important you always have music. Get some of those big drum CDs. That way, next year when we come get you, you'll know all the songs."

Zeus took the broken gift and then stood and watched this fragment of his family pile back into the car. When Jimmy turned the key, the music blared and they drove down the street and out of the community to Northern Cree singing a round dance song about beautiful women they couldn't ignore. *Heya, heya, ho.*

Joan had come to a potluck dinner that night—potluck was Bee's style. Zeus wasn't in the front room when she got there and, since he was the main reason she came by for meals, she went to find him. She walked past the bathroom with its mountain of towels on the floor, past the twins' bedroom with the bunk beds wrapped in duct tape and padding so they wouldn't kill themselves or each other, and finally stood outside his closed door, hand raised to knock. But she paused, because she heard soft sobbing. She opened the door slowly, hoping he was watching TV, wondering who, if anyone, was in there with him. Instead she found him cradling a shitty old Discman to his chest like it was a person and crying, his eyes shut tight.

She closed his door quietly and went back to the kitchen, where Bee told her about the visit. She waited for him to come out on his own. When he did emerge, Joan took him down to the docks for ice cream and promised him she'd never let anyone make him cry like that again. She'd cut off Jimmy Fine's nuts and hang them from his rear-view mirror with all the other crap.

Since they got back from Hook River, he and Joan hadn't been able to find any sign of a tent-up. So Joan had gone back to work and Zeus had distracted himself with school, both of them checking online every time they stopped for a meal. Now it was Friday afternoon and he was hiding out in the library, checking everywhere he could think of, but still no luck. He really wanted to get out on the road again.

His phone dinged. Joan.

Dinner at Ajean's? I'll pick you up at 6

He texted back.

K. I'm at the library.

K

He opened Facebook on his phone and went to the ministry's group page again, like he had every day since they came home. The page had the same images from the pamphlet they got in Hook River. There wasn't much posted: some quotes, small articles on the founder, Mr. Thomas Heiser.

"Dammit." The most recent still only gave directions for the Hook River meetings. Nothing since. He went to the members section and a list of profiles lined up down the screen. Who were all these people? He began browsing.

Joan picked him up an hour later and they drove over to Ajean's, who fed them tuna sandwiches and beet salad. A cold rain began, plinking on her windows like impatient fingers. Zeus watched it collect in the rutted driveway in untidy pools shining in the street lights.

After dinner, Ajean set cups of sweet tea and a small saucer of hard oatmeal cookies on the table. "Any news on the travelling Jesus show?"

"Nope." Joan went to the front window and slid it open a crack, then lit a cigarette. "Nada."

"I found their Facebook page when I was at the library," Zeus said around a mouthful of cookie. "No upcoming meetings. But I got looking at some of the individual profiles."

"What do you mean?" Joan asked. "Show me." She flicked her smoke out the window and slid in beside him on the bench seat.

He fished out his phone from his pocket and opened Facebook, clicking on the ministry. "See, you just go to their members list and then click on the one you want."

"Her." Joan stabbed her finger at Cecile's listing.

"Okay." He clicked. A profile picture beside her name, which was *Cecile Ginnes*. "Hmn," Zeus said. "Her posts are set to private."

"Fuck."

He scrolled back. "What about this one? The one with the red hair who stopped us from going to see Victor."

He clicked on the small, pale face. In the picture, she looked serious, her red hair gathered into a high bun that emphasized the roundness of her face.

Ivy Johanssen
Dedicated to My Lord and Saviour, Jesus Christ
Birthday August 17, 1998

He started scrolling through prayers and motivational sayings she'd typed in curlicue fonts with glitter effects.

"Good job, my boy," Ajean said, giving him a little congratulatory rub on the shoulder.

Joan was leaning so far into the screen her head was in front of Zeus's face. He gently pushed it back with a finger.

"Does she say where they're headed?" Joan asked.

"No. But we can see where she's been."

"How the hell is that going to help us?"

Ajean clucked her tongue. "Simmer down, there. Give him a chance."

"Thank you, Ajean." Zeus cleared his throat dramatically. "To answer your question, Ivy Johanssen likes to post pictures." He went to one of her photo albums and began flipping through a series of black-and-white images.

"Are there clues to where they're headed?" Joan could barely keep her bottom on the bench.

"Not exactly. Her photos are mostly art shots." He clicked through them, one by one. They were not very good.

A deflated balloon still attached to a string like a celebratory umbilical cord.

A field with a decaying fox in the foreground.

A ditch filled with discarded pop cans.

A stormy sky that reflected nothing.

Joan almost growled. "There's absolutely nothing here! A dead fox? How are we supposed to figure out anything from this shit?"

Zeus tapped a photo and turned it so she could read the text at the top. "She's tagged them with location markers."

"Genius!" Joan jumped up and paced the kitchen. "You, sir, are a friggin' genius!" She pointed at Zeus, who smiled with his full face.

"Here's the last two," he said. "Hook River and then Sturgeon Falls. Looks like they're heading north."

"Okay, we need to leave as soon as we can," Joan said. "I don't know about you coming, though. You have school on Monday."

"I can take a few days off. My marks are good and my mom won't care. Less for her to worry about."

Joan pulled a fresh cigarette out of her pack and went back to the window. "I'll think about it."

After they left, Ajean put the cookie plate and the teacups in the sink and used the damp rag that hung over the faucet to wipe everything down. Something wasn't right. The wrongness draped over her like a blanket, making her tired, making her slow. Yet it also cut into her like sharp sewing scissors so she couldn't sit still. It was fear, she finally realized. Ajean was not accustomed to dealing with fear. Not anymore. She'd spent years pruning and nurturing herself so that there was nothing left for her to be scared of. But she had grown complacent, had forgotten that there was always room to be afraid. All fear had to do was let doubt do the dirty work and then it could move right in, past the rubble of a person's defences.

She thought about grating some salt off the bone still in the tin on top of her fridge. She even grabbed it, the contents rolling around inside.

"Not yet, you," she told herself. "Don't go jumping to no conclusions, wasting Angelique's medicine."

She put the tin back and went into her bedroom. She picked up the small Virgin Mary figure from her dresser and kissed it on the face, at the spot where the paint had long since worn off. By now her Mary had one eye and just a bottom lip remaining. She tossed the figure on the bed. Next she grabbed the square ceramic jewellery box that held her best rosary and put it beside the statue. Back in the kitchen she got a blue plastic Canada's Wonderland tumbler, a silver serving spoon and a broken watch she'd been meaning to get fixed and brought them all back to the bed. She retrieved seven more items from around her house: a spool of thread, an empty beer bottle she'd kept because she drank it on the night she beat old Elsie Giroux at euchre, a pocket Bible with gilt edging, a toothbrush she used to clean her shoes, a picture frame with no picture in it, a beading needle and a hundred-dollar casino chip she'd found on a walk one day, so scratched she couldn't read the casino name and cash it in. Then she grabbed a plastic bag from the shelf under the cupboard that exploded plastic bags when you opened it, packed all her items into it and went out onto her porch.

The rain was still coming down hard. She watched it, bag in hand. Someone told her once that chickens could drown, mesmerized by the rain, heads turned up to the leaking sky, beaks open and taking on water. She imagined that slow, stupid death. She'd prefer to have her head chopped off: clean, easy, even with the indignity of the after-death jog around the yard. Ajean placed the bag on her welcome mat and upended it, the random things rolling until they settled.

No matter which community claimed them, rogarous were known for some specific things. They smelled odd, like wet fur and human sweat. They were men turned into beasts for any number of reasons—each one unique to the storyteller. They were as notoriously bad at math as they were obsessive. A rogarou, try as he might, could only count to twelve. Put thirteen things by your door and he would be inclined to stop and count them. But since he could only get to twelve, he could never count the entire pile, so he was doomed to start again and again, stopping at twelve and returning to one. Eventually, he'd give up and go away, forgetting he'd ever intended to enter. At least that was the theory.

She pointed to each object on the mat, as she counted them. Then she counted again. "Une, deux, trois" to "treize."

She clapped her hands together when she was done. Her wolf alarm system was set. She hummed the alarm company jingle again as she went back inside her small, warm home.

Ajean was glad for all the ways she knew to keep herself alive. She'd learned how to flip a man who was trying to get into her pants and kick him right in the nutballs. She'd been taught that at the Friendship Centre self-defence class. The flyer said to wear athletic clothes, so she'd tucked her best long johns into wool socks, put on the Molson Canadian T-shirt she got in a two-four box last summer and wore her sportiest kerchief. Boy, could she ever flip and kick by the end of that class.

She also knew the old ways, things some people called superstitions. Pfft. See who they all come to when someone gets medicine put on them or when they need to know how to cure an infection. Ajean knew how to survive.

Still, she was worried. She could smell the doubt that hung around Joan like a sickness. (Bronchitis smelled like clay, pneumonia like wool.) Joan wouldn't get Victor back if she went at him with any doubt in her—about him or herself. She had to forget any doubt if she was going to get past that rogarou to get to her man.

"Damn wolf." She opened the door to spit outside. She looked once more at her thirteen objects and then closed both the screen and the wooden door against the night.

She turned off the kitchen light and headed for her bedroom. Then she stopped. Just to be safe, she went back to the door, slid home the deadbolt and crossed herself.

"Name of the Fadder, the Son, and that Holy Ghost."

14

ALL THE POSSIBILITIES

Flo's truck was in the driveway. Junior was parked behind her and George's SUV leaned on a flat tire in the front yard now covered in fallen leaves. Indian summer was gone.

Joan almost drove by. She wasn't sure she wanted to deal with her family tonight. But at the last minute, she decided to pull in. She really needed to tell them all she was about to take off again in search of Victor.

"Hey," she said, opening the door.

"Well, well, if it isn't Noodles McGee." Junior waved his own arms, teasing her for her back-to-work soreness. She never should have mentioned it or, worse, admitted she needed an extra break.

"Who needs two breaks for one shitty roof?" George, who was sitting on the couch with a cold beer, pointed a finger at her and laughed.

Flo came out of the kitchen and snapped both sons in the

leg with a twisted dishtowel. "Enough, enough. You two were more than happy your sister was back on the job. Don't be bugging her about it."

"No, I deserve it." Joan flexed. "I mean I can still take you both, but go ahead, take your jabs now, while Mom is around to save you."

George went to the fridge and grabbed her a beer. She settled on the couch beside him to watch a round of *Jeopardy* with her brothers and kicked their asses on the trivia front.

Afterwards Junior carried their empties to the kitchen. When he came back, he said, "Georgie and me were talking. We'd feel better if you let us put some traps at your place near the edge of the woods. They never did catch that wolf."

This was the second time traps had been brought up since their grandmother's death. "I don't want anyone's pet getting caught," Joan said. "That's the last thing I need."

"No one should let their pet go loose, especially not now," Junior said. "Your safety is more important than anyone's cat, anyways. You're out there all on your own."

"I know you mean well," Joan said, "but I can't stomach the idea of traps." She got up from the couch and went to sit at the dining room table.

"Anyone want tea?" Flo flipped on the kettle. She wasn't ready to go anywhere near the subject of Mere's death.

"What's on the schedule this week?" Joan asked.

"Gotta finish Longlade's before winter," Junior said. "Frost is already here."

"That's not a very big job," Joan said.

"Big enough," George answered. "Especially for you."

She returned his smirk. "Babies could do that reno, so should be about your speed, Georgie boy." Then she took a deep breath. "Okay, well, I wanted to tell you I have to be somewhere this week."

Junior, so concerned a minute ago, gave her a death stare. "What the fuck, Joan? More time off? This is why we're behind!"

"It's about Victor."

"It's always about Victor."

"Junior, you're not my boss."

"Someone has to be," George chimed in from the couch.

"No, but I am," her mother said, giving her a meaningful look.

"Fuck, forget it." Joan stood up from the table. "Thanks for the beer." She walked to the front door and grabbed her coat from a hook on the wall.

"Is this about that religious group?" Flo asked. Joan turned back. She saw pity on her mother's face. She'd rather deal with her brothers' exasperation—she wasn't sure she could handle pity.

"What religious group? Joan, did you join some sort of cult?" Junior asked. He pushed his hand through his hair. "Frig it, Joan, that's not gonna help you."

"I think I found Victor."

Her mother sighed, dropping her chin to her chest. "Here we go . . ."

"Where?" Her brothers spoke in chorus.

"Remember when you came to get me after Mere . . . when I'd been at Travis's? The day before I'd gone into a church tent set up at the Walmart and Victor was there." She left out the part about him being the preacher.

"What the fuck?" Junior said. "Why didn't you say? And why didn't he come home with you?"

"He didn't know me. He couldn't remember anything. He has amnesia or something."

"Amnesia? Is that even a real thing?" George asked. "I thought that was just for movies and shit."

"It's real—he really didn't know who I was. And he had a different name, different friends, a different . . . job. He even looked different. His hair was cut."

"Are you sure it was him?" Junior asked.

"Pretty sure."

"How sure?"

She made eye contact with him. "Pretty sure, Junior."

Flo cleared her throat. "Joan, dear, I'm going to say something here that you're not going to like, but I'm just going to say it, because you need to look at all the possibilities." She softened her voice, as if that would make what she had to say less of a blow. "If it was him, maybe he isn't lost and maybe he doesn't have amnesia. Maybe Victor just left you."

George suddenly found his feet interesting. Junior held Joan's gaze, slowly nodding his head. And her mother kept that pity firmly affixed to her face. Joan felt tears well—how were there still more tears—and pulled her arms through her coat sleeves. She turned away, then paused with her hand on the doorknob. She said over her shoulder, "I won't be in this week. Hopefully I'll be back with Victor by the weekend. And you can ask him whether he abandoned me yourselves."

She slammed the door behind her.

❦

She wore her red coat and the cream heels she'd bought for their wedding. She never did wear them; she was too worried about losing her balance and maybe wrecking her eight-hundred-dollar shoes to put them on. She kept them in a box in the closet, each one in its own special bag. But in the dream, they were firmly on her feet. They made it difficult to walk across the field, but she had to, because the tent was just there, up ahead. Every few feet she came across a dead fox, teeming with maggots and swarming with flies. She stepped over each new corpse, unable to stop looking down at them, watching the way the maggots were running on a sped-up loop so that the bodies were melting under their labour. The tent was so close she had to keep going, pulling the slim heels out of the muck each time they sank.

But something wasn't right up ahead. As she got closer, the tent seemed like an empty plastic bag, with nothing inside to crisp up its shape. And it was quiet—no music, no loud prayers, just the low hum of a woman softly sobbing as if exhausted with grief. She stepped over another fox, whose dead eyes looked like scratched taxidermy inserts. She had the urge to stick a fingernail behind the orbs and pop them out. She could carry them in her pocket.

The tent was just ahead. Except she couldn't get to it. So she kept walking, through the field with the foxes rotting into the dirt around her pretty shoes. And then she heard a scream, so high and loud it hit her like a cramp in her thigh. She fell to her knees in a mushy pile of snapped ribs and decomposing flesh, the soupy mess splashing up her legs.

"Zeus?"

A distant howl answered her.

"Zeus!" She yelled so loud her eyes closed. "*Zeus!*"

She opened her eyes, gasping, and then clutched her thigh where pain twisted her muscle. The bed was a mess of sheets and sweat. She sat up, knocking the last bits of the dream away, rubbing her skin to make sure there was no blood, no maggots. Then she got up to walk the last bit of the charley horse off.

"Fucking Ivy and her art photography." Saying it out loud into the room made her feel better. And proved she was awake.

She used the washroom, then came back to sit on the edge of her bed. She was rattled. The worst part of the dream hadn't been the decaying animals but the crying she'd heard from the tent. The sound of it, even in memory, made her chest ache. Before Zeus had screamed, he had been crying, and the sound woke something in her that she wasn't sure was supposed to be awake. It made her feel powerful and vulnerable at the same time. She thought maybe this is what it felt like to be a parent, and she wasn't sure she liked it.

VICTOR IN THE WOODS: CHRIST IN THE CLEARING

He felt her terror like a weight on his chest and bolted upright, clambering to his feet.

"Joan."

The clearing was illuminated by a hollow grey light, which revealed the chair. He examined it frantically, throwing it on its side and upending it, and then with meticulous care. The screws were silver and cheap, and the seat cushion was new enough to not yet be indented from people sitting on it. There was nothing miraculous about the chair, save for the miracle of it showing up here.

He pulled a crescent moon of fingernail out from between his bottom front teeth. His mouth tasted like he'd been sucking on a penny: Joan's fear and his own, he realized.

He righted the chair, sat down, then wrapped the hem of his T-shirt around his right pointer finger and rubbed at his teeth and gums. Ugh. This was not helping. The metal tang grew so that his silver fillings sang a cruel note. He stopped, unwound his finger and breathed as shallowly as possible. A thin blanket of scent crept over him. He inhaled, his head tilted. He could not tell where it was coming from, besides suddenly everywhere. It was wild and refined at the same time, like a corpse dressed in fine linen. It stirred him.

He scanned the space around him. Sharp evergreens, heavy spruce, the delicate veins of thin birch branches against the grey light. The ground rose at the outer edges of the clearing in a ridge topped with scrubby grass and a luxurious fan of ferns like filigree against the backdrop of trunks. Nothing out of place. Every leaf and blade accounted for.

What was this smell? He sniffed at himself. Nothing. No smell at all. Maybe he was a ghost. What had he done to deserve this? He'd been a good son, coming back home to care for his mother until the cancer took her, burying her beside his father with the knife she always carried in the fold of an apron. He'd been a good husband, like his father before him. That was easy. He loved Joan with a ferocity that scared him.

He felt a twinge in the back of his head. Something he couldn't quite remember. They had fought, he knew that much, but he'd left the house rather than be angry in her presence. Surely that couldn't be held against him. He pushed his fingers into his tangled hair and tried to massage the twinge out of his scalp. Impossible.

No. He was not dead. He was afraid, and what would there be left to fear if he was dead?

He stood up and walked the perimeter of the clearing, sniffing the air. The smell grew stronger and the grey muslin light was fading.

"No, please no," he said to the darkening emptiness around him.

He heard a low cracking sound.

He turned, the light pushing shapes into shadows. A figure was now sitting in the chair, calmly regarding him with that same tilt of the head. It held its upper body stiff, perfectly straight from the waist up, and its chaotic hair looked like spokes against the darkening sky. It reminded Victor of a stained glass Christ wearing a dangerous-looking halo. Perhaps he was dead after all.

"Jesus?" he asked.

The seated figure gave a deep laugh. The sound filled the clearing like vomit, like a menacing growl. And the sky grew darker for it.

If he were capable of regular functions, this is when Victor would have pissed his pants.

15

MEETING GOD

They were headed south for a change, so Cecile should have been happy. Except Ivy had been the one to suggest it, which rankled. So she slept most of the trip with her head on a folded MNR fleece propped against the cool van window. Let the others take care of navigation and choosing pit stops and keeping receipts for a change.

"Cecile."

Someone was shaking her by the elbow.

"Cecile, wake up." It was Greg.

"What?"

"Ivy says we're still about two hours away from the retreat, so we're going to stop for a quick picnic here. You hungry?"

Goddamn Ivy. She answered him with a sigh, unbuckled her seatbelt and climbed out of the van. He was already unloading the coolers from the back. "Great," she said. "Sandwiches and warm juice at a cold rest stop."

He ignored her sarcasm, just kept whistling "This Little Light of Mine" while he stacked checkered blankets on top of the coolers at his feet.

Cecile stretched, getting out the kinks that came from being cramped in a back seat with other bodies and duffle bags for hours. She looked around. The lot was almost empty, except for an older model camper, a grey sedan and their three blue vans, parked side by side. It was late in the season for road trips, and there wasn't much to recommend the spot. Only a thin row of pines protected it from the highway. Beyond the locked-up visitors' centre was a map of the area on a wooden post; a few metal picnic tables hunkered at the edge of an open field that ended in a patch of woods. She walked over and studied the map. It showed a small body of water called Lord's Lake on the other side of the trees. Lord's Lake: What were the odds? So that's where she headed, passing the others who were laying food out on the picnic tables.

"Cecile, aren't you going to eat with us?" Ivy called. "We could use some help, you know." Cecile kept walking, savouring the exasperation in the younger woman's voice. *Good. Be frustrated. Let me be the cause of your frustration.*

She followed a narrow dirt path into the woods, worn smooth by the sneakers and sandals of travellers seeking respite from the road. The trees closed in on both sides like an evergreen cross-stitch. At last she popped out of the dark onto a small beach lit grey and brown by the water and the clouds collecting chill over her head. "Lord's Lake." She said it out loud, like the beginning of a prayer.

Cecile spotted a flat rock near the water's edge and sat

down, pulling her knees up and wrapping her beige sweater tight around them. What now, she wondered. She wasn't afraid of fighting for what she wanted. She knew how to fight and win—she'd figured out that no one else would do that for her by the time she was ten years old.

❦

Little Cecile had been good at keeping her adults happy. She knew what to say and when. After her mother was gone, she lived with her daddy and his mum, Grandma Pat, and wore the gingham dresses and little aprons the old woman sewed for her on an old sewing machine she set up on the kitchen table.

"You look like Holly Hobbie," Grandma Pat would coo around a Marlboro Light after she'd dressed the girl in her latest creation. Cecile didn't know who that was, but she twirled on the linoleum in her sock feet anyways.

She had no memories of her mother but pretended she did because her father liked that. At least most of the time he did.

Sometimes he cried, holding her tight as if she might blow away. "Such a small thing," he'd whisper into her neck. "Such a tiny little thing you are." Other times he refused to look at the girl, growing angry when she came to find him. "Jesus, Cece, don't you have anywhere else to be?"

On those days, Cecile closed her bedroom door and let her gerbil, Bella, out of her cage. She built mazes on the carpet out of books and Lego pieces and prodded the little creature along pathways and around corners, pushing it into the rooms of her dollhouse, pinching it when it lingered too long. "Get out of the kitchen, Bella. Jesus, don't you have anywhere else to be?"

Cecile's mother wasn't dead. She'd left them when Cecile was three. Her father would sometimes make a point of reminding her that he wasn't the only one her mother had abandoned. "She walked away from us both. Can you imagine a woman who would leave her husband and kid to go to Florida to be an actor?"

"To be a whore, you mean," Grandma Pat would always say. She was smug. She'd warned him.

"Don't people run away to California to be actors?" Cecile had once asked.

"Don't be a snob," her father answered.

One night, Grandma Pat came into the living room to find her son weeping into his daughter's narrow neck while he held her down on his lap by the shoulders. Her grandmother walked out again without saying a word. The next morning at the breakfast table she told her son, "It's time to find a mother for that child." Cecile's stomach suddenly felt too heavy to carry. She didn't want a new mother.

But her dad took the hint. Women of all kinds started showing up. Women with limp bangs and adult acne. Overweight women with rouged-on cheekbones and soft voices. Women who smoked with Grandma Pat and gave Cecile side-eye. Women who moaned through the walls and left her father's bedroom smelling like an aquarium. But none of them stuck, until Karen.

Karen wore her hair clipped short to her head so that she looked like she was wearing a helmet. She had a thick waist and muscular calves and a voice that rang like a porcelain bell. She bought cartons of menthols for Grandma Pat and six-packs of Coors Light for her father.

Grandma Pat approved of Karen. So did her father. After a while he invited her for an introductory family dinner, where she showed up with the dessert, behaving as though the next time she'd be coming with her luggage. There were more dinners, a few outings with the kid tagging along, lunches, and then, after a few months, a weekend in Niagara Falls.

Grandma Pat and Cecile were left at home to fend for themselves. Grandma drank a glass of whisky after they shared a frozen pizza, and toasted the happy couple. Cecile went to bed early. "Shut up, Bella," she hissed at the gerbil, which ran and ran on its plastic wheel.

To Cecile, Karen smelled of onions and old blood, like a pocketful of pennies. She couldn't live with that smell. She would die. She got on her knees the night before Karen was to babysit her for the first time so that her dad could take Grandma Pat to the dentist, and asked God to step in, beseeching the ceiling for help. She fell asleep waiting for an answer.

The next morning, Karen showed up in her burgundy minivan with a canvas bag full of half-used colouring books. *What a cheap-ass*, Cecile thought. *Couldn't even buy me a brand new one.*

As soon as her daddy and Grandma Pat pulled out of the driveway, Cecile went to her bedroom and shut the door behind her. She poked the eraser end of a pencil into her gerbil's shredded paper nest, prodding Bella awake, then opened the cage door and picked up the sleepy pet. She flopped on her bed, sitting Bella on her chest. "Go back to sleep, numbskull," she ordered. The animal was just starting to settle down, the rotations of her whiskers growing intermittent, when Karen barged in without knocking.

"Shut that door!" Cecile shouted, surprised by the volume of her own voice.

Karen was also surprised. She stood in the open doorway, with her plucked-thin eyebrows arched. "What did you say to me, missy?"

"I'm not a missy." Cecile sat up against the headboard, and Bella toppled to the bed.

"You're not polite either." Karen held her ground.

"Shut it! Bella could escape."

"But she hasn't. She's right there." Karen pointed to the gerbil, who was now pissing on the white comforter. She paused, then regrouped, saying in a calmer tone, "Besides, I would help you find her."

"I don't want your help." Cecile pictured this ridiculous woman sleeping on her father's chest. Rage made her limbs itchy.

Karen put a hand on her hip. "You would rather Bella got lost?"

"I would rather she was dead."

Karen gave a small, nervous laugh. "You don't mean that."

Cecile picked up the gerbil, tucking the tiny, warm body into her right palm and closing her fingers around her. Looking Karen directly in the eye, she tightened her grip.

Bella squirmed, let out a quick chirp that stuttered at the end and then, in desperation, dug her long front teeth into the meat of Cecile's thumb. The girl squeezed harder and Bella stopped squirming.

Karen backed out, closing the door. Cecile heard the front door click, the minivan start and gravel spitting on the driveway. Karen didn't stick after all.

Looking out at Lord's Lake, Cecile thought, once again, about how people could only make themselves small for so long. She had spent too many years pretending to be small enough to crush. She was bigger than that, and she deserved more than that. She used to think the way to do it was to serve at the Reverend's side, but that dream died in the woods. Now she understood that little episode was God's way of reminding her that only He deserved her obedience and sacrifice. The lesson was clear now.

She unbent her legs, pulled off her desert boots and socks and dug her toes into the cold sand, which soothed the still healing cuts on the pads of her feet. She felt at peace. It had been so long since she felt this way, she almost didn't recognize it.

The Reverend had a weakness in the form of a woman. Cecile, at this moment, was strength in the form of a woman, and she could use that strength to deliver him unto temptation. She could be the Eve to his Adam, with Joan as both apple and snake.

She needed to do it in such a way that she was blameless, though, so she remained the best and most obvious choice to replace the Reverend. She wasn't Native, but she could transcend that. She could prove to Mr. Heiser that she was truly chosen. After all, there was no such thing as race in the eyes of the Lord.

She closed her eyes, steepled her hands and prayed. God would show her the way.

She registered a change in the light through closed eyelids and shivered as she felt the presence of a divine ear and a loving heart. It was better than the rewards of humble service performed in His name, more touching than a full tent of raucous prayer, more powerful than a meth rush. She breathed deep, attempting to be fully in this moment. The air grew cold against her hands and neck, and she felt the zing and clatter of electricity. She was heard and so she would also hear. God would let her know what was to come next.

Just as she opened her eyes, the sky was torn open by blue light and the wind rushed to fill the gap. The clap of thunder that followed was so loud it rippled the water and shook her bones. Cecile turned her face upwards and smiled into the rain that fell hard, solid like wet sheets on a clothesline. She scrambled to her feet on the rock, opened up her arms and was baptized anew. Purposed. Bigger than ever before. Maybe just big enough.

16

DECAY IN THE NORTH

Joan lifted the newspaper and stared at the small picture of Heiser in a line of men until his face was a dot matrix. She was parked outside a diner, smoking and pacing under a street light in front of the Jeep. The night was cold and she shivered in her thin sweater. She reread the headline:

New Development Announced for Northern Region—Local First Nations Sign Agreement on Consultation

And there he was, Mr. Lying-Ass Heiser, grinning for the camera from his spot tucked in beside a broad-shouldered man in a grey suit who was shaking hands with a shorter man in a ribbon shirt. She imagined him with paws tucked into his shiny brogues, fur covering his straight back.

"My, what big teeth you have," she said aloud.

She crumpled the newspaper with hands stiff from gripping the steering wheel across county lines, around the Bay and into Precambrian rock. She crunched and folded until it was an uneven ball and threw it, in a perfect arc, into the metal garbage bin.

Her phone vibrated in her pocket. She'd left Zeus back home, and he had spent the evening sending her angry texts. His messages crowded her screen and, when she refused to open them, pinged intermittently. She'd read the bulk of them after she'd placed her order, guilt making it impossible to text him back. But no matter what Ajean said, and no matter how much she loved the kid, she couldn't bring him on this trip. Her desperation was wearing out her frantic hope and she didn't want Zeus to see that.

She ground her cigarette butt under a heel and exhaled, pulling her keys out of her pocket. It was time to get back on the road.

By eleven o'clock, she'd made it past Sturgeon Falls to the town called Rice Creek, population 784, the last location they'd been able to track on Ivy's Facebook. There hadn't been any online updates since.

There was one motel in town, a throwback to the 1960s with Magic Fingers beds that ate your quarters and rattled your teeth, orange carpets that smelled like mould and industrial cleaner, and a small, round, empty swimming pool out front.

The registry was an actual paper ledger. Printing the date beside her signature, she asked the clerk, "Sir, do you happen to know if there is a church revival mission in town? Maybe even staying here?"

The man at the desk, who must have always been the man at the desk, had a long, Yosemite Sam style moustache of pure silver. His head was haloed by long wisps of white hair that he may have tried to push over his bald dome at some point earlier in the day. His Wrangler jeans sagged so far off his flat ass, the full upper half of his grey long johns were visible. Luckily they were in good repair, with newer plaid patches over earlier striped ones.

He paused so long Joan thought he hadn't heard the question. She was opening her mouth to repeat herself when he said, "No, no. It's all mining guys right now. Someone came in here from the local church and told me to expect some revival people to book in soon, but I haven't seen any of them fellas yet. Good thing I didn't hold any rooms for them." He shuffled to the desk behind him and passed a dangling hand over the surface, scattering papers like he was setting up for a game of memory. Then he selected a blue pamphlet and carried it back to the counter.

"These fellas." He put it on the counter in front of Joan. A glowing cross. MNR.

"So they haven't shown up, then?"

The man regarded the pamphlet, then the counter for a while. At last, he seemed to catch himself drifting and reached under the counter for a small envelope with shaky numbers—104—written across the front in thick black marker.

"Your keys." He held it out.

Joan took the envelope and drove the Jeep around the side of the building and parked in front of room 104, which was in the middle of a long, low wing. Every other space was taken by newer model F-150s and a couple of Cadillac SUVs. Her brother was right: looked like the pay for jobs in the mines was pretty decent these days.

As she got out of the car, she heard laughter and the high twang and low bass of country music. She turned to see a small bar, hanging like a comma off the end of the motel wing. Outside, a small group of men stood smoking. A long, narrow sign in neon tube letters spelled out *The Drunk Tank* over double doors painted to look like saloon shutters.

She was slamming the back hatch closed, her bag by her feet, when she heard her phone ding. Zeus again, she thought, heaping more abuse on her solo mission. But it wasn't a text; this time it was an email.

It was from Resource Development Specialists—Heiser's company. The subject line read simply *For Joan*. There was a JPEG attached. Should she open it? What the hell would he be sending her? Maybe it was a virus. *Sure, Joan, that's the extent of his evil-doing. He's going to give you a computer virus.*

She clicked and watched as the file downloaded and an image popped up on the screen. She stared at the lit square, trying to stack and restack the colours and lines so what she was seeing made the kind of sense she could live with. She needed it to be different, so her heart could continue to pump.

Holding her breath, Joan carried her bag to her room and unlocked the door. She turned on the lights, closed the door behind her, put on the safety latch and then set her bag down on the bed. She let the air in her lungs go, took another breath and held that one too. She raised her phone to look at the picture again. There was a buzzing in her ears, angry and steady. She sat on the bed and then, exhaling, slid all the way to the floor, her phone falling out of her hand onto the rug beside her.

The muffled music from the bar, the laughter of the smokers, the crunch of the gravel, the roar of cars on the highway—all of it filled her ears like salt water she might drown in.

The photo was taken at night, the colours grainy and the edges too dark for specifics. There were a dozen ways you could look at each shape. Trees on all sides threw shadows like the bars of a cage. But really, there was only one conclusion. In the centre, on the ground, was her husband, stretched out on a sleeping bag beside a small fire, with a blonde woman on his chest.

She put both hands on her forehead and rocked, softly knocking her skull on the bed frame. She had to get up, now, or she'd never get up again.

It was busy in the Drunk Tank. Joan couldn't find a seat, so she leaned against the bar, shot the first vodka and sipped the second. Then someone noticed she was an actual woman and offered her his stool. Even though she was clearly distressed and monosyllabic, it took him almost twenty minutes to take the hint that she was in no mood for a chat.

After he moved off, she ordered a third round and set her phone on the bar, the image centred on her screen.

She wanted someone to explain this away, to tell her it wasn't what it looked like. But who? Not-Victor acted like he didn't know who the fuck she was. No way was she showing Zeus, or Ajean, who would just rant on about tricky wolves and trickier Europeans. For the first time since she saw him again at Walmart, Joan was angry. So angry she wasn't sure she wanted to save him. Hell, if Victor called her right now, she wasn't sure she'd even pick him up from the Greyhound station.

She clicked her screen off and swivelled around on her stool to survey the room. Anything for a distraction.

The bar was a sausage party. There were easily four men for every woman, and some of the women looked like the kind you paid for. There was a stage for a live band, a small dance floor and high, round tables packed with drinkers. The place was lit with a hundred different neon signs hung on the walls. Every beer company she knew and some she'd never heard of; open and closed signs; puns; rudimentary pictures drawn in neon of beer mugs, women, pool triangles and sticks. There was no need for more illumination, except for the spotlights on the stage and two small lamps behind the bar so the bartender could check IDs and make change. Everyone in the place looked frighteningly cubist and excitingly attractive in the neon glow.

She rubbed the lighter in her pocket, flipping it lengthwise a few times. She checked her purse. No smokes. Fuck. She got up and went outside. There were two choices: a group of three men and two women who were well beyond tipsy and having some sort of flirt party, or a single guy in a cowboy hat. She went for the cowboy.

"Hey, sorry to bother you." She motioned to his lit cigarette with her chin. "Can I buy one off you?"

"How could I say no?" He pulled a pack out of his front pocket and handed it to her. She tried to give him a loonie and he waved it off.

"Thanks," she said.

He offered her a light, but she used her own.

"So, why are you hanging out in the finest establishment in town tonight?" he asked.

"Oh, just the usual bullshit." Her bullshit was anything but the usual. But right now she wanted to smoke and she wanted to be mad.

"Well, I am happy to be your nicotine dealer for the evening. I'm Gerald."

"Joan." They stuck their cigarettes in between their lips and shook hands.

"What's with the hat?" she said.

He tipped the brim with a finger, just like she imagined he would. "Homesick, I guess. I'm from Alberta. Setting up this new project out here for a few months."

"People in Alberta actually wear cowboy hats?"

"Only the good-looking ones."

She surprised herself with a laugh. And oh, laughing felt good. They smoked in silence for a few minutes. Then he flicked his butt into the parking lot and it hit the ground with a tiny explosion of orange sparks. "I need a drink. You need one, Joan?"

"I do. Unless you can just hook me up to a Grey Goose IV out here."

He looked at her with mock surprise. "Jesus, I better hit the ATM if it's going to be that kind of night."

An hour later they had commandeered one of the high-top tables and were leaning in to talk over the three-piece band. Joan had danced, and now her T-shirt was stuck to her sweaty back. That felt good too.

Gerald was telling her about the mine. "I mean, the work isn't always glamorous, but I do get to stay in awesome places like this."

Joan found she had to ask. "Hey, have you seen any church people around here?" The drinks had loosened her up but hadn't yet shut down the obsessive part of her brain.

"Church people? Well, my guess is you wouldn't run into them at the Drunk Tank."

She sipped her beer. There was sure to be a hangover tomorrow. "True. This place is only for champions like us."

"Are you a church-going woman, Joan?"

"Me?" She laughed. "No fucking way. I'm just looking for someone travelling with some missionaries. Hey, you think they only do it in the missionary position?"

The band finished up its unrecognizably slow rendition

of Nirvana's "Smells Like Teen Spirit" and launched into something a hell of a lot faster.

Gerald slammed his empty onto the table. "Oh my god. We have to dance to this. Come on." He held out his hand to her.

"What the hell song is this?" She screwed up her face, trying to decipher it.

He closed his eyes and started singing along. *"There's a man going 'round, takin' names . . ."*

Johnny Cash. Yes indeed, she did have to dance to this. Zeus would approve. On the full dance floor, Gerald put a hand on her lower back and pulled her in close, holding her other hand out and up.

"Oh shit, are we gonna do this cowboy style?"

"Almost. I won't make you line dance."

She'd forgotten the feel of being held, of being pushed and pulled in a small space with nothing else to be concerned about. The band was horrible and the crowd was the kind of drunk that made people clumsy and sure of themselves at the same time, and this man was a stranger, but near the end of the song, out of weariness or gratitude, she laid her head on his damp chest, which felt odd and comforting at the same time. He pulled her tighter so she was held there, then he picked the steps, he cleared the way. And she allowed it. As if it were safe to allow a man control even for a second. She knew better, but she was so tired. So fucking tired.

Back at the table, they stood close, the heat of him reaching her skin. At one point, while discussing the merits of mullets in the work of natural selection, he put a hand on her hip. She let it stay, as experiment. And it did cause a tightening in her crotch—a feeling she forgot existed outside the context of Victor. She waited for it to make her sad, the same way she cried after masturbating. But it didn't. Anger is a strong temporary blocker and she was still very angry.

Why not kiss someone? Let someone kiss the hell out of you? Why the fuck not. Just to make it even.

Gerald leaned down. If she turned and tipped her face up a bit, they would be kissing. Anyone looking at them—him leaning in so close to her face, a hand on her hip, asserting possession—would think a kiss was inevitable.

Fuck, her head spun. And suddenly she had so many tears her face hurt and she didn't have the strength to let go of them. This was not what she wanted. This man wasn't Victor.

She had to get rid of Gerald for a minute so she could breathe. "Can you grab me another beer?" He stared at her for a moment, but then he nodded.

She pushed her hair out of her face and muttered a heart-felt *Fuck* as he walked away.

She watched him at the bar. He was good-looking, that much she gave him. Brown hair, smooth skin, great build from a lifetime of labour and taking care of himself. But he was not Victor. Even if Victor was fucking Cecile. Even if he couldn't remember Joan. Even if he was lost to her forever. Even then, she didn't want anyone else. She snapped an elastic she'd forgotten she'd stuck around her wrist and tied up her hair in a low ponytail. Back to work, Joan.

Gerald returned with two sweating bottles of light beer, put them down on the table, then tried to move back into his cozy spot up against her. She stepped out of reach and he moved toward her again. She moved once more and this time he stopped where he was. It took him a minute, but he settled at a safe distance, noticeably sulking.

They listened to the band massacre "Love In an Elevator" by Aerosmith—or was it "Carry on Wayward Son" by Kansas, who could be sure? She noticed him noticing the blondes who sashayed by their table, bumping into him or each other, all tipsy-clumsy cute. He smiled his appreciation at them, even tipped that fucking hat. Well, that didn't take long. Also, who the hell orders Miller Lite when there's Labatt 50?

Just as she was thinking about getting out of there, he leaned toward her again. "So tell me. Who is it exactly you're looking for?"

"My husband."

"Ahh. I see. And does he know you're looking for him?"

"He does."

"So if he's expecting you, how come you don't know when they'll be here?"

"Things are complicated, Gerald. And also none of your business."

"True." He took a long pull on his beer. "Well, maybe some of the guys from work will have an idea." He used the neck of his bottle to point around the room before taking another swig. "There's always one of those mission tent things popping up on projects."

"For the workers?"

"Nah, for the local communities, Indians mostly, I guess. But it's also kinda for the workers. Makes our jobs easier." He finished off the bottle and pushed it away from him. "We call them the clearing houses."

She let that *Indians* slide for now.

"How's that?" She sipped her beer, regretting now how alcohol made her dull, made them all dull. The whole bar was a cutlery drawer full of spoons, not a tine or a blade in sight.

"You know all these projects have to go through approvals, right?" he said.

Why would she know that? But, "Yeah."

"The only real threat to a project—to our jobs—are the Indians. They're the ones with the goddamned rights, I guess. Always protesting and hauling us into court."

Okay, clearly he had no idea Joan was Native. Maybe he thought she was some hot Italian mama or fiery Latina, both of which she had been mistaken for by douchebags in bars.

"It's the ones who have traplines or who do ceremony out on the land." He actually put air quotes around *ceremony*. "Those traditional Indians, they put up the biggest fight. They can stall work for years. But when the missions come through?" He snapped his fingers. "They're too busy praying to protest. The missions are good at changing the way people see shit. Course it helps if you can hook one or two of the powerful ones—chiefs and whatnot, especially the ones willing to take the company cheque and give speeches about moving on with things, doing things like actually working." He laughed and shook his head. "Mission tents are an important part of mining, of any project really—mining, forestry, pipelines. That's what's going in up here next, a pipeline conversion. Maybe that's why your guy is coming to this shithole."

"Missions are *part* of the project?"

"Yup. The only thing more effective than an Indian priest is a kid preacher. They have those down in the States now. Craziest thing." He reached for his bottle, then remembered it was empty.

"Holy fuck."

"Exactly." He laughed so hard all his teeth shone in the glare of a hundred neon lights.

She saw the Reverend Wolff then for what he was, leading the people like some kind of Anishnaabe pied piper. Heiser's role made sense too. He was a rogarou, and the rogarou is doomed to eat the people, to wander the roads leading us into temptation. It made sense, then, that he was also filling the church tent.

The image of Victor and Cecile in the woods came back to her and rage bubbled under her skin. The idea of Victor and the rogarou tearing the people from the inside out, fucking up whole communities, made her ball her hands into fists. And then there was this dickhole, still laughing at his own racist commentary. She watched his eyes squint, his mouth open wide, the glare of his overdone veneers. And she pulled back and punched him right in that fucking mouth.

He bent in two, his empty bottle crashing to the sticky floor.

She yelled into the top of his hat like it was a microphone: "We're not from India, jackass."

Then she turned and hauled ass out of there, not stopping until the door of her room was locked, with her safely on the inside.

⚘

"I'm okay, I'm okay," she whispered to herself in the empty of her room, water filling her eyes. "Everything is okay. Victor isn't Victor. He can't cheat on me because it isn't him right now. He's crazy, I am not."

She filled a plastic cup with water and drank it all down, then refilled it and brought it to the bedside table. She peeled off her clothes and slipped naked between the rough sheets. She wished more than anything she had quarters for the Magic Fingers. Instead, she found small solace in small words, chanting them like Ajean would.

"Name of the Fadder, the Son, and that Holy Ghost."

Then she uttered a different kind of prayer. "Dear Victor, please, please don't be gone. Please."

VICTOR IN THE WOODS: RUN BOY, RUN

The pressure in the air made it hard to breathe. He wanted to run, but instead he was rooted, eyes stuck on the figure still seated in the chair, its laughter fading. Then it was quiet and the silence was terrifying. His feet broke free and he ran, arms out in front to avoid collisions with the trees. The thing vaulted from the chair and came after him, its movements fluid with muscle and magic.

"I am going to wear you," the thing said. "The tearing will be a horror but the fit will be couture."

It sounded gleeful, unbothered by the usual strain of running. In a sing-song voice, the creature called, "Fear just makes the meat tougher and then it will take even longer to remove the outer layer."

Jesus Christ, who said such things? Victor flashed on every horror movie he'd ever seen, and none of them had anything reassuring to tell him about the situation. So he kept running. He'd spent enough time in the specificity of this leafy prison to know when to jump, when to duck, and how to find purchase on the steeper bits. But apparently, so did his pursuer.

And so they ran. Victor felt as though he were being chased by his own shadow. It never got closer, never fell behind, and seemed to know his next move before he made it. But there was nothing familiar about the shape or tone or even the smell behind him, though now he knew what was responsible for the scent of rotting flesh in fresh linen.

"Joan!" Victor realized he was screaming, spit parachuting out of his mouth. "Joan, come get me!"

He'd heard her—when was that? He had no idea how to measure time, not here. What was that line? *I have measured out my life with coffee spoons.* Who said that? Some poet, probably dead—they all are.

What the fuck was he doing thinking about buried poets and cutlery, while being pursued by something out of a horror show?

Where was Joan? He'd heard her last year or just a moment ago, saying that she was on the way. She'd better find a quicker route, because Victor wasn't sure how much longer he could run. The thing behind him wasn't even panting. It might as well have been twirling a stick and whistling a tune.

There was nowhere to hide here, not any place that he wouldn't be caught. He called over his shoulder. "Who are you?"

The thing laughed. "Just someone."

"Who?!"

"No one you know."

Victor tripped over a root and went sprawling on his face. He lay there on his stomach, hearing the figure approach and then come to a stop above him. There was that laugh again, like a growl or an old engine rumbling. But nothing else. No attack.

Fuck it. Victor flipped over onto his back. Might as well see what the hell was after him. Rather, what he had been caught by.

The creature was indeed wearing a well-tailored linen suit, brogues, with the chain of a pocket watch tucked into a vest pocket. But its head was in shadow. Victor squinted.

"What do you want from me?"

The thing reached down with gloved hands and pinched the fabric of its carefully cut pants above each knee to allow it to bend, and then it lowered itself so Victor had a clear view of its face.

It rubbed its fingers together like it was asking for money while it regarded him. "Well, hello there, human."

Victor screamed into the trees, but there were no birds to take flight. There was nothing but him and the rogarou.

17

WOLVES IN THE SOUTH

The last thing Cecile wanted was to be stuck at some retreat with the Reverend and a collection of idiots. And yet, here they were, pulling up to a cheesy off-the-grid community lodge, even farther off the beaten path than they normally travelled. They were somewhere near the US border in the middle of a national park.

Cecile slung her weekend bag over her shoulder and rushed through the pouring rain into the lodge. After her moment of communication with the Almighty by Lord's Lake, she was back in control. No one was going to call dibs on shit until she had picked her own space, especially since Heiser was staying off campus. That obviously meant she was in charge. The Reverend could keep tending to the souls for now, but she was the one who would keep the group in line.

The lodge had one huge, central room, a kitchen, gendered washrooms, a small office with a computer and a printer, and a closet area with hooks and cubbies, but no bedrooms, no beds.

There was no upper floor, either. Instead, the ceiling arched up forty feet to a pointed roof dotted with cloudy skylights.

Great. No privacy? Surrounded by morons? She'd just have to take over the office.

"This place is beautiful!"

"Right?"

Ivy and one of her ponytailed sidekicks were high-fiving each another, kicking off their sneakers and twirling in their socks on the hardwood floor. A part of Cecile still wanted to feel this joyous over the small crumbs life offered. But that wasn't her lot anymore.

"Let's get the kitchen stocked and the bedding and pillows inside," Cecile ordered, even though the others were already doing just that. She rounded on Ivy and her friend, who stifled themselves and shuffled off to the vans, though they couldn't help bursting into laughter just outside the door.

The Reverend's vehicle pulled up outside. Garrison was driving him, treating the job like he was a member of the secret service, if that secret service agent drove around a small-town preacher in a Dodge Journey that smelled of joint cream and hand sanitizer and had belonged to his mother.

Then the front door opened, the rain clapping in the trees, and the Reverend walked in with a smile on his handsome face. Garrison followed, laden with bags.

"Good, I am so glad we're all here. Now we have a full set of apostles," the Reverend said, grinning, his skin glowing, his hair perfect. The others giggled, yet even so, felt important in the light of his attention. He turned and smiled at Cecile, like that night in the woods had never happened.

"Cecile, our rock, our strong guiding star," he said, and he reached out and took her hand in both of his, squeezing it gently.

She felt a quick beat of hope. Maybe things could go back to the way they were? But it faded fast. She wasn't the woman who had sought him out so shamelessly. Not anymore. What was his attention in comparison to holding private audience with the Father Himself? Still, she smiled back at him. He was inconsequential. They'd all see it soon enough.

The Reverend moved on, and Cecile went over to Garrison, who was standing by the kitchen door, a jam sandwich already in his hand. "I need a lift into town please. We're low on feminine hygiene products."

"Now?"

"Yes, dear. We wouldn't want any of our sisters to go without, would we?" She turned and headed for the door. He was left with no choice but to follow. He couldn't let a high-ranking member wait for him in the pouring rain while he ate.

At first they drove in silence, Garrison concentrating on the road through the rain and Cecile composing a message in her head. How much would someone like Joan—a pagan, obviously, drug-addled more than likely—even understand? She'd have to keep it simple.

When they hit the highway, Garrison relaxed. "Oh, thank Jesus that's over. Whew!" He shook out one arm at a time, then looked over at his passenger. "You okay there, Cecile?"

"I am better than fine. I am truly blessed."

"I hope Mr. Heiser has the same bright outlook. I've heard

the weather has made for some traffic delays. He won't be here until tomorrow, looks like."

"I didn't realize he was coming at all."

"Well, he is. He wants to make sure we don't lack for anything."

"I can take care of us." Heiser was their sponsor, their advocate, but not their spiritual leader. This retreat was meant to be a spiritual one, after all.

"Clearly." Garrison chose his next words carefully. "I think maybe he just also wants to spend some time with us, Ivy in particular."

"Ivy, why Ivy?"

"Well, because they've been spending more time together lately. Personal time."

He arched his eyebrows and lifted his shoulders and looked at her knowingly. Garrison loved gossip, the big old gay. When she was leader, she'd get him some conversion help. But for now, she would squeeze him for every drop of juice he had to offer.

"Really?"

"I saw her leaving his room myself, just three nights ago."

Only the seatbelt was holding her back from literally shaking him. "Did you ask her what was going on?"

"Not in so many words. But when she saw me in the hall she gave me the *shh* finger." He lifted his own fat finger to his lips.

"Oh my."

"Yup. And then she did this little wiggle move to pull her skirt down." He wiggled in his seat to demonstrate. "Pretty incriminating, if you ask me. Not to mention a sin." He was thoroughly enjoying himself.

"I *am* asking you. I'm asking if you're sure about it?" The blood rushing in her ears was making it hard to see straight. She'd thought Ivy was after the Reverend, but it turns out the little tramp had gone straight to the top. Fuck!

"Uh, yes. I mean, Lord, Cecile, that's all I know."

She tried to calm down—to remember the light and love she'd been so damn full of. She uncurled her fists and put her middle fingers to her thumbs, invoking a small prayer for patience. "I'm sorry, Garrison, dear. It's just—it's just that I heard she was aiming for the companionship of the Reverend, not Mr. Heiser, is all."

He looked away from the road for a moment, checking her expression for sincerity. "Heavens, Cecile. Why would she do that? Everyone knows you and the Reverend are made for each other."

She shut her eyes against a fresh wave of humiliation. So all of them were watching, waiting for her and the Reverend to get together. What would they think when they didn't? Now she really had to make sure the Reverend checked out, and Ivy with him.

She checked her phone to see if she had service. Two bars. She quickly logged on to Facebook. "How much longer to town, Garrison?"

"Lord Almighty!" He swerved in his lane and she almost dropped her phone. "Did you see that?"

"What?" She hadn't seen anything. But then came another clap of thunder, this one so loud it shook the car.

"The lightning. It hit the ground, I'm sure of it." He leaned forward, peering around her.

"If it's this bad, maybe Heiser won't make it." She was calm.

"It did hit, look!" Garrison pointed out her window and she turned.

In a farmer's field, a tree had been split down the middle and was smouldering. Its bark had exploded off the trunk with the strike, the exposed wood ragged and pale. Flames licked up and were tamped back down by the rain, the sky fighting with itself to bring heat and water at the same time. She watched until they were over the next hill, until all she could see was a single plume of smoke still rising through the rain.

That smoke was a message as clear as if He'd leaned through the foggy glass and whispered in her ear. Cecile now knew exactly what she had to do.

VICTOR IN THE WOODS: THE AGE OF REASON

"**I** am just as trapped as you are, brother," the rogarou said. "And just as miserable about it. Maybe more." It rubbed its chin with a thoughtful hand.

Its eyes were distracting, flashing between yellow and green like a traffic light. *Caution, stay still,* they shouted. *Get the fuck out of here!* they screamed.

"The truth of it is, I was tricked here." It lifted its arms level with its shoulders and turned a slow circle. "I don't want to be here." It spoke slowly, as if Victor were himself slow.

Victor was backed up against an elm trunk, where he had wrapped his shaking arms around himself in a weak attempt to stay calm.

"I am used to being a free agent, so to speak. I don't like to follow anything but my own heart." It tapped at its chest with the head of its walking stick, the rounded knob carved into a snarling wolf's head. "And yet here we both are."

"Who are you?"

"My dear child, you know who I am." It rested the stick on Victor's shoulder like it was knighting him. "You know in your bones." As it uttered the word *bones* its eyes flashed in the dark. Victor held his breath.

He did know. This was the creature from one of his moshom's stories, the dog from the road, the dancing trickster who didn't fuck around. "I do."

It smiled. "I have a bit of a reputation, don't I?" If it really was trapped, it seemed pretty calm about it all.

"Normally, I would slip right *over* you." It ran the stick up one of Victor's arms, across his chest and down the other, as if measuring him for a suit.

"But then I ran into a stranger somewhere." It rubbed its forehead. "It's the damnedest thing, I can't really remember . . . Regardless, I ended up slipping *under* you instead."

The creature sighed and lifted its head toward the moon, which had managed to cut through some of the pervasive gloom. Victor stared at its long snout, at the dark fur that covered its cheekbones and brow. Not man at all, though it spoke like one and wore a man's clothing.

In its presence Victor felt the certainty of his end and he remembered his moshom taking him out on an overnight hunt when he turned seven. In the church and at his Catholic day school, the priests called seven the age of reason. Moshom called it the age of learning how the hell to survive. Same thing, really. So the day after Victor's birthday party, held in his grandparents' kitchen with a dozen cousins and not enough cake to go around, Moshom took the boy into the woods.

"People think it's the hurt things you gotta worry about. The hungry ones. The crazed ones." Moshom settled on a large rock and lit a filterless Player's. "But they don't think, them. Hunger and hurt makes an animal do things he won't do regular. Makes him irrational. He'll make mistakes. You can live to see tomorrow because of those mistakes."

Victor sat on his packsack watching as his grandfather coaxed a fire out of kindling. The flames, as they grew, turned everything kinetic. Even his grandfather's face, usually stern and smooth, was animated. Shadows poured out of the crooks of branches. They slid along the leaf-strewn ground. They formed solid figures just beyond the first trees and teased the boy from there.

"It's those healthy ones you gotta look out for when you're tryna stay alive. The ones who know what they're doing. They got their job and they're damn good at it. An animal's not lazy like a man. He'll kill because it's what he's supposed to do. He'll eat every part that's not poison. A creature who understands his own damn self and isn't distracted by fear or pain: that's the creature you don't turn your back on." The old man tapped his smokes in the breast pocket of his flannel jacket, indicating his heart.

So here, in the clearing, Victor kept his back against the tree while he unwound his arms and stood. He cleared his throat, trying to keep his voice from wavering. Which was impossible, because he already knew the answer to the question he was about to ask.

"You're going to eat me, aren't you?"

The rogarou laughed so hard it howled. And then it said, "In a manner of speaking, yes, and also quite literally." It crouched to seek out Victor's eyes and stared yellow into them: *caution, caution.*

"Only the parts that aren't poison."

18

HURRY

Her head hurt like an open wound. But that was minor compared to the operatic pain in her hand. She waited in bed with her eyes closed, a pillow pulled over her face. It would come back to her. It usually did. Yup, here it came . . .

The email.

The Drunk Tank.

The cowboy.

The truth.

The punch.

She threw off the pillow, then winced as she checked out her hand. It was swollen, the entire rack of knuckles split and bloody. Those damn veneers.

She swung her legs off the side of the bed and waited a moment for the nausea to settle. Then she tiptoed to the bathroom and ran the water as hot as she could stand and held her hand under the stream to clean it, swearing steadily. Then she switched it to cold for the swelling.

She wiggled each finger, relieved that nothing was broken. She dried her hand as best she could, then patched it up with an alcohol wipe and gauze from a small first-aid kit she carried in her purse. She carefully dressed, wincing when anything touched her hand, then had to take her time as she repacked. The ministry wasn't here. Victor wasn't here. And after the email and the fucking bar, all she wanted was to go home.

When she slid the keys into the ignition of her Jeep, she had a moment of fear that it wouldn't start. Fingers crossed.

She turned the key and there was too much silence and she was sure she'd been jacked again. But then came a rumble and a rev and the Jeep gurgled to life.

Thank god.

She backed out of her parking spot and drove slowly across the lot, keeping her head down in case the cowboy was around. It would take her a few hours to get back to Arcand, so she paused at the end of the driveway, reached into the glove box and grabbed a bottle of Aspirin, shaking three directly into her mouth and chasing them with last night's cold coffee. Then she turned right, toward home.

Zeus's bike was sprawled on her front lawn.

Fuck.

All she needed right now was a nap and a new plan, and maybe some better painkillers, not an angry twelve-year-old. As she parked and turned off the car, she saw him in the front window, a scowl on his face. Jesus, he looked like his mother right now.

She was too tired to get her bag out of the back of the Jeep, so she left it and trudged toward the mudroom door. He confronted her as soon as she walked in, leaning in the doorway of the kitchen with his arms crossed over his chest. "Real nice, Joan. Real nice."

"I don't need this right now, Zeus. I'm exhausted. And aren't you supposed to be in school? It's not even two o'clock." She pulled off her sneakers and tossed them at the rack.

He pointed at her. "*You* don't need this right now? *You?*" They stood there for a few seconds until he dropped his hand. "You know what, fuck it." He turned and walked away from her.

"Hey! Don't swear at me. Not in my own house." The curse shook her into movement and she followed him. "Are you listening to me?" She grabbed his shoulder, wincing at the pain in her hand but holding tight, and turned him around.

He wriggled out of her grip, stifling a wet sniff. She pulled off her sunglasses and looked at him. "Zeus, are you crying?"

"No, you big jerk, I am not."

But he was. New tears were starting to fall, following the shiny trails the old ones had left on his dark cheeks.

"Zeus, listen, man, I had to go alone." She reached once more, this time with her left hand, rubbing his arm gently. He pulled away from her again.

"I'm fine," he said. "I just—I had a bad day."

He sat on one of the high stools by the counter that separated the kitchen from the living room. Joan put her sunglasses and phone down and filled two glasses with cold water from the tap. She slid his over like a bartender, leaning toward him from the kitchen side of the counter. "So, what happened?"

"You first." He wiped his face with his sleeve. "Did you see him? Victor?"

"Nope. They weren't there." She pushed out her lips and slowly shook her head. "And I have no idea where they went."

"Bummer."

"Yeah, bummer. But that's okay. We'll keep trying." She took a long drink from her glass, rubbed her forehead where the hangover lingered. "Now you. What happened?"

"Fought with my mom."

Joan nodded. That wasn't so unusual. "Well, you and Bee have a bit of a tumultuous relationship."

"Yeah, but this time was different. It, it went too far."

"What do you mean, it went too far?" Dark, red images moved into her brain. She wasn't above driving over to her cousin's and smacking the shit out of her if she had laid a hand on this kid.

"I was really mean."

"How so?"

He flushed red to the tips of his ears. "I told her I hated her."

Joan wanted to laugh, she was so relieved. She thought of all the times she'd said the same thing to her own mother. But Zeus, even at twelve, was more thoughtful than she'd ever been. So this was different.

He continued. "I was late for school this morning and she started in on me. I tried to walk away from her but she just kept following me. *Zeus, why are you so lazy? Why can't you be more responsible? You're more like your father every day. Maybe you should go stay with him instead, maybe that'd teach you to listen.* She followed me out to the backyard, even. I kept telling her to stop, to leave me alone, that I was sorry, that she didn't have to drive me, that I'd just ride my bike to school—it was fine. But she wouldn't stop." Water blurred his eyes again.

"It's okay, man. Bee can be a little much. I'm sure she knows you didn't mean it."

"That's the thing, Auntie." He looked up at her with sombre eyes. "I do mean it."

Just then, her phone buzzed, shuddering against the countertop. Zeus glanced at the lit screen. "It says you have a new Messenger request from . . . Cecile Ginnes."

"Who the hell is—" Joan froze. It couldn't be. The phone buzzed again and this time she jumped.

"What's it say?"

Zeus picked it up. "Same request, same person."

"Fuck. Oh fuck." She pushed herself away from the counter and nervously shook out her hands. "What do I do?"

"It's easy. Just swipe the notification open. What's your passcode?" Zeus tapped at the screen.

"Don't touch it!"

Zeus put the phone down and raised his hands like he was at gunpoint. "Easy, Auntie. She won't know you saw it unless you accept the request."

"Oh God, Zeus, it's the woman from the ministry— remember? The blonde one." Joan paced in the small space between the fridge and the doorway. "What do I do? What could she want?"

"Well." Zeus slowly picked up the phone again, eyes on her in case she lunged at him. "You can open it up and look at her message. Then you'll know what she wants. Problem solved."

Joan rounded the counter and came to stand beside him. "Okay. Okay, go ahead."

Zeus clicked Messenger open. When Joan saw Cecile's name she tried to slap his hand away. Her phone had become a time bomb. What if Cecile was watching them? What if she was messaging from the 5 Star Motel, the cowboy by her side, his bloody mouth full of laughter? What if she were sending another picture of herself with the Reverend?

Instead, the message opened to a small map marked with a red pin. Somewhere near Leamington, Ontario, right near the perforated line of the US border. Underneath the image was a single word that was both instruction and request and suspect as all hell. It jumped into her ribs and set her heart thrumming. It could be misdirection. It could be a cruel joke. But what if they didn't pay attention? What if they ignored it and Victor disappeared forever? Maybe the ministry was crossing into the States as Joan stood here, maybe Victor would be all the way to Mexico by week's end. She saw him getting smaller and smaller, pulled away down unfamiliar highways.

The clock was ticking. Her bag was still in the Jeep. She moaned. What should she do?

She reread the message and paced the linoleum, Zeus watching her in unusual silence.

HURRY

This time there had been no leaving Zeus behind.

It was after seven when they finally arrived at the Leamington Deluxe Motel, its neon lights already lit and buzzing. Stepping across the threshold of their room, Joan felt some of the stress leave her. They were here—close to the ministry and whatever that meant. As Zeus settled on his bed, she went for a shower. And as soon as she got out, they began to argue over whether he should go with her to rescue Victor.

"It could be dangerous, is all I'm saying."

"It was always dangerous," Zeus said. "I want to come. You need me—you're practically crippled with one hand."

She turned away from him. "I should go alone."

Zeus protested, "But we're a team."

"Yeah, and you're too young to lose. Ajean, me? We at least have had some life."

He stared at her with narrowed eyes. "I'm not ten years old, you know. You don't have to be condescending."

"I do know." She sat heavy on her bed and picked up a brush to attack her hair, buying time.

"Well then, what?"

She threw the brush down and slid to the floor in the space between their beds. "Okay look, here's the truth. Ajean told me that to rescue Victor I would have to seduce him. I might have to seriously Sleeping Beauty him, but like, without clothes."

"Really?" Zeus pulled his legs up and tucked them side-ways.

She nodded.

"We came all the way here, through all this, so that you could get into his pants?"

She nodded again.

"That's the shittiest end to an adventure I've ever heard."

"Could be worse."

"Not really." He picked at his big toe nail, deep in thought. "I could stay in the Jeep."

"I have to ditch it so no one in the mission will spot it and then walk in. I don't want to leave you alone in the park."

"What if we just do a recon mission tonight? Figure out if he's actually there or not."

It was a decent idea, but she felt like she couldn't be careful that way. Not anymore. "We don't even know if this is real. I don't want to waste any time. We might have to book it back up north if this was just Cecile misdirecting me."

"Exactly, and it'd be faster to leave directly from the park. We shouldn't take the time to come back here." He swung back to stubborn. "I'm coming. I'll close my eyes if it gets weird. But I'm not letting you do this alone. We're a team, for god's sake."

He leaned over, feeling for his shoes under the bed.

She was pretty sure that if she didn't have to have sex with Victor, she might at least have to break Cecile's arm. She didn't want Zeus to witness either.

"Alright, alright. Go grab a shower, though. I don't want to go until it's dark, and you have road stink." She pulled herself off the floor and grabbed the brush again, turning her back to him and starting back in on her hair.

Since he'd got his way, he simply said, "Okay." He fished around in his bag for clean clothes and disappeared into the bathroom, which was still steamy from Joan's shower.

When the door clicked shut, she moved fast. Her phone. Her bag. She left behind her red coat and her wallet; she didn't want him to think she'd abandoned him completely.

She was wearing a black stretchy skirt and a black sweater Mere had knitted, proud of herself for making her grand-daughter something "goth." Joan gave herself a once-over in the mirror: the real Victor thought she was hotter than hell in her work clothes, so this should be good enough. She threw a tube of red lipstick into her purse just in case. Then she slid into her boots and opened the door, closing it softly behind her.

She waited until she was out of the parking lot, down the street, and just about to take the ramp back onto the highway before she texted him.

> Sorry, my boy. I can't risk you. I'll check in ASAP. STAY THERE and keep the door locked. This could be a trap.

She felt a sick lurch in her stomach as she pushed send. Zeus would be pissed—maybe for months, maybe forever.

Twenty minutes later her phone started buzzing. She looked over: *Zeus, King of all gods*. She flipped it over onto its face and ignored it. When the texts started pinging, one after the other, she flicked the volume button to mute.

❦

She turned off at the exit for Great Heron National Park just after nine thirty. She followed the road into the park, past the official welcome sign and the closed ranger's station. She stopped to check out the wooden post with the colour-coded map for campers and day trippers. She snapped a picture of it with her phone, guilt making her lungs hurt when she had to swipe past the string of texts from Zeus:

How could you do this?

Answer your phone!!

I'm calling Ajean!

THIS IS SHIT

You're as bad as my parents

She didn't have service out here so she couldn't text him back even if she wanted to. That gave her a bit of relief. It was out of her hands.

She turned right toward the campsites, which were closed to the general public this time of year. According to the map, there was a stretch of forest between them and the community lodge. The lodge was where he was supposed to be. Adrenaline made her face numb, made her ass all pins and needles.

She parked the car in a circle of pines near an old firepit, easing the nose under the lower branches. When she got out, she pulled some of them over the roof. Good enough. She would go the rest of the way on foot. Between the weight of her bag and mud from the rains, it wasn't an easy trip.

But soon enough she saw lights peeking through the trees. The lodge. She dropped her bag by a fallen log and edged as close as she could get to the clearing. Parked out front were three blue vans and a minivan with a white decal on the back of a stick-figure woman with four stick-figure cats.

The door opened and she crouched among the branches as her heart jumped into her ears. She couldn't hear anything but its thudding. It was a young woman in a long, yellow T-shirt that went to her knees. Might have been a nightgown. She came down the front steps, looked around, and took two quick hits off a vape, blowing the clouds above her head and waving them away frantically. She went back inside.

Joan's eyes filled. That did not look like someone from the mission. Of course not. She'd fallen for it. She'd been a fucking idiot. Why would a woman who was sleeping with her husband help her? *Honestly, Joan? You're a moron. You fucked this whole thing up. It's over.*

Then the door opened again. This time, it was him. Actually him.

She sprang to her feet, ready to run to him, when a large man with a white beard appeared behind the Reverend and put his hand on his shoulder. The Reverend turned and the two began to chat. Then in the window just to the right, a figure moved. A woman . . . Cecile. She and Joan locked eyes and for a moment Joan was sure she would scream. But she didn't. Instead, she lifted a finger to her lips, then mouthed one word: *Wait.* She dropped her hand but stayed in the window, watching. Joan crouched again, once again out of sight.

Eventually, she heard the Reverend and the big man go back inside. She stood slightly to get a better look as, one by one, the lights winked out until only the light in the small window where Cecile had stood remained. Oh, it was torture. Joan could hear time shedding itself into memory all around her. She couldn't just stay here and wait.

She ran through every possible scenario in her head. They all dead-ended in the same problem: How would she get him to come to her, or stay with her, long enough to change him? Heiser would be sure to give chase. She couldn't outrun a rogarou, especially not while she was dragging a full-grown man along with her, most likely against his will.

Then she remembered the little bag of bone salt. She went back to the log, dug around in her bag, and pulled out the fabric pouch. She picked her way back through the brush to her lookout spot, took a deep breath and ran softly toward the building. She crouched by the wall and untied the pouch. In the soft light from that single window, she sprinkled salt as close to the front door as she dared. Then she walked backwards, toward the woods, shaking a faint line of salt on either side of her, making a path, almost invisible to the naked eye, that ended in an uneven circle she drew on the ground. She'd made a small holding cell for Heiser. If Ajean was right, that is.

She took just one more little moment, praying to her mere for this to work, and then she crouch-ran back to her hiding spot. She bounced the small weight of the pouch, estimating what she had left, her mouth dry with nerves. If Heiser did get trapped in this circle of salt, she couldn't be sure she wouldn't run him through with her blade where he stood.

From the lodge, someone yelled: "Fire!"

She jerked in shock and the salt bag dropped, spilling dust at her feet. Fuck! She pinched what she could see back into the pouch and jammed it in the front pocket of her sweater. Then she snapped open the blade of her knife. She was ready. Or at least as ready as she could be.

"Everybody out! The centre is on fire!"

She recognized the voice. It was Cecile.

19

CLEANSE ME WITH FIRE

After dinner everyone had taken a turn in the showers, and now the group was settled down in sleeping bags on the floor in the big main room, fanned out in a circle like a flannel daisy. Except for Cecile, who had taken over the office as her due. She had been keeping watch out the window for almost an hour, but so far no Heiser and, worse really, no Joan.

And some of the volunteers were still restless: one of Ivy's girlfriends had just tiptoed out the door and within a minute or two, Cecile smelled marijuana coming in through the office window, which she had opened just a crack. Yet another reason why the group needed new leadership, and fast. "Godless hippies," she muttered to herself.

The girl crept back in, coughing into her fist, and climbed back into her bag. And then another body moved in the darkened room. God, would they never just go to sleep?

This time it was the Reverend, heading for the door with his sleeping bag under his arm. No, tonight he couldn't wander away to sleep among the trees. She had plans for him.

She crossed the floor on sock feet to where Garrison lay on top of his sleeping bag, reading a pamphlet on speedboats by the light of his phone.

"Garrison?"

He sat up quick, tucking the brochure under his bag, as she crouched beside him. "I need you to persuade the Reverend to stay indoors tonight," she said. "You heard Mr. Heiser. We have to keep a close eye on him in case someone comes to tempt him back into his old ways."

"On it, boss." Garrison was on his way in his pyjamas before she could even stand back up. Garrison was one of the good ones. There would definitely be a place for him in her ministry, after his conversion therapy, of course.

Cecile went back to the office so she could watch the men out the window. And just then she spotted her at the edge of the clearing: Joan. The woman was pacing a tight line, visible to anyone who looked her way. What was she doing? Did she intend to run straight for the Reverend, even with Garrison there? She really was crazy.

Cecile waved her hands and, thank god, got Joan's attention before she screwed everything up. *Wait!* she mouthed at her, and after a nerve-wracking minute that tried her Christian patience, Joan slunk back into hiding among the trees. Soon enough, Garrison was leading the Reverend back inside, having persuaded him that being in a building in the middle of the woods was almost as good as being in the woods proper, or that, given that they were on retreat, they needed their spiritual leader among them, or something, because soon they both settled down again on the floor.

Cecile gently closed her office door, then watched for any movement through the frosted glass panel. Nothing. She went back to the window. No sign of her, but she had to trust Joan was still waiting in the bush like the coiled snake she was.

Softly humming "Victory in Jesus," Cecile reached under the desk and pulled out the two bags of stuff she'd bought in town. One was full of store-brand maxi pads and tampons. The second contained four cans of lighter fluid and a box of barbecue matches. She swivelled in the cracked pleather chair, still humming the hymn under her breath, while she read the precautions on the back of one of the cans and tested a match against the strike strip on the box. What a satisfying snap from friction to fire! She stopped for a moment to regard the spent match, then dropped it. Yes, everything still felt right.

Cecile waited a few more minutes and then went over to the door, opened enough that she could listen. The silence was broken only by punctuating snores. She closed the door again and said a quick prayer before tucking the matches into her back pocket. She wedged one can under her right arm, another under her left and carried the third in one hand, leaving the fourth on the desk as backup. Then she stepped out into the big main room.

She walked carefully around the perimeter, squirting the lighter fluid in wide arcs onto the walls and nearby floor, drenching the drapes at each window, until the can wheezed air. She placed the empty container on the floor near the kitchen door, and began again with the second can. She soaked the kitchen and doused the bathroom, hitting the extra rolls of toilet paper and paper towels in the cabinet, leaving its doors open. The third bottle painted the cubbies where their jackets hung. It all stunk so much she was amazed no one woke up.

She was about to start on the front door when she remembered she needed an unimpeded exit route. When the fire department made their determinations, it would be clear that the fire had been set on purpose. That was fine because it would also be clear that a stranger had been hanging around that night, one with a motive and the kind of instability of character that looks bad in court. Cecile had a receipt on her Visa for the pads, but it was a woman in sunglasses and a hat who paid cash for the lighter fluid and matches. *That woman was probably Joan Beausoliel, officer.*

She walked back the way she'd come, lighting matches and tossing them into corners and puddles. The flames popped into life with a deep whoosh she hadn't anticipated, and travelled with such force that as she threw the final match, she yelled: "Fire!"

When hardly anyone stirred, she waved her arms frantically, shouting, "Everybody out! The place is on fire!" Then she kicked at a few of the bundles on the floor who were crawling too slowly back to consciousness. Soon billowing smoke made it impossible to see the other side of the room. Someone at last ran for the front door, screaming for the others to follow. The person threw it open and the flames leapt as he ran outside. She spotted Wolff shepherding members of his flock out onto the soggy grass, where they collapsed. Above her, the ceiling collected individual columns of fire and squirmed, alive with roiling flames. It was time.

"IVY!" Cecile screamed. "Ivy, where are you?"

Ivy was hauling Nancy to safety, one of the older woman's arms looped over her shoulder. "Here, I'm here," she called.

"I need you, quick. Someone has collapsed!"

Ivy handed Nancy over to Greg and turned back into the fray, crouching under the smoke. "Here," Cecile yelled, grabbing her arm to steer her into the office.

Even though she had been careful not to douse it, the small space was suffocating with heat and smoke. Soon the flames would find their way in. This bird had to be taken care of, and Cecile only had the one stone and maybe three minutes left to throw it.

She closed the door behind them, the heat almost unbearable now.

Ivy was coughing and gasping while she stumbled around the small room, searching. She bent to check under the desk, clutching the edge with a shaking hand. Behind her, Cecile picked up a paperweight—a solid glass sphere with a giant moth trapped in the centre, its wings marked with eyes to keep predators at bay. She hefted it above her shoulder and brought it down on the side of Ivy's head with as much force as she could gather, and the girl went down like a snapped branch.

"For he is the servant of God, an avenger who carries out God's wrath on the wrongdoer," Cecile intoned before a cough doubled her over. Time to get out of here.

She felt her way to the door and pushed it open. Fire and brimstone everywhere. At her feet, the plastic bags from her shopping trip melted and warped, the pads smouldering, the boxes turned to ash that twisted and flew only to be batted back down by heavy smoke. The insides of her mouth and nostrils were cooking. She put a protective arm over her face to try to keep the heat away and took a step to leave. Then rethought. The window—it would be faster to climb out through the office window.

She held her breath, closed her eyes and turned back, feeling for the far wall. She would be outside in a moment. She just had to stay focused. Then she would rush to the Reverend and beseech him to go find Ivy. "Please," she would say. "Please, Reverend, surely the Lord will spare you among men." He would run in, she knew him that well. And even if he didn't, well, then he was a coward. She could spin it either way.

And then as she groped blindly for the window—so near—she stumbled over Ivy's body and came crashing down. Whatever air was left in her was hammered out and she gasped for more, choking on smoke.

Above Ivy's dead face, sitting where she'd left it on the desk, was the last can of lighter fluid. The label had burnt off and the sides were bulging dangerously.

She took a deep breath, steepled her hands and gave it all she had. "Surely the righteous will never be shaken; they will be remembered forever."

The can was a balloon, stretching grotesquely, and then it popped.

Oh, it was glorious to Cecile: an explosion of red and blue, lightning and heat, reprieve and forgiveness—fireworks to celebrate the righteous, a new burning bush struck to flame by the hand of God. And there in the hot centre of it, burning brighter than the sun itself, Cecile saw Jesus Himself while she lay burning on the cheap carpet of a wilderness lodge, fighting a dying battle to honour His word. She moved toward Him, toward the light, the bright, glorious light.

And found that it was just flame, abundant and eternal, after all.

VICTOR IN THE WOODS: CEREMONY OF DEVOUR

It was hard to keep his eyes open against all this new brightness.

The rogarou was undressing, slowly, folding each piece of clothing it took off and draping it over the back of the armchair. Unbuttoning its pants, it noticed Victor watching and started singing the classic striptease song—"Ba da-da da, da-DEE da da . . ."—exaggerating its movements. It was enjoying this far too much. And even though Victor was terrified and sure this was the end, he still found something so alluring about this creature, something so beautiful, he was humiliated by his interest, and also angry.

Its chest was bare now. From one angle, it was all fur, shiny and thick. From another, it was skin with tattoos covering every inch, Victor's tattoos. Except where Victor had *JOAN* just under his collarbones, the creature had *VICTOR*.

Rogarou felt his attention and rubbed a hand over it. "You like it? I do." It stared back at him with cruel yellow eyes that flashed from desire to disinterest. It sighed and held its hands out to indicate their surroundings. "I mean, there's not many options for artists out here."

Victor actually laughed at that. What the fuck was he doing?

Now, pants open, shoes kicked off, the beast sat in front of its prisoner. It propped its face in its hands and leaned toward him, an elbow on each knee. "Tell me about her. Please. Before we begin."

"Who?" Victor did not want to talk about Joan. It would be like pouring a gallon of water out on the ground while he was still so thirsty.

"The person who makes you so resistant, of course."

Why did it seem to be closer than when it first sat down? Victor could feel its breath on his face. He was so warm now he wanted badly to take off his coat, but he felt rooted in place.

"Take it off, then," it said. And Victor was free to move, stripping off his coat and letting it fall to the base of the tree.

"Better?"

"I guess."

"Take the sweater off too if you're still uncomfortable. Here, let me help you." It reached out and undid the three buttons near the neck, then held out its hands, motioning for Victor to raise his arms above his head—which he did without really thinking about it. He wasn't sure if he even wanted to. No, he was sure. He wanted to.

Rogarou yanked the sweater over his head and Victor was left in his camouflage pants and thin undershirt, his boots heavy with mud.

"Can you . . . can you help me?" he said.

The rogarou tilted its head. "Help you with what, my boy?"

"To understand."

It reached across and smoothed Victor's hair, then ran a finger down the side of his face. "Perhaps I can, if I want."

"What is this place? I'm not in the woods, am I?" Saying it out loud, Victor realized he knew this to be certain. He was not on the land where he hunted, the place where he laid and checked traps. Well, he was and he wasn't.

Rogarou shook its head, maintaining eye contact. "You are wherever the betrayal happened."

"What betrayal?"

"Whatever you did that brought you into my arms. That's where you are. And this is where I'll bury you." It tapped Victor's bicep like it was checking a maple for sap. "Time's almost up. No one's coming for you. It means you're mine, only now it'll be forever. Isn't that swell?" It leaned in so its forehead grazed Victor's.

Victor was even more uncomfortable now, because he could feel himself getting hard. What was wrong with him?

The creature tilted its head back. "So, tell me about her."

"Who?" This time he meant it. Victor didn't know who. Who was he supposed to be talking about? He knew only this place and this creature and what forever might be.

Rogarou smiled.

My, what big teeth it had.

"That's perfect." It put a hand on Victor's stomach and he felt it there as heat and want.

"What happens now?" he asked.

"Oh, this is where I devour you." It leaned in; its breath was sweet. "Slowly. We have hours yet."

And then its eyes narrowed to a pinpoint. And it pulled back, jerkily, as if its limbs were attached to strings. It dangled there for a moment on unseen hooks, then spun on a heel. It walked back to the chair, its smile changing to a snarl. It walked around the chair once, twice, and again and again . . . It couldn't stop its circuits.

"Stop this at once!" The words careened into a howl.

Victor watched the creature wearing the ground under its feet into a shallow circle.

"Tabernac!" it screamed, snout pointed toward the moon that now showed itself over the tops of the trees. "Stop!"

Victor was torn between wanting to run to the beast, to grab its arm and help somehow, and wanting to get the hell away. But where? What was happening? He was as confused as he'd been at the beginning of this whole thing.

And then, all at once, her name came back. And her face. And her skin. Oh, her skin. *Joan.*

He turned from the beast, who was howling now without words. He searched the trees and was able to see them again as individuals and not as a woven fence penning him in the dark. There! Just there, he could see something, in the birches. But what was it? He couldn't tell. The sky began to pull itself inside out and rain threatened.

The rogarou was trapped, maybe even in pain. Now was the time to take advantage of it. So Victor walked into the trees with his eyes wide open, trying desperately to see.

20

THE ACE OF SPADES

When Joan saw the flames, she almost ran into the building. Where was he? She cut the palm of her hand trying to close her knife so she could go to him. Even if it meant getting caught. She took a step into the clearing, and in the confusion and smoke, no one saw her outlined in black against the white birch trunks. And then there he was, dragging a man in one-piece pyjamas out the door. Two people came forward to take the man from him and lay him down on the grass. She stayed where she was as the Reverend began counting the ministry volunteers sprawled on the lawn, sitting on rocks, standing around weeping and consoling each other.

"Two missing," he called at last. "I'm going back in."

"It's Ivy and Cecile," someone shouted. "They went into the office!"

As he reached the steps, the office window blew out in a spectacular shower of glass and flames that dropped him to his knees. The big, white-bearded man ran to him and dragged him away from the building.

Then the walls buckled and rippled as if under a great weight. The roof creaked. From the rear of the building came the smash and tinkle of another window blown out.

The guy with the white beard waved everyone farther away from the building. "Get back right now! This thing's going down."

Joan had no idea what to do. She already felt woefully unprepared for this mission with her strange tools—a playing card, a knife, a fucking bag of salt—and now there was a raging fire on top of it all. Joan watched as the Reverend picked himself up from where the bearded guy had laid him, arms hanging at an odd angle. As the others moved back from the fire, seeking a safe distance, he turned on a heel, pushed by a force she couldn't see. And then he was facing her direction, held still at an awkward angle. She caught her breath. Could he see her past all the smoke and fire?

He walked on bare feet over the wet grass, each blade reflecting the flames clawing out of smashed windows, the open door, the growing gap between walls and roof, so that even the ground seemed consumed. Twice the Reverend tried to walk toward the others, and twice he was stopped by an unseen barrier. Each time he was turned back on unsteady legs. One foot jerked in front of the other and then he was making his way toward the trees where Joan stood waiting.

She watched, confused. What was wrong with him? His face was so strained he'd bared his teeth. He looked like he was struggling against his own movements. And then she remembered—the bone salt. He was caught by the trap she'd laid for Heiser.

He uttered a growl full of menace and fear, like a trapped animal. Because that's exactly what he was.

The Reverend Wolff—no, Victor—Victor was a fucking rogarou.

Moving like a wooden puppet, he walked between the lines of salt, staggering to the circle at the end of the pathway, where he stopped. After a second, he walked the perimeter of it once, twice, and then again. She could feel her heartbeat in the cut on her hand. She pressed it against her thigh. A rogarou keeps the man trapped inside, his ribs like the bars of a cell. What was Victor's heartbeat like now? Was it quick and heated? Were there two of them, the monster's and the man's, thumping an anthem in his familiar chest?

"No. No. No," she whispered. Should she grab him? What if he called for help? Those volunteers would run to rescue him from the knife-wielding halfbreed. She looked over at them. They were all holding each other, watching the building burn.

Then came a tremendous crack and the roof caved in, disappearing into the fire, which jumped and spit in triumph. The crowd cried out and none of them were looking her way.

She walked out to where the Reverend stood trapped in the circle of salt and kicked at the line until she'd made a small opening. She slipped a hand under the waistband of her skirt and pulled out the ace of spades, the most magical of cards. Carefully she slipped it into his collar so that it slid inside his shirt. He couldn't make the moves to resist her.

She took a step back, once again opened her small blade, and gestured to him. "Come." And he did, unsteady on his feet. He was still the Reverend or maybe a rogarou, but definitely not Victor.

When at last he stepped into the dark of the woods, she had backed up against a tree, holding the knife in front of her. She looked at his face, and at last thought she saw signs of Victor poking through around his eyes. She lowered the blade.

"What is happening to me?" he said.

She bit her cheeks to keep from saying too much too soon. "I'll explain everything," she said, "but you have to follow me."

"My friends." He looked back at them, still weeping and praying.

"You can't help them right now. But I can help you."

She slowly turned her back to him and took a step farther into the woods. At first all she could hear was the crackling of the fire and the prayers of the terrified, but then she heard a footfall right behind her. It almost sent her to her knees. He was following. Oh, sweet Jesus, he was following.

Calm.

Calm.

She walked on steadily, trying not to look back. After a minute, she couldn't help herself, glancing over her shoulder just to make sure he was still with her, that he hadn't changed into something with fangs and fur. He was a wreck, clutching his stomach or maybe the card he carried now against his skin. Since he was shoeless, he had to pick his way carefully. But he followed. And he still looked human.

When they got to the log where she'd left her bag, Joan sat and patted the spot beside her. He lowered himself shakily, obediently.

"Let me get you something for your feet." She dug around in her bag. "I don't have shoes that would fit you, but here." She handed over a pair of wool socks.

"Thank you." He took them but held them as if he wasn't sure what came next.

She took them back. "Let me do this for you." She got on her knees in front of him and picked up one foot, setting it in her lap. She brushed the twigs, dirt and leaves from his sole, slowly, the way Victor liked. Then she unrolled the sock over his foot, watching his face for a sign that he recognized her. There was none.

She brushed off the second foot and then rubbed it a bit, taking her time to run her fingers between his toes. His hands unclenched and fell to his thighs. She took even longer unrolling this sock, and when she was finished she remained on her knees, looking up into his face.

A crash from the direction of the fire distracted him, another part of the lodge falling in, and she took advantage of it, placing a small kiss on one knee.

"There's nothing more you can do for them here. Let me take you to my car. We'll go get help." She slid her hands up his legs to his thighs, then took his hands in her own. He allowed it, even squeezed back against the pressure of her fingers.

As she stood, she pulled him up, and then they were still for a moment, leaning against each other in the dark of the woods. She held on to his hands for as long as he allowed it, which was another few seconds. Then he backed away.

"Please, let me carry that." He held his hand out for her bag and she passed it over.

"Thanks."

Victor was always such a gentleman. But maybe so was the Reverend. She took out her phone and used it as a flashlight to light their steps. The farther they walked, the more she shook. So close, so close . . . Every part of her sang a song of absence and need. It was terrible to be this close, yet to be this alone. She wanted to drop to her knees again. Only this time, she would take him in her mouth, push her forehead up against his stomach. She would take off her panties and climb him like a fucking tree. She would kiss his beautiful mouth until his lips bled. She would remind him who he really was.

"Is that it?" he said. A headlight was reflected in the beam from her phone through the trees.

"That's it."

"A Jeep. I love Jeeps."

"So does my husband."

"I think I know him," he said, confused. She picked up his hand and they followed the path into the campsite, surrounded by its circle of pines. She released his hand to push the branches off the roof, unlocked the door and took her bag from him. And then, there he was—this Victor-looking motherfucker with Victor's tattoos peeking out the top of his T-shirt, leaning against Victor's Jeep. She dropped the bag.

"Fuck it."

She pressed up against him, resting her head in the crook of his neck, the Creator's spot. She put her arms around his back and felt all the good curves and angles of her love. She was shaking so bad. But it wasn't all her. He was shaking too. She looked up into his face and he was staring off into the trees, still not quite Victor but not quite the Reverend either. She picked up his arms and wrapped them around her. When one dropped, she picked up that hand and guided it up under her skirt.

"Wait . . . ," he stuttered.

"No." She held his fingers against the damp cotton of her underwear, then pushed the fabric out of the way so she could slip his fingers further in. She felt him respond against her hip. Oh God, yes.

"Wait . . ." He was breathing hard; she was barely breathing at all.

She wiggled against his hand, moaned just under his ear. But he was pulling away, pushing her off.

"No!" He held a trembling hand up in front of him. "Heiser, just wait!"

21

REMIND HIM

Joan turned and there Heiser was, hands in his pants pockets, a hard smirk on his face. She hadn't noticed the black Town Car parked just up the gravel road. But the Reverend had.

"So, Joan, you found him after all." Heiser shook his head slowly. "There is just no keeping you away, is there?" His tie was crooked and the suit jacket was missing. He looked almost dishevelled.

She stepped in between him and her husband. "Fuck you, Heiser."

"But I didn't expect this." He pointed back into the woods, shaking his head. The smell of smoke was everywhere. "I really underestimated you."

"I didn't have anything to do with that fire."

He kicked at the ground, still smirking and shaking his head. "Right—you're totally innocent."

"I did not do that. I came here to get my husband." She pointed behind her. "*My* husband."

"And the lodge just happened to catch on fire right when you show up."

"Why don't you ask Cecile what happened? She's the one who told me where to come."

"You expect me to believe that?" He stepped forward. "And you're not taking the Reverend anywhere. He is coming with me."

"She wasn't there." The Reverend stepped around Joan. "Cecile woke us all up. She discovered the fire. And she called Ivy back inside. They . . . they didn't make it out."

Heiser paced a small circle in his thin-soled shoes. "Okay, okay. Eugene, you come with me. We'll get you all tucked in and settled. And you," he pointed at Joan. "You get in your car and you drive away and never trouble the Reverend again. Or there will be consequences."

"I can't," the Reverend, not quite the Reverend, said.

"Pardon me?"

"I can't go with you, Mr. Heiser." He slumped to the ground and leaned back against the Jeep.

Joan moved in front of him again, blocking Heiser from making direct eye contact. "Yeah, fuck off, *Rogarou*." She said it like a curse uttered in church, half whispered and with a lot of venom.

Heiser stopped pacing, lifted his chin and seemed to gaze over the treetops.

"Yeah, I know what you are," Joan said. "And I know you've made him into one too. But you can't have him back."

Heiser laughed so loudly it echoed around the campsite. "Rogarou? Oh, you know everything, do you? Such a smart girl. Smart, smart girl."

He came toward them now. "If you know everything, I am surprised you want him back at all."

"I saw the picture you sent me. I don't care what he did while he wasn't himself." Joan was growing frantic. She had to get Victor up off the ground and into the Jeep and away from this dangerous creature.

"The picture? Ah yes, well. A minor thing." He slid around her so quickly she couldn't stop him and laid his hand on Victor's head. "Come now, Wolff!"

Joan threw herself on Heiser, hitting out wildly as they tumbled to the grass. She couldn't come this far, be this close and be widowed again. She'd sooner die.

Strong arms pulled them apart. The Reverend or whatever the hell he was right now pushed Joan behind him and held his arms out to keep Heiser back.

The man got to his feet, brushed off his pants and straightened his tie. Joan reached into the pocket of her sweater and opened her small blade. Now she was ready to use it.

Heiser said, "I see you really are not listening anymore, Wolff. Never mind, we'll soon fix that."

"Just get in your car and go back to Germany or wherever the fuck you came from," Joan hissed. "You know what, before you go, I have a question for you."

"Anything." He smiled wide.

"Why? That's my question—just why. Why would you do this to him? To us?"

"That's what you want to ask? Really?" He paused, then began to giggle, and was soon doubled over in laughter. "I didn't do this. That's what you don't get. I can't turn anyone into anything." He pointed to the sky. "I am not God. Only He decides what creatures to set padding across the Earth. I merely inherited a set of talents."

And as he said that, she saw him change, grow taller, grow colder. "Joan, my dear," he prodded. "Don't you have another question? One I can answer. How about this one: Whatever happened to your grandmother?"

"What are you talking about?"

"She died, yes?" Heiser lifted his shoulders. "But how did she die?"

"Shut up. You shut up now." Rage boiled up her spine.

"Did she pass away quietly in her bed?" He smiled and clapped his hands together, giving them a congratulatory shake. "Ahh, that's the dream, isn't it? To meet your maker surrounded by loved ones. No stress. No violence."

He mimicked the horror on her face. "Oh wait, I can tell by your reaction that's not the case. What happened to your beloved granny, then, Joan? Was she attacked?"

"Stop it." It was the Reverend.

"Was she maybe even murdered?" He lifted a hand to his mouth in fake shock.

It really had been Heiser. She should have known there was no way a random wolf had attacked Mere. Wolves around the Bay were few and far between.

"So tell me how it feels to stand so close to her murderer." He put a finger under his chin, in mock contemplation.

"It was you, you son of a bitch. Why Mere?"

"Me? Oh dear me, no." He laughed again.

"Stop it now," the Reverend said, his voice shaking.

"What's wrong, Wolff? Why don't you want me teasing your poor wife?" He clucked his tongue at him. "Okay then, I won't. Here's the truth. Joan, it wasn't me who ripped your poor old grandma to pieces. That's not my style at all. It was the man you came here to rescue."

She stepped back and bumped into the Jeep. "No, that's not true."

"Oh, I'm afraid it is."

"Why would he do that?" She looked into her husband's face. He refused to meet her eyes.

"Well, you see, a newly minted rogarou is like a big puppy, very hard to control. Sometimes they try to go home. This puppy had a really strong sense of smell and made it back. Lucky for you, but not so lucky for your grandmother, he ran into her before he made it into the house."

Joan leaned on the hood, trying very hard to breathe. "I don't believe you." He had found her softest spot, her rawest wound. She put her hands over her ears, but that didn't stop the feeling that she was being invaded. "I don't believe you."

"Don't you? Doesn't it make sense?" Heiser clasped his hands behind his back and paced a bit, showing her his ease, his sense of command. "I mean, I found him before anything too drastic happened and I probably could have stopped him, but why?" He shrugged. "The old bird had been kicking up quite a commotion in the community about one of the projects I'm working on. So I just let nature take its course."

She looked at the creature wearing her husband's body. He was slouched in the bones that normally did not slouch, small in the muscles that did not contract that way. He was holding his own shaking hands.

And she knew in that moment that this creature—whatever he was right now, whatever he had been over the past year—had been capable of it, had ripped Mere apart. Vomit bubbled in her throat and she retched up a mouthful of bile. Once the nausea passed, the rage in her spine spread across her back, into her lungs, into the tremble of her thighs, her calves, into her fingertips cold against the knife in her pocket.

"Are you fucking kidding me?"

"Afraid not." Heiser's response was lilting.

She looked then at the Reverend, this shell of a man she once knew, watched his back curve into a question mark, watched his knees buckle. He crouched there on the balls of his feet, rocking himself, holding his face. "The blood on my hands. The fingernail in my mouth . . ." His words were slimy with snot and tears.

In that moment, two different voices reached out from her memory to speak to her. One was Ajean's, from the day she met the rogarou out on the road. *Remind him he is a man under it all. You can do it by making the thing bleed.* And the other was Victor's, from the night he came home with a broken tooth. *If you're gonna fight, then fight like hell. Otherwise you're just dancing. And nobody ever defied death with a waltz.*

And then she raised her knife, watching the ladder of his ribs expand and contract under his thin shirt as he began to pray. A Catholic prayer from his childhood. "Holy Mary, Mother of God . . ."

"Wait now, Joan. Is this really what you want to do?" Heiser took a step toward her.

Joan was trying to understand, to remember that Victor wasn't Victor, that he was something else entirely, but her anger was making it difficult to comprehend. She told herself, "It isn't him. It isn't him."

Her first blow was a slash, cutting him deep and red like a zipper unzipped. That one was for Mere. It was shocking how he opened up. Before she could truly consider it, she raised the knife again and stabbed him, then dropped the knife, her mouth opening in a silent cry. The Reverend had not stirred from his crouch as she struck him, had not cried, but only bled into the grass, filling his wife's wool socks with sticky red, as Heiser watched. She dropped to her knees beside him and pulled him to her until his head rested in her lap. He was so still. Someone had died. Someone had been killed. The sounds of murder leaked into the woods.

"Oh, Victor." She rocked him slowly and kissed his forehead, his nose. She looked up at Heiser through tears and asked, "Why? Why would a rogarou need him?"

Heiser leaned down to her. "You really are slow, aren't you? I'm not the rogarou. I am the Wolfsegner." He held a hand out to her to shake, once more mocking her. "Nice to meet you, finally."

"Wolfsegner?"

She was so intent on Heiser, on her bleeding husband, she didn't hear Robe stealing up behind them. She didn't see the rock in his hand. And then the blow came and she folded over Victor into the dark. She didn't hear Heiser laugh as he walked toward his car, confident that it was he who had killed two birds with one stone. Didn't hear him say to his driver, "I barely had to aim."

22

LOSING CONTROL

The ministry tent was filled with candles, like an illuminated belly bloated against the sky. The sound of a thousand small tongues of flame licked the inside of her ears. She was dressed in her wedding gown, standing alone at the bottom of the aisle. She turned in a circle, the ivory layers spinning with the movement.

"Over here, my girl."

At the top of the aisle, in front of the stage, backlit by the illuminated cross, was her grandmother.

"Mere!" She dropped the bouquet she didn't realize she was holding, grabbed the front of her skirt and ran. But in that obnoxious dream way, it took hours to get past the first row of chairs, empty of worshippers or guests.

Mere watched Joan with an indulgent smile, raising her hand to wave her on, her lips shaping words that had no volume. After a while, when Joan made no progress, she shook her head and turned her back on her.

"Mere, wait!"

The old woman walked to the side of the stage and began climbing the stairs, lifting one foot onto each step and then the other, turning back once to smile at her granddaughter.

"Mere, don't go up there!"

Mere waved back at her and carried on. When she reached the stage, she moved toward the cross.

Blood pounded in Joan's head. Her ears began to ring like church bells.

"Wait!"

She yelled it so loud she woke herself up.

"Oh goodie, you're back." The voice was Heiser's.

Joan was in the front seat of a moving car. She tried to turn toward the voice but not only was she restrained by a seatbelt, her hands were zip-tied and so were her ankles.

"What's going on?" She struggled to shake off her grogginess, the bells still knocking together.

"We're just going for a little drive," Heiser said.

In the driver's seat was a man she'd never seen before, a dark Native man with shaggy black hair and a gently lined face, a serrated slash healed to keloid on the side of his neck. She swivelled as best she could to glance in the mirror, and finally made eye contact with Heiser, sitting in the back seat behind the driver. He wiggled the fingers of one hand at her.

"Where's Victor?"

"Don't worry about him," Heiser answered. "He's right

here beside me, resting for now. We're going to get him patched up and then he's going to kill you."

"What the fuck?" She was having a hard time putting the pieces together. Outside the trees were a solid wall, the road a black ribbon unfurling in their headlights.

"You were the one who cut him," Heiser went on. "If our man here kills you himself, the magic might stick. Also, you won't be skulking about our tent meetings anymore. As fun as it's been, Joan, I have to tell you, I won't miss it. I wanted to take care of you in the park, but with all the commotion and sirens . . ."

She was crying now, the tears running off her chin and into the folds of her neck. Victor was responsible for Mere's death, her horrible, horrible death.

"Oh, don't worry. We'll take good care of him. Just as we were doing before you showed up. He'll be fed and adored and maybe even married." Heiser was silent for a moment as Joan sobbed. "Yes, I think that'll be the first order of business— to marry him off. Though I guess since the prime candidate for Mrs. Wolff is dead, we'll have to look around. What d'you think, Robe? A winter wedding might be nice."

"Yes sir." The driver's voice was deep and graceless. When he smiled, Joan saw the brown outline of a snapped front tooth.

"Everything is going to work out just fine, Joan," Heiser carried on. "Sure, we lost some people, but people are easily replaced. Rogarous, on the other hand? Those don't just show up on your doorstep every day."

"What are you?" she whispered.

"I told you, I am a Wolfsegner." She heard pride in his voice.

"What the fuck is that?" She lifted a shoulder and wiped her face on it.

He laughed. "Oh, where to begin? In Bavaria, back in the old days, my ancestors were burnt at the stake along with the witches. Like your own people, Joan, we were persecuted for what we were. We are the carriers of wolfssegen."

"Wolfssegen?"

"Charms." He leaned toward the front seat so that his voice easily cut through the steady ringing in her ears. "We control the wolves."

He settled back in his seat. "Back then, wolfsegners were wealthy men, revered, even. We were the ones who could bring prosperity to the right farmer by culling the stock of his rival. A useless power, I thought, until I discovered the rogarou.

"I've come to learn that if you can control the darkest part of a community, you hold the key to the entire thing," he said. "No excep—"

His breath sputtered and Joan felt a kick in the back of her seat. The car swerved as Robe tried to drive with one hand and reach for Heiser with the other. She heard desperate gurgling and strained to see in the mirror. Victor's hands were white from strain as he dug them into Heiser's neck.

Robe turned back for a moment to correct their course as the car veered wildly. Then Heiser's foot came over the seat and kicked the driver in the head. The car turned horizontal on the road, then slid fast toward the trees, tires screeching, Robe limp in his seat. Joan screamed. And then, for the second time that night, everything went black.

VICTOR OUT OF THE WOODS

He ran. His legs ached, his breath stung his throat, his eyes fought to close against the strain, but he kept going. This time, somehow, he knew he was getting somewhere.

Behind him, the rogarou howled and kicked the chair clean across the clearing, where it smashed against a tree. Another howl, closer now. Fuck, it was after him again. But this time it wasn't toying with him, so sure of its tempo and direction it practically skipped along. Now it dug claws into the soil, ripped bark from passing trees, leapt over crevices and got turned around in the fading dark. There were no more words or songs or games. It was wild, vicious and hunting. It had a job to do.

Victor zigzagged to throw off the beast. But it had his scent. If it caught him there wouldn't be a chance to reason or barter or delay: it would bring him down and tear out his throat. He had to get out of there, so he just kept running.

The air was growing so cold his panting breath clouded in front of him. It was getting lighter too, like a pre-dawn morning, except this light flickered. And then he saw it, up ahead, in a circle of pines—a white car. His Jeep! He doubled his pace. If he could just make it to his Jeep.

There was a crack from above like sudden thunder, followed by a shower of leaves, and then the rogarou jumped out of a tree. It landed right in front of him, with a thud he felt in his own kneecaps, blocking out the Jeep and the dawn and survival.

He tried to stop but pitched forward, landing in a heap within reach of the thing. He couldn't stand. He tried but his legs wouldn't hold him. Instead he curled up as small as he could, put his arms over his head and shouted, "Wait!"

He kept his eyes closed so he couldn't see exactly how it would happen, how the rogarou would take him apart. He imagined his skin coming off like a lady unzipped from a gown. There was a long pause and then came a blow that launched him into a tree, and he fell to the ground, snagging on branches, landing on rocks. He screamed, but it was as if the volume was turned right down.

He tried to crawl away, grabbing at shrubs, yanking grasses out of the loose soil. But it was on him. It bent down, and its breath wasn't sweet anymore, and it grabbed him up in its jaws. There was pressure and then sick release as a long incisor popped through his skin like a blade, sliding through fat and muscle to stop at the bone.

He came close to losing consciousness, dangling there in the mouth of the rogarou on the edge of his forest cell. It wasn't all bad. He felt each tear in his flesh and was glad that he could feel, if only to know this terrible rending.

And then he heard her. Joan was crying. When he opened his eyes, he was in the back seat of a moving car, bleeding through his shirt.

23

A DIRT-LIFTING JIG

This time it felt like no time had passed before she opened her eyes. When she inhaled, there was a breath-snatching pinch in her chest.

"Ow. Oh, fuck." Joan tried to lift her bound hands to rub the spot but couldn't get them past the airbag that had shot out of the dash and trapped her.

"Just wait, hold on." Victor, crouched by her open door, found her knife on the floor and picked it up. He slashed the airbag, releasing a cloud of acrid powder, and then cut the zip ties. She licked her lips and tasted the chemicals on her tongue. "What happened?"

"We crashed. Can you move?" He dropped the knife and took her head in his hands, gently turning it right, then left.

She realized the seat beside her was empty and the door left open, which is why the alarm was pinging rhythmically. "Where's the driver?" Then more frantically, "Heiser? Where's Heiser?"

"Just a minute. Let's see if you can stand." Victor took her hands and helped lift her from her seat. She placed her feet on the dirt, and he steadied her.

"My chest hurts when I breathe in."

"Probably a broken rib. Everything else feel okay?"

"Maybe." She put weight on one leg, then the other. "Yeah, I'm okay."

She turned back to look at the car. The front driver's side was completely smashed, though the headlight on the passenger side still shone, tilting into the trees that bordered the road. Both airbags drooped in the front, the black interior coated with fine, white dust. Heiser was slumped over in the back, still belted in, his head touching the seat beside him at an odd angle.

"Is he . . ."

"I think so."

She turned away. "Victor?"

"Yes?"

"Are you really you?" She searched his face, then reached out to feel his cheeks, his ears, the shape of his skull. He smiled at her, and yes, it was all him. She took little sips of breath, trying not to cry—it would hurt too badly to cry.

"I think so," he said.

She fell into him then, and he held her, loosely, so her chest wasn't crushed. She felt around his back for the wounds she had given him.

"I'm fine," he reassured her. "The bleeding's almost stopped."

"We've got to get you patched up."

Someone began clapping. For a minute she couldn't make out where it was coming from.

A few feet in front of the car was Robe. He stood in the beam of the one remaining headlight with blood thick over a swollen eye so that his damaged face mimicked the car's.

"Congratulations." He smiled real big, each tooth outlined by a frame of bright blood.

"For what?" Victor asked, moving toward him.

"I can't see him anymore. Just you, now." His smile flattened. "Too bad. He was a good one."

"Are we talking about Heiser?" Joan grabbed Victor's shirt and tried to pull him back. This man could be dangerous. He was Heiser's man. He might want to finish them both himself, right here on the side of the road.

"Lord, no. Heiser was an ass. He should know better than to play with magic that doesn't belong to him." Robe licked his hands, palms to fingertips, passed them over his face, and then ran his fingers through his hair. "I'm referring to your rogarou, of course."

Something clicked for Victor—a memory or a recognition. He tilted his head, made his voice soft and moved slow, like he was approaching a dangerous animal. "Your name— Robe. Is that short for something?"

Robe pushed his hands in his pants pockets and rocked heel to toe. "I used to go by Guillaume Robitaille. Heiser called me Robe, though I suppose that's all I could manage to communicate by the time we found each other."

"Guillaume, I—"

"It's Robe now."

Victor put his hands up, placating him. "Fair enough. Robe, I think we can help you."

He laughed. "You do, do you?"

"I think we might have the same problem, friend."

"Which is?" Robe sounded amused.

"You're being hunted by a rogarou." Victor tapped his own temple with his forefinger, then tapped his heart. "In here."

Robe pulled his hands out of his pockets and copied Victor's movements. "In here." He tapped his head, eyes wide. "And here?" He pointed at his chest.

"Yes," he said. "We can help."

Joan pictured Robitaille's wife somewhere in this night, curled up on a couch in a crocheted blanket, crying in a room lit by an intrusive moon. Alone. Hurt. "I got Victor back," she said. "Maybe I can help you too."

"You can?" Robe stepped forward, his hands beseeching. "Really?"

"Yes, I can."

Robe bent over, resting his hands on his knees, head hanging, and his back began to shake.

"Hey hey, it's okay." Joan took a step toward him and Victor's arm came out to bar her from getting any closer.

A low whimper, then a whine and soon Robe's laughter filled the entirety of the night like a howl.

"What the fuck?" Joan watched as he stumbled around under the force of his mirth, shuffling into the road and then into the ditch.

"*You?* You want to help *me?*" He held his stomach and after a few more chuckles, finally grew quiet. "You want to help me, kwezanz, or you want to help Robitaille."

It had been years since anyone had called her a little girl in the language. It made her feel small. She didn't answer.

He straightened. "Because I don't need help from anyone. I'm kind of a free agent, a self-made man. And good old Robitaille? I left him buried in the field where he forced himself on his little cousin. He don't need anyone's help anymore."

"Joan, he's not human anymore," Victor said. "Human Robe got lost in his own woods and he's not making it out."

"And thank the Jesus for small mercies!" Robe yelled, and lifted his arms up to the sky, then dropped them. "Man, it'll be good to take a break from all this praying now that Hitler over there is out of commission. I was getting sick of *Driving Miss Daisy* too." With an exaggerated movement, Robe bent to one side and curled a hand around his ear. "Say, can you hear that?"

Joan strained to listen through the ringing. There it was, a small moan. Coming from the car.

"We'd better skedaddle, friends. I need to get away from that one while the going is good." With that same dramatic flair, Robe spread his arms straight out at his sides, bent his hands at perfect ninety-degree angles and snapped them onto his waist. Then he picked up his knees and began to dance. His feet moved so fast they became a blur, kicking up small clouds of dirt. And with graceful jumps and extravagant reels, the rogarou jigged out of the light, down one side of the ditch and up the other, and leapt into the woods. Only the stars knew which direction he took once under cover, and they weren't talking.

"Joan, we gotta get out of here too." Victor pulled her arm. "Come on, before Heiser wakes up."

"Should we leave him like that?" She could barely think.

"We can't help him. And we can't finish him off. Neither one of us is a murderer." His face changed when he said it, his eyes filling with tears. "Joan, I'm so . . ."

From somewhere in the trees came a pulse of small barks that sounded a lot like more laughter. Joan started walking back in the direction from which they'd come. "You're right, Victor. Neither one of us is a murderer. Let's get the Jeep."

After a minute, he followed.

24

SWOOPING IN

Broken and weak, they carefully climbed into the Jeep and drove. All they left behind was a pool of cooling blood making mud out of the dirt, and on the other side of the trees, fire trucks dousing the blackened frame of the lodge. Soon enough, they would find the bodies.

They drove in silence until they passed the wreck of Heiser's car, its one headlight still beaming and no signs of life from inside. The door alarm beeped its tiny emergency into the night with no one left to take notice. When they turned onto the highway, both of them broke open. Joan knew she sounded like a madwoman, laughing and then crying, spitting out the horrors of the night, of the past year, and of her big, sad love. She couldn't stop.

"I can't believe you're here. You're not close enough." She reached over and grabbed his hand, putting it on her thigh, between her legs, under her arm, in her mouth.

In Leamington they stopped at a drugstore and she bought

the things she needed to patch him up, and then they sped to the motel. She texted Zeus while waiting at the red lights in town.

Hey boy, we got him!!!!

Nothing. She doubted he was sleeping, so he was probably still angry with her. She tried baiting him.

Showdown with Heiser . . .

Waited a minute.

Car crash.

Another minute.

Found another rogarou. He got away, but WE GOT VICTOR BACK!

I had to stab him though

Shit, this kid was tough. She sent one more message.

Twice . . .

No response.

Between town and the motel, it rained again—a dying sigh at the end of the passing storm.

The parking lot was wet, and the neon *T* in *MOTEL* stretched out over the puddles like a cobalt cross, ending on the hood of a Miata that had parked in Joan's spot.

They backed the Jeep in by the front office and clambered out, all adrenaline and touch, stopping near the trunk to kiss. "Let's get Zeus and get the fuck out of here," she said.

And then, because a movement drew her eye, she looked up at the sign. She watched a large, dark bird alight near the green *M* screeching electricity from a frayed circuit. It dipped its head as if to read about the *ICY AC* and the *COLOR TV IN EVERY ROOM*.

Her smile faltered. Odd for a crow to be active at this hour.

Then the second crow arrived.

In moments like this, it is hard to know if crows are a delay tactic or a true warning. The two regarded her from their pedestal, and she was judged. They each called out their verdict and then waited for a response.

"It's rare to see crows at night," Victor said. Under his feet, the reflection of the neon *T* pointed to the room. Joan turned toward the door.

"Oh. Oh, Jesus."

Joan was running. She careened off the Miata as she dug the key out of her purse. And there, leaning against the door like a pitched tombstone with a gold epigraph, was a small, black Bible.

"No."

She kicked it and it caprioled down the walkway, landing hard.

Key in the door, shoulder against wood, and she was in. A lamp on the nightstand threw yellow light on the crumpled bed, the uneaten snacks torn from the bag, the clothes pushed to the carpet. Joan fell to her knees and the crows cackled from across the lot, watching Victor sprint through the neon puddles.

Zeus was gone.

She could barely breathe. She had no hymns, no prayers. Hymns only work if you can sing past the constellations named for pagan deities—Orion's Belt, the Chained Maiden—to reach a Creator willing to listen. And what is prayer when your own god has been plucked out of the wing-dark sky? All she had was prophecy, and she placed it there, on the threshold:

"I'm already on the way."

25

ZEUS IN THE WOODS

Zeus was not going to wait around until his auntie came back. This was his mission too, dammit. He strode along the road with the possession of a man about to deal with impertinent employees who'd slept late too often and forgot to clean the grease trap. When he got to the highway, he walked on the verge, passing clusters of trees and the reflective yellow signs where side roads splintered off like skin tags, sticking out a thumb whenever a rare car passed. The wind was up here, rustling the leaves, so he missed the footsteps. And then his feet left asphalt.

Sleep, or something like it.

He knew he'd been taken because he hated his mother. He tried to explain it—the hows and whys of the feeling—but there was no mercy to be had. The creature put a gloved hand on his shoulder and said, "There are no exceptions, Little Big Man." And then laughed like there were bees trapped in its throat.

He was hungry and then he was angry and then he was nothing. Sound existed only as echo. His eyes saw only layers of black and navy thatched over an empty space. He blinked but had to touch his eyelids with his fingertips to see if it had actually happened. He thought he heard the screech of a rusted swing set, like the one he knew sat at the back of his own yard.

Someone was coming. At first he knew who it was: pictured the grooves between her eyebrows when he wasn't coordinated enough with the playlist; smelled the Earl Grey and cigarette smoke of her shirt. But now, after hours or maybe just a minute, she was gone. Her name—he knew her name. It was important to remember her name. So he ran his palms over the dirt to smooth it into a tablet, pushed in a finger, and drew out the letters. *J O A*— From somewhere there was wind, carrying scent and humidity, and then hidden bugs built symphony out of scuttle and punctuated the dark like so many audible stars.

He knew himself. He closed his eyes and knew him to be himself. And he was bound to her and she was coming. The certainty made him smile, even here.

But by the time he finished the *N*, he had already forgotten. He was supine and he was lost, and the thing that sat just out of reach sang all the bees trapped in his throat back into the sky.

HOME

"Ajean." He sat up in bed and nudged her shoulder, bare where it peeked out from the heavy quilt. "Hey, Ajean."

"Mon Dieu, let a woman sleep."

"Ajean, wake up."

She rolled onto her back, flopping her arms down by her sides so hard they bounced on the mattress. "Rickard, you're my booty call. Know what that means, eh? Means I don't have to be nice to you. Go home if you can't be still. Or else get that thing back up." She slapped his leg under the sheets.

"You know those pills don't work like that." He pushed a hand through his thin hair. "I keep telling you. Anyways, that's not it. Listen."

"What?"

He lowered his voice. "I think there's something moving on your porch."

She opened her eyes then and stared up at the low popcorn ceiling, striped from the street light coming through her bed-room blinds. She stayed very still and focused. Her hair was a grey starfish on her red pillowcase.

Since Joan had called her about the boy, she'd been listen-ing real good. She'd even recounted her alarm system. Some asshole had taken the empty back to the beer store for the deposit. She replaced it with a Johnny Cash CD in a cracked plastic case. Oh, that Johnny Cash, he was a man she could snag in half. At least until his fat days, when he got too churchy and found out he wasn't a real Indian.

Shuffling. Scratch against wood. A heavy thud, which she knew was her marigolds in their planter boot tipping over.

"Alright then." She pushed the blankets off and stood up, smoothing down her nightie. She shushed Rickard and fixed the blankets, lifting them back to the pillow. She told him to stay put. Before she got to the bedroom door, she turned back. "Next time you bring an extra pill or don't bother to stay."

She tiptoed into the kitchen and reached on top of the fridge, sticking out her tongue for balance. She felt around until she found the tin and pulled it down. She really should have prepared the salt before. Now she couldn't turn on the kitchen light and she couldn't open the drawer where she kept the grater and her knives without a lot of rattle and bang. She turned, looking for something that would work to shred some bone, a diminutive ghost in a thin, white nightie, wavy hair down to her waist.

"Merde."

She remembered the careful way they had to handle Angelique's body while dressing her to meet the Jesus so that the holes they'd stitched up wouldn't crack back open. She remembered old Elsie Giroux tucking both lips inside the pressure of her clenched teeth to stop from talking about things that hunt the road. Ajean would have popped her in the nose if she'd upset Flo and Joan with those stories. She'd told her so straight out. Angelique didn't die with a pleasant look on her face; Ajean remembered having to coax the muscles to ease the tension from her jaw. Angelique didn't die nice. Ajean wanted to pass in peace—at bingo with the winning card, or lying out all stately-like in buckskin on the dock, or under Rickard like a proper lady who'd lived a good life right to the end.

On the counter was a thick crystal glass reflecting the small bulb above the stovetop like a faceted lighthouse beacon. Inside, in lukewarm water with a full Polident tab, was Rickard's top plate. She didn't give herself time to reconsider, just fished out the teeth, pried open the tin and scraped herself a small pile of salt. Then she dropped the denture back into the glass where it smiled at her like an overbite, some grains sinking to the bottom to join the cleaner residue. She'd take care of it later.

She held the pinch of bone salt in her small, brown fist. With her other hand she grabbed a wooden spoon she kept on a hook by the telephone for just this kind of thing. On second thought, she went back to the counter and retrieved the yellow bag of oatmeal cookies, tucking it under her arm. Now she was ready, and she wasn't fucking around.

"Oh my girl," she whispered as she stood before the front door with the street light through the window casting the shadow of wild fur over her face. "I hope you're almost home. He is. And I don't know how long I can hold him."

She opened the door, just a crack, and made clucking noises like she was calling in a stray. Silence. And then the shadow strained and flexed, blocking the street light, the moon and any god pulled away from the contemplation of silent stars to watch the choreography of a damn good fight.

acknowledgements

I AM THANKFUL to my husband, Shaun, and our children, Jaycob, Wenzdae and Lydea, for putting up with me disappearing into this world for days at a time, locked away in my office.

To my longest-running fans and supporters—Hugh, Joanie and Jason Dimaline—I love you. You are the reason I am fearless, and so damn full of words. Thank you for making me believe each of them had value.

To my agents, Rachel Letofsky and Dean Cooke, and all the amazing souls at CookeMcDermid who I love to burst in on and hug, you are truly the best. You make it possible to continue publishing and allow me the time and space to dream up new ways to speak my truth. You guard the road so that I can spin around and sing and pluck memory to braid with wonder. I cannot thank you enough.

Sometimes you meet a person and know that they will make you the best version of yourself. It doesn't happen often and when it does, you need to hold on to it. Anne Collins, you make me a better writer; it is a gift I will never be able to properly repay. A special thank-you to little Olive for allowing me time with her grandma to put this fever of a book to bed.

My thanks, also, to Kristin Cochrane for our first lunch and the ones yet to come, and most of all for changing the world so that we writers have a steadier place in it. Your belief in me makes me work harder. I guess that's why you're the boss.

This story, and every story, is from and for my mere, Edna Dusome. I am grateful to Mere and to my great-aunt Flora for telling me scary tales of giant black dogs on the road, for keeping me safe and for filling me with community and story and the kind of love that sticks. I carry you every day and know that you carry me right back.

CHERIE DIMALINE's young adult novel *The Marrow Thieves* shot to the top of the bestseller lists when it was published in 2017, and stayed there for more than a year. It won the Governor General's Literary Award, the *Kirkus* Prize in the young adult literature category, and the Burt Award for First Nations, Métis and Inuit Literature, was a finalist for the Trillium Book Award and, among other honours, was a fan favourite in the 2018 edition of CBC's *Canada Reads*. It was also a Book of the Year on numerous lists, including that of the National Public Radio, the *School Library Journal*, the New York Public Library, *The Globe and Mail*, *Quill & Quire* and the CBC. Cherie was named Emerging Artist of the Year at the Ontario Premier's Awards for Excellence in the Arts in 2014, and became the first Indigenous writer in residence at the Toronto Public Library. From the Georgian Bay Métis Community in Ontario, she now lives in Vancouver.

Help us make the next generation of readers

We – both author and publisher – hope you enjoyed this book. We believe that you can become a reader at any time in your life, but we'd love your help to give the next generation a head start.

Did you know that 9 per cent of children don't have a book of their own in their home, rising to 13 per cent in disadvantaged families*? We'd like to try to change that by asking you to consider the role you could play in helping to build readers of the future.

We'd love you to think of sharing, borrowing, reading, buying or talking about a book with a child in your life and spreading the love of reading. We want to make sure the next generation continue to have access to books, wherever they come from.

And if you would like to consider donating to charities that help fund literacy projects, find out more at **www.literacytrust.org.uk** and **www.booktrust.org.uk**.

THANK YOU

*As reported by the National Literacy Trust